SWEET SURRENDER

THE ISLAND SERIES - BOOK ONE

EROTICWRITERGIRL

KINKY INK PRESS

First paperback edition May 2025

Cover design by eroticwritergirl

ISBN 978-1-968079-01-7 (paperback)

Published by Kinky Ink Press

www.kinkyinkpress.com

For every woman who desires
freedom to be true to herself

ONE

I knew what I was getting into and I had no idea what I was getting into. I showed up in a soft silk slip dress that barely graced my thighs with no bra and no panties as instructed. I struggled to walk in my five-inch Lucite platform heels but figured they wanted me a little off balance. This was what I had signed up for, I reminded myself, as the nerves rattled through me, making me edgy and hyper-aware.

They led me through a heavy wood door back to a waiting area, putting a glass of what looked like wine in my hand but I knew better. They had told me they'd be giving me something to relax, something to make the evening more enjoyable, to help me accept my place in this new world.

I signed up for this, I told myself again as I drank the dark burgundy liquid, aware that I was stepping into the unknown, giving myself over to a dark calling that had been scratching to be let out.

My best friend was the only person I told where I was going in case anyone asked. I didn't want a missing person report filed or anyone to worry. My parents were older and out traveling the world. I rarely talked with them but let them know I'd unreachable for six months, telling them I'd be volunteering somewhere in the Bahamas. I didn't have siblings so, besides my friends, no one would miss me.

I drained the last of the liquid, finishing it in a few gulps, grateful for the way it buzzed in my head and made my limbs seem fluid. I knew I wouldn't resist anything they wanted to do to me—that thought aroused me. I welcomed the sense of surrendering full control.

"All set?" a young woman with fiery red hair and killer green eyes asked once I'd finished. She wore a similar silk slip dress but hers was green. I wondered if she also wore nothing underneath. They told me I'd be lucky to be wearing anything at all during my time on the island and to get used to being naked and exposed.

I nodded, my heart racing. "All set."

She gave me a knowing smile.

"It'll get easier. I'm sure you'll be happy here. Not everyone who applies gets accepted."

I was aware of this. They told me that several times during the interview process and, although I felt pleased and honored to be here, I also wondered what the hell I was doing. I had signed my rights as a person away only a few days ago, accepting my place as property in this new society they started on a remote island in the Bahamas. No one would know where I was and the only way off was by boat or plane, both of which were controlled by the society.

"Let me escort you to the plane," she said.

She ushered me through the rest of the building, vacant except for a few men in suits situated around a bar. The jet waiting outside was compact, only space enough for ten passengers. I didn't have bags. I wouldn't be needing them. I would be auctioned off as soon as I arrived or else I'd become part of the island's brothel which I was told wasn't where I wanted to be. I said a silent prayer hoping I'd be bought by some compassionate man but knew there'd be no guarantees.

The men at the bar joined me on the plane a few minutes after I was situated towards the back. They chatted without acknowledging me, my first lesson in how little I would matter. I knew I couldn't engage them in conversation. I was only allowed to speak when spoken to and it was a punishable offense to speak to a man first. I'd be able to converse with other women freely when men weren't present but until I met one, I'd need to remain silent.

I'd never been a fan of flying and closed my eyes during takeoff, escaping into my mind. I thought back to what had started this craziness. I had seen an article online about a new society one man created where women were considered inferior and would be under full control of the men. He called it the natural order and got together with other men to buy a remote island off the Bahamas to start their new society. He put a call out to recruit interested men and women, offering to compensate the women for their time. The men needed to be self-sufficient.

I had been intrigued and kept going back to it. Something within me resonated with this lifestyle, wanted to live in a place where everyone knew their role in life. I had recently graduated with a Bachelor of Arts degree in communications and had no idea what I wanted to do with my life. This sounded like the perfect distraction while I figured it out. Plus, I got turned on by the thought of giving up full control.

I signed up without overthinking it which was unusual for me but it had felt right. Something about it clicked. I signed over the consent papers before I knew it, giving myself over to this lifestyle for the next six months, committing to be considered property.

The plane touched down a short while later, pulling me out of my thoughts. The men exited without a glance my way. I waited in my seat as instructed. My heart raced, my nerves a mess, despite the calming drink. This would be the start of turning my life over to someone else.

An older, clean-shaven man with short sandy brown hair entered the plane once the men and the pilot left, his eyes landing on me.

"Let's go," he said, his voice stern.

I immediately stood up, swaying a moment before regaining my footing. I followed him off the plane and across the tarmac to a waiting golf cart. He put me in the back without a word before slipping into the driver's seat. Part of me screamed that it was foolish to be trusting him, to be here at all, to have put myself in this position. I took in a few deep breaths and reminded myself for the millionth time that I wanted to experience this and needed to trust that it would work out.

He didn't say another word as he wound his way through a stretch of houses before it opened up to a busy downtown. I settled back in the seat, taking in deep breaths to calm my nerves. This is what I wanted. This is what I chose. I wanted this experience. I needed to give in to it.

He pulled up to an office building before escorting me out, his hand strong around my elbow as if I would flee. I had no idea where he thought I would go. There was no way off the island unless I intended to swim. Plus, I signed up for this.

The office interior was bright and minimalist with white everything. A receptionist nodded to the man as we walked by. He led me to an open elevator and pushed 12. I held my breath as the doors closed, trapping me inside. I watched the numbers grow larger as we went up. He didn't touch me or talk to me. He simply stood in front of me as we waited.

The doors opened upon our arrival. I followed him out. This time he stopped to talk with the receptionist, letting her know that he had a new arrival. She smiled and thanked him, telling him to put me in room four and that someone would be around to tend to me.

He deposited me in a windowless room that resembled a doctor's exam room and left without a word. Thankfully, I didn't have to wait long before another man came in, this one in a white lab coat. He smiled at me.

"Please have a seat," he said, directing me to one of two chairs.

I sat, tucking the slip dress underneath me as much as I could, aware that most of my underside was sitting directly on the rough fabric.

"I'm happy you decided to join us," he said. "My name is Dr. Jones and I'll be conducting your exam today. I am also your primary care physician while you're on the island. If you have any health concerns, schedule an exam here. Your medical expenses are covered during your stay so there are no concerns about that. You will need to request permission from your owner but it's in their best interest to make sure you stay healthy. This includes your mental health. Do you understand?"

"Yes," I said, my voice quiet as I sank into my new role.

"Very good. Now let's start with your exam. Stand up and take off your dress. You can hang it on the hook over there."

Heat rose in my cheeks as I stood up and slipped the dress off, leaving me in nothing but the platform heels. Even though this felt clinical, I knew there was more to it. This was my life now.

I had a slim figure with rounded hips and ample breasts. My nipples hardened against the cool office air. Anticipation crept up my spine as I tried not to think about what he'd do next.

He took out a stethoscope from his pocket and listened to my heart and lungs, instructing me to take in deep breaths. He took my temperature and blood pressure, looked into my ears and mouth, before running his hand down my back and over my ass, stopping just short of my pussy.

"Bend over," he said. "Grip your ankles if you can."

Embarrassed, I did as he said, knowing I was giving him a full view of my underside. I had waxed before I arrived, as instructed, so I knew I was clean and bare. It had taken some getting used to but I didn't think I'd ever go back to not waxing.

I felt him inch closer, his thighs grazing the back of mine, before he slid a finger into my wet pussy. The invasion startled me but I knew better than to say anything. He pushed a second figure in and then a third, stretching me as if testing my capacity. I breathed through the discomfort, careful not to squirm, careful not to show anything.

"Not bad," he said before pulling out. He went over to the desk to type something on the computer.

I stayed bent over until he came back. This time he thrust a lubed finger into my ass, rocking me forward. I steadied myself as he pressed in deeper, wiggling around, making me want to move away from the invasion but I forced myself to stay steady.

"Nice control," he said before pulling out and slapping my ass. "You can stand up."

I slowly uncurled myself until I was standing upright, my arms hanging at my sides, as I watched him type on the computer. I wondered what he was recording about me. Once he finished, he stood in front of me and examined my breasts with his hands, holding them before brushing lightly against the hard nipples, sending a jolt of arousal through me. He squeezed each nipple tentatively before increasing the pressure, watching my reaction. I squirmed a moment, not meeting his eyes, until he released me.

"Not bad," he said as he returned to the computer and typed some more.

My eyes went wide as he pulled out a large needle, sinking it into a small jar, pulling liquid up into it. He chuckled at my reaction.

"One last thing," he said as he came near me with that thing, "I need to give you a high dose birth control shot that will keep away unwanted pregnancies during your stay. It's 100% effective and will allow you not to have to worry about who uses you."

I gritted my teeth as he sank the needle into my ass. It stung as the liquid entered me. I wondered what else was in that needle besides birth control. I had given myself over completely so they could do whatever they wanted with me other than anything that would cause permanent harm.

"Good girl," he said when he pulled the needle out. I sighed with relief. "You'll go through your orientation with Chelsea next. She will give you the rules and expectations for your time here. Again, reach out to us if you need anything."

With that, he left. I wasn't told to get dressed or to leave or anything so I stood there worried that I was doing everything wrong. I felt a little calmer than before but I was swimming in a sea of over-whelm. I was grateful I had told a friend where I would be but she had no way of contacting me and I had no way of contacting her that I knew of so I wasn't sure at that moment what good that was doing me.

A moment later a woman came in carrying a clipboard. She was dressed how I imagined secretaries dressed in the fifties, in a thin black pencil skirt that skimmed her full hips, a proper white blouse that gaped open at the top revealing unadorned full breasts. Her chestnut brown hair was pulled up in a loose topknot with a few stray strands curling around her heart-shaped face. She wore bright red lipstick and her upper eyelids were heavily lined with black. It was only the white collar around her neck that hinted at something different.

She smiled when she saw me standing there like an idiot.

"Hi," she said, her voice sweet and upbeat. "I'm happy to see you didn't move and didn't bother getting dressed. That will put you a couple of points above the others which is exactly where you want to be."

I blinked at her, not quite understanding what she meant, and hoped she'd be able to guide me through this crazy society.

"You may sit," she said as she took a seat in one of the chairs, crossing one slim leg over the other.

I slowly sat down, the fabric rough on my ass.

"I see you're with us for six months. That's a perfect length of time. Not too short and not too long. You can always renew your commitment to stay once your six months are up. A lot of women do that."

I nodded. Six months felt like forever.

"Today I will go over all the rules and expectations for you while you're here," she said. "They gave you some indication of what would be expected of you during the interview process but this is where we get more specific.

"First off, you won't own anything while you're here. Everything you need will either be provided for you or you will go without. You are considered property and property doesn't have ownership rights. Do you understand?"

I nodded, my voice escaping me. The severity of what I signed up for started sinking in.

"Good. Next, you need to understand that as property, you have no rights. The only right you have is to not be permanently harmed. Men are considered superior and they can do and say whatever they want to you without reprimand. You signed your consent when you agreed to come here and that's all the consent they need. They do not need your further consent. With that being said, if you refuse or talk back to any man for any reason, unless he is causing permanent harm, then you will be punished and I can guarantee you you won't like it. Understand?"

I nodded again, my eyes wide, as I considered what this all meant.

"We do not have safe words here since we are not a club but a lifestyle. However, if you feel in danger of being permanently harmed, you can say the word red and you will be brought to this office immediately to be examined and fixed up if needed. You can do this without punishment except if it's found that you used the word without the imminent threat of being permanently harmed. Then you will be shipped off the island and will not receive any compensation for any time spent here. Do you understand?"

"Yes," I said, my heart hammering. What the hell had I agreed to?

"Good. A few more simple ground rules and then we can get to the next steps of your intake. Do not initiate conversation with any man. You may talk with women but not when there's a man present. When a man's present, all your attention needs to be on him. However, you cannot make eye contact with him unless he requests it.

"They will auction you off this evening to your new owner. Most men have multiple women under their ownership so don't be surprised if this is the case. There is no hierarchy among women inside a household since all women are inferior and none rank higher than another. Do your best to get along with the other women inside your new household. This will make your life here easier.

"If you're not purchased during the auction, which sometimes happens, then you will be sent to one of the brothels until someone wants to claim you as their own. Also, if you displease your owner in any way, he can drop you at the brothel and release his ownership of you. The brothels are not a fun place to be so do your best to keep your owner happy.

"Your owner will give you a collar representing his ownership over you. This will alert other men of your ownership status and whether your owner will share you. Different color collars represent different rules of ownership. A white collar means hands-off, that only the owner may touch you. A yellow collar means the owner allows groping only. A green collar means the owner allows others to fuck you any way they want but cannot cause any pain. A black collar means the owner allows others to do whatever they want with you without restriction. Girls at the brothels are not collared and are free use for whatever without restriction, including being taken overnight or for days at a time. All collared women must be returned to their owner by midnight unless other arrangements are made."

I started to feel unsettled, like the world was shifting beneath me, as I took in the rules. It was feeling too real.

"I know it's a lot," Chelsea said, "but you'll get used to it. Your owner may have you work if they wish. They will receive a list of your skills and may want you to be a productive part of this society. All your wages will be deposited into his account since property cannot own anything. But working is a wonderful way to meet people and to acclimate yourself to being here. Any questions?"

I wouldn't even know where to begin. It was too much.

"No? Well, you might. Make your way back here if you have any questions in the future. It's better to ask them here than in your new household. The other women might not always give you the most truthful answers. It can be in their best interest for you to fail and to be shipped out of here. Never ask your owner any questions unless he asks you for them. He shouldn't be bothered with your confusion.

"You are to present yourself however your owner wants. This could include being clothed or unclothed. Your owner will provide you with clothes if that is his wish. Brothel girls are to be unclothed at all times since they own nothing. Meals are provided for the brothel girls since they are part of the community and we don't want anyone to starve. Your owner will dictate your meals for you. If you are to work, your owner will decide what you wear to work as well. Don't be shocked or surprised if you see that most women are unclothed or displayed in some way. You'll get used to it. Women are considered ornaments and are often displayed regardless of their collar status.

"I know this is a lot to take in. Again, reach out to us here if you get confused. We want this to be a pleasurable experience for you as much as possible. We intend to create a permanent society here and that can only happen if the women want to stay. We don't keep anyone here against their will. If at any time you want to leave, come to this office and let us know. We will ship you out as soon as we can.

"You will be given new rules by your owner that you must abide by or you will be punished accordingly. Do your best to follow all the rules and you'll be fine. Any questions?"

I swallowed the lump in my throat. This was too much but also everything I needed. I needed to be here, to experience whatever this was, to get it out of my system before I could return to the real world. Not to mention that the compensation would set me up for a couple of years and allow me time to figure out what I wanted to do with my life. I needed to be here.

"No questions," I said.

"Good," she said. "Leave the dress here. You won't be needing it. Follow me to the waiting area. You'll stay there until the auction this evening. Lunch will be brought to you but, since you're the only new arrival today, you will be alone. This will allow you to start learning patience and the ability to do nothing for long periods."

Without another word, she was out the door. I followed her wearing only my platform heels, clicking down the hallway after her like a lost puppy. My mind swam as we walked down a long hallway filled with closed doors. We turned the corner, past the receptionist who didn't bother looking up, and down to a room off to one side. The room had a full-length window open to the hallway and reception area with no windows to the outside, a table with two chairs and an uncomfortable-looking orange couch.

"You'll be here for the next few hours," she said. "Get comfortable. Remember, don't initiate conversation with anyone except other women and only when no men are present. I would hate for you to be punished before you're auctioned off. That would lower your ability to be bought."

She opened the door for me, closing and locking it once I was inside. I stood there a moment, staring back at her, staring out into the empty hallway and reception area, wondering what the hell had I done. I felt like a prisoner awaiting my sentence even though I already knew what my sentence would be.

TWO

She walked away without looking back. I could see the receptionist but she wasn't looking my way either. I felt comforted that there was someone who could see me if she wanted—that I wasn't totally alone—but I somehow knew she wouldn't be looking this way during the duration of my stay.

With nothing else to do, I sat on one of the chairs, the wood cold against my wet pussy. I couldn't believe that through all this, I was wet and aching. I already felt used and I had barely been touched. How would I feel once the six months were over? Would I want to stay? I couldn't imagine it now but a small part of me whispered that this could be what I'd been looking for my entire life.

Time crept by. The receptionist never looked over and no one came down the hall. I tried not to overthink things but all I could do was think. I tried meditating, something I had learned from one of my friends, but my mind refused to stay still. Instead, it wandered through all the questions I had about this place and what I had gotten myself into.

After what felt like forever, a woman dressed in a simple white sundress with a white collar brought me chicken noodle soup with crackers. I wanted to talk with her, since no men were around, to ask her questions, to hear my voice, but all I did was nod thanks and she was gone.

I savored each spoonful of soup, wanting to stretch time. I had no concept of time since there weren't any clocks and I had no idea how much longer I needed to wait. I had access to a simple bathroom, providing me with water and a toilet if needed. I contemplated going in there to study my face but was afraid of what I'd see.

I had dozed off on the sofa sitting up when the door opened. A sizable man with a broad chest dressed in a black t-shirt and dark jeans entered.

"Up" was all he said.

I jumped to my feet.

"Follow me."

He was out the door and halfway down the hall before I caught up with him, stumbling on my platform heels.

I was feeling more comfortable being naked in front of others, not that I had much choice. He led me down a series of halls until he came to a closed door. He pulled out a blindfold from his pocket and secured it around my eyes without a word. I heard him open the door before he grabbed my wrist and pulled me.

"Walk," he commanded.

I did my best to keep up with him, feeling disoriented without being able to see. I heard the low rumble of voices and knew we were no longer alone. Fear spiked through me. I had never been naked in a room full of people and the blindfold made it worse. I felt out of my element and at their mercy. I hoped I hadn't made a terrible mistake coming here.

"Steps," the man barked, alerting me to the steps in front of me. "There are three."

I took my time climbing them, not wanting to fall. He moved me to a spot then told me not to move. The hum of voices grew louder. My nerves crackled along my skin as I suspected I was on some sort of platform waiting to be auctioned. I prayed I went to someone kind. I knew I wanted this but I couldn't believe I was doing it. My heart hammered, refusing to calm, as I waited.

The voices quieted as I heard someone come up beside me. Someone smacked my ass, causing me to jump, before he cleared his throat.

"Welcome men. Thank you for coming out to view our latest acquisition. This gem is only 22 years old, fresh from college, and wanting to experience life as an inferior slut. She signed on for six months but I'm sure her new owner can persuade her to prolong her stay.

"She's five-seven, 135 pounds, a 36D and a non-virgin. She's only had three sexual partners, all male. She was brought up in a traditional household where the father worked and the mother was his secretary until she had children. She shouldn't need much breaking in and has shown extreme responsiveness during her exam. She'd be a desirable addition to any household.

"As you know, this auction is electronic. We will show the current bid on the overhead screen along with that bidder's paddle number. Once the bidding stalls for more than 10 seconds, I will declare the winner."

I felt mortified as I stood there hearing about myself as if I were a used car or a horse to be bred. The murmur in the room escalated as the bidding started. The male voices grew louder, a mix of laughter and conversation I couldn't understand.

The auctioneer pulled on my nipples, causing me to gasp and lean into it.

"Look how responsive she is," he called out. "Imagine tormenting and playing with these wonderful tits."

The voices grew louder and more excited as the auctioneer pinched and pulled on my nipples, causing me to squirm. He slapped my breasts a few times, the sting reverberating through me, causing a pool of warmth to spread throughout my lower half.

He pulled and slapped my nipples while he egged on the men. Shame washed over me as he manhandled me, embarrassed that I found it incredibly arousing.

After more pulling on my sore nipples, he turned me around and forced me to bend over at the waist, showing my underside to the audience. Cheers went up as the auctioneer spread my ass cheeks and pushed a lubed plug into my ass, causing me to gasp.

"She's an ass virgin so think of all the fun you'll have breaking her in there," he said as he slapped my ass. He slipped two fingers into my wet pussy. "Look how wet she's for it. This slut can't wait to be fucked and to serve you. You don't want to miss out on this slut."

He fingered me, pushing in deeper. Shame overwhelmed me as an orgasm began to build. Oh God—don't let me come in front of all these men. The auctioneer found my clit with his thumb while he continued to pump his fingers in and out. It was too much. I let out a scream and gushed as an orgasm rolled through me. The auctioneer laughed before pulling out and smacked my ass, wiping my wetness on my leg.

"This one is super responsive," he said, his hand still on my ass. "She wants to be put in her place. Look how turned on she is from being displayed in front of all of you."

He slid his fingers through my wet pussy as if to prove his point. The voices grew louder as the auction heated up. The auctioneer kept his hand on the small of my back, forcing me to stay bent over. The blood rushed to my head, making dizzy.

He played with my pussy, spreading my labia to give the audience a better view. I had no idea how many men were in the room but knowing they were examining me like I was nothing did something to me. I felt on edge and more aroused than I'd ever felt. My mind didn't know what to do with that.

After what felt like forever, the auctioneer announced that the bidding had slowed. He called out a crazy large number and asked going once, going twice, before throwing down a gavel and declaring me sold to Mr. Lance Wood.

I sagged against my knees, grateful it was over but knowing it had only just begun.

The auctioneer straightened me up as he conversed with Mr. Wood about me as if I wasn't there. Since everything was done electronically, Mr. Wood had already paid and was free to take possession immediately.

I felt a collar slip around my neck and lock in place. I heard another click then felt a tug at my neck as they pulled me forward. As I started to walk, the realization hit me that I was on a leash walking away naked in front of God knows how many men.

No words were exchanged as he pulled me forward. I had no choice but to follow, still blindfolded, having no idea where I was or where I was going. I had given up complete control and it terrified me.

We took an elevator down and then we were out on the street. I was still naked, only in heels, and he hadn't said a word to me. I guess he didn't need to—I was only property to him, like a used car, nothing to converse with.

The warm ocean breeze wrapped around me, warming my skin. I tried not to think about the countless people who could see me, thankful I was blindfolded so I didn't have to witness it.

He helped me into the backseat of a car, ducking my head like a cop would do to someone they arrested. In a way, I was a prisoner but a prisoner of my own making. I heard car doors slam and felt the car pull away. I tried to calm my nerves as I waited for something to happen, for hands to reach out and touch me. I didn't dare move. I knew punishments could be severe and I wanted to avoid one for as long as possible.

The car inched along for what felt like forever but was probably only a few minutes. The silence and uncertainty had me on edge. I was surprised this man hadn't jumped on me the moment we were alone but he kept his distance, making it that much more intense. Once we stopped, he pulled me out of the car by the elbow, up some steps and through a door.

"Make her presentable for the party tonight," Mr. Wood barked to someone once we were inside. "I want something sheer with easy access. She will be a delight to my guests."

My heartbeat quickened at the thought of being paraded around in front of his guests but swallowed my fear as my I heard a female respond, "Yes, sir," and felt a tug on my leash.

I followed like the pet I had become, still blindfolded, through the house which stretched on forever. The female didn't talk to me and I didn't dare say a word. Being blindfolded didn't allow me the luxury of knowing if any men were present and I didn't want to be punished my first day.

"Stop," the female commanded.

I stopped without hesitation. She pulled off my blindfold, revealing a white-washed bedroom with a white covered bed and white furniture. It was minimalist but plush. Nothing was extraneous. There were no knickknacks or unnecessary ornamentation. It made sense since a man designed it for men. Women were no longer a consideration.

The female in front of me was gorgeous. Her thin, petite body highlighted her perky breasts that were more than a handful and long blond hair that cascaded like gold down her back. Her baby blue eyes were rimmed with dark eyeliner and her lips were stained red. She wore nothing but a yellow collar and Lucite platform heels, letting the men know that they could grope her but not fuck her.

"This is your room for now," she said. "Mr. Wood will decide where he wants you once you're more settled. He likes to keep his new acquisitions separate from the rest of the household until he has time to mold her to his liking. He doesn't want you to be influenced by the other women here."

"How many other women are here?" I asked, curious about how this society worked.

"That is not for me to say," she said. "Mr. Wood will tell you everything you need to know. My only job is to prepare you for his party this evening. He is entertaining his friends with an elaborate dinner party and wants to show you off."

I wasn't sure whether to feel honored or horrified but reminded myself this was why I came. I wanted to give up control and be submissive to the men on this island.

"What do I need to do?" I asked.

"He will direct you," she said. "Your only job is to obey. Obey without question and you should do fine. Hesitation will imply questioning so respond immediately. Your backside will thank you."

I wondered if I would ever be friends with this woman as she went into the bathroom to draw a bath. I didn't follow because I wasn't sure what the protocol was for interacting with other women. I assumed I didn't need to obey them but perhaps I was put in her care and needed to follow her instructions. Either way, I planned to obey every command they gave me regardless of who gave it to me. I wanted to make my transition into this society as seamless as possible. I already felt out of my element.

"Come here," she ordered.

I entered the steamy bathroom, taken in by its opulence. Everything was white marble with floor to ceiling mirrors. There was no escaping myself in this bathroom. The tub was massive, complete with jets she had turned on.

I caught sight of myself in the mirror for the first time as property. I looked like myself but different. It wasn't until I saw the black collar around my neck that I stopped breathing. He had given me no restrictions, which meant any man could do anything with me as long as he didn't cause permanent harm. Fear gripped me. I felt faint.

"Soak in here for 20 minutes," she said before turning to me. She must have noticed how white I had become because she shook me and asked if I was OK.

I nodded, not sure what else to do. This was my life now.

She must have understood because she said, "Everyone starts out in this house with a black collar. That's why you're freaked out, right?"

I nodded.

"He starts every female at this lowest position until she proves herself to him. He believes it helps remind them that they're inferior and must obey any man. It's part of your training. If you're obedient and responsive, you'll be moved up to another collar soon. Be patient and go with it. It's part of the experience."

I took in a deep breath as I let her words sink in. It made sense but I didn't like the idea of being trained. What did that mean? I didn't like the idea of any man being able to do anything to me. Sure, I expected some men and definitely my master to have full control over me, and that's something I craved, but I wasn't sure about every man. I didn't know how I was going to cope with that.

I sank into the warm water, letting the jets wash over me. I didn't have access to a tub like this at home and wondered how often I'd be able to take a bath here. I prayed it'd be daily. This tub could seriously work out all the kinks in my muscles and then some.

"I'll be back in 20 to collect you," she said. "Try to relax. This is the calm before the storm."

I wish she hadn't said that.

THREE

I must have fallen asleep because the next thing I knew I was being shaken awake.

"You could have drowned," she snapped. "Never fall asleep in the tub again."

She was draining the water before I could put together what she was saying, leaving me wet and cold.

"You're my responsibility until the party tonight," she said. "Don't screw this up for the both of us."

She handed me a plush white towel as I stood up. I wrapped it around myself, happy to shield myself if only temporarily from her wrath. Even though she was small, I didn't want to get on her bad side. It was obvious she had been in the house a while to be wearing a yellow collar. It made me wonder if anyone got to the coveted white collar in this house. I guessed I would soon find out.

"Come sit," she said, directing me to a settee in front of the vanity. It was a crushed white velvet and felt smooth against my skin. She brushed out my auburn hair before pulling it up in a loose chignon.

Once she had my hair secured to her satisfaction, she came around to my front and started applying makeup. Her breasts dangled in front of my nose as she focused on my eyes and lips. It made me wonder if the women ever played among themselves, if that was allowed. I had always been fascinated by the female body and, although I had never had sex with a woman, I had kissed one.

She stood back, looking satisfied, before putting the makeup supplies away.

"Everything in this bathroom and room are yours to use while you're here," she said. "Mr. Wood will let you know when and if it's otherwise. Once you're more integrated into the house, you'll probably share a room with another female. Mr. Wood will decide that."

I blinked at her, not sure what to say or if I should say anything. I wanted to ask how long I'd be in the black collar but was afraid she'd shut me down again. Instead, I kept my mouth shut and took in my transformation in the mirror.

I resembled myself but a more seductive and sultry version. My lips appeared fuller and swollen, like I had been thoroughly kissed. My eyes looked bigger and more green, making my skin almost translucent.

"I can see why Mr. Wood purchased you," she said as she looked me over. "You'll fit right in."

She dressed me in a short sheer dress with a low v neck that grazed my nipples, leaving them mostly exposed. She added a couple of strands of long pearls that hung to my navel and two-carat diamond studs in my ears. She had me slip into platform Lucite heels before strapping them on. She spritzed me with floral perfume. I smiled at the smell of it. It reminded me of something but I couldn't put my finger on it.

"Remember, no eye contact with any of the men, don't speak unless spoken to, including any females since you'll be in the presence of men, do what you're told and don't hesitate to obey." She paused as she considered what else she may be missing. "Mr. Wood will test you tonight so be even more accommodating than you think you need to be. Don't overdo it but do more rather than the minimum if you get my meaning."

I nodded. I think I did.

"There will be other females there but treat them as nothing more than ornamentation. Don't engage with them. They won't respond and you'll look like a fool and possibly be punished.

"I shouldn't be telling you this but I feel like it'll be my ass on the line if you screw this up. Mr. Wood knows this is your first foray into this society but don't expect him to be lenient. He is a stern master and expects perfection. He isn't afraid to break a female so let this be your warning to go along with whatever happens this evening. Consider it your initiation."

With that, she left. Like before, I didn't dare move. I longed to check out the rooms that were to be mine, to open and close drawers, to see what this new life included but I knew better than to look.

I had spotted a massive closet and a sleek white dresser in the bedroom and wondered what type of clothing would be made available to me. My current dress left nothing to the imagination, a simple yet elegant covering to highlight my curves.

I felt like I had on a costume, had stepped into a role, and decided that's how I was going to approach the evening, like I was trying something on. I knew I could leave at any time which offered some comfort. I'd lose my compensation, which I desperately needed, but I liked knowing I had an escape route. I reminded myself that I had come here to experience a new way of living, to discover if this was how I wanted to live my life. I knew they were hoping to develop a new society here, one where women would want to stay, so I hoped that meant they wouldn't be too horrible to me, especially on the first night.

I realized after she left that I hadn't gotten her name. It sounded like the house was full of females. I'm not sure how I felt about that. In a way, I knew I should be relieved because the attention would probably be off me most of the time. I wondered how he'd allow me to spend my free time. Would he want me to get a job? I went to college, graduated with a communications degree and had no idea what I wanted to do with my life. I wasn't sure what that would qualify me to do here. I guess I'd find out.

I FELT RIDICULOUS STANDING THERE. It felt like forever but my intuition told me not to move. Being part of this society meant being at the whims of the men here, something I deeply craved but that also meant practicing patience.

I wiggled my toes in the new shoes, trying to adjust to them. I rarely wore platform heels. I leaned more towards comfort over fashion but knew that wouldn't be the way here. I wouldn't have a choice over my clothes or anything else in my life. I needed to give up control, to be of service, a role I had always desired but that also scared me.

I was used to having full control over my life. I had always been intrigued about fully surrendering that control but I had assumed I'd do it within the confines of a safe intimate relationship. I never imagined giving it up completely, if only for six months. Six months felt like forever.

I had answered the call for women almost without thinking, like a deeper part of me had taken over. I had answered their detailed questionnaire and sent in a head and body shot even as I blushed doing it. I had found it in a chatroom online that discussed how women were inferior to men. I had joined on a lark, curious while also intensely turned on by the thought.

I considered myself to be just like all the other women I knew, financially independent, in control of my life, not looking for a man to complete me. I wanted a long-term relationship, possibly marriage, but rarely gave it much consideration. I was still young and felt like I had forever to make that happen. In the meantime, I wanted to have some fun and explore my sexuality, engage these deeper parts of myself, see what worked and what didn't.

It had shocked me when they had reached out to me, telling me they wanted me to come in for an interview. Butterflies exploded in my stomach as I reread that email a million times, wondering if I was brave enough to do it, take such an enormous risk. I was placated by the six-month term and kept telling myself that it was such a small slice of my life. I was single, didn't have a job I loved, so if I didn't take the leap now, I'd probably never do it. Plus, the compensation was outstanding and something I needed.

I sucked in my breath when he walked in. His tall frame filled out his black tux. A crisp white shirt stretched against his broad chest, making me want to reach my hands out to touch it. His square jawline ticked as he looked me over, his dark green eyes menacing, causing me to stand straighter.

I held my breath as he circled me, evaluating but not touching. The room hummed with an electric charge as the sexual tension filled the room. I was already drawn to this man, felt commanded by him, and he hadn't even said a word.

"Kneel," he said when he circled back in front of me.

I dropped to my knees without thinking. I kept my eyes locked on his shiny dress shoes as he studied me. My nerves crackled. My breathing got shallow. I felt on edge, having no idea what he'd do.

"You are to be the guest of honor tonight," he said, his voice deep and surprisingly soothing. "What that means is that you'll be expected to obey what any man asks of you without hesitation. You will also allow your body to be used in any way my guests wish including but not limited to being touched and penetrated.

"I know you're here because you have a deep desire to submit and surrender yourself to men, to see yourself as the inferior female that you are. I applaud your ability to give in to this deep desire. Most women don't and that's to their detriment.

"I want you to be happy here and ideally I'd like you to want to stay after your six-month commission is complete. With that in mind, the men on the island don't hurt or cause pain to the women unless they require punishment and then it is used only for their own good, for correction. You will not like any of the forms of punishment so I recommend you avoid them.

"You've been given the black collar because this is the level I start all my females. I believe it helps you to learn your place quickly here and keeps you from thinking you're better than anyone else. I advance the collars as I see fit and I have no hesitation putting or keeping a female in the black collar if needed. This is the only area of your life where you will have some control.

"When you're at rest, like you are now, you will always kneel. I will let you know if I want it any different. Being modest for now is OK. The only time you may use furniture is when I tell you or the man present tells you it's OK at that moment. The floor will be your default until you're told otherwise.

"Don't make assumptions about anything. Your old life is gone, at least for now, so keep that in mind while you navigate this new society. We expect you to obey without hesitation and to make our lives easier, not more difficult.

"When addressing me or speaking of me, you will call me Mr. Wood. I am not your master or your dom. We don't use that terminology here. This isn't a game but a lifestyle. Do you understand all that I've said?"

I nodded, keeping my eyes lowered, afraid to speak.

He lifted my chin so I was forced to look at him. His green eyes pierced through me, igniting something deep in my soul.

"When I ask you a question, I expect you to answer."

"Yes, Mr. Wood," I squeaked out. "I understand."

He caressed my cheek with his thumb before trailing his fingers down my neck. The light touch sent sparks through me. I wished for a moment that I had this beautiful man all to myself, that I was his alone and that he wouldn't let anyone else touch me, let alone use me. I wanted to be his only.

"Good," he said as he straightened. "Zoey will be back to direct you to the party. Although your duty here is to serve and bring pleasure to men, I also want you to enjoy yourself."

FOUR

My head swam with conflicting thoughts as I waited for Zoey to return. I couldn't believe the pull I felt towards Mr. Wood already. He captivated me, making me yearn to please him which surprised me. I couldn't believe how much control he had over me in such a brief time. It thrilled and terrified me.

What if I succumbed to this inferior female philosophy and remained an inferior female forever? What would that mean for me? Would it make me happy? A deep part of me screamed yes, this was my true purpose and to allow myself to surrender to it, while another part felt mortified by the idea.

Zoey returned quicker this time, pleased to see that I was on my knees. She attached a leather leash to my collar and commanded me to stand. I uncurled myself as gracefully as I could.

"It's time," she said as she led me out.

She walked me down a long hallway with a bunch of closed doors which I assumed were bedrooms before leading me down a massive staircase that curved and opened up to a marble foyer with an impressive crystal chandelier. My heels clicked on the marble as she led me to two massive carved wood doors with wrought iron handles.

She turned to me.

"Remember, you are here to please and obey. That's it. Don't look anyone in the eye, not even the women for now, and don't speak unless directed to do so. Mr. Wood will probably circulate you to show you off but don't be surprised if he gives you over to someone else. Try not to think too much. Turn your brain off and give yourself over to the moment. Act demure and respectful and you should be fine."

My nerves felt like they were about to explode as she opened the massive doors to reveal an opulent ballroom filled with men dressed in tuxes and women dressed in elaborate sheer gowns. I noticed that all the women wore collars, a mix of whites, yellows and greens. I quickly realized I was the only black collar in the room as Zoey pulled me deeper into the gathering.

Zoey did a lap around the room as if showing me off to Mr. Wood's guests. The men gave me appreciative looks, some grabbing my ass while others brushed against my erect nipples. Electricity zinged through me with each touch. I felt like a show pony and in a way I loved it. I took in the women who stood or kneeled near their men, allowing their man's hands to wander over their bodies while the men conversed among themselves as if it were nothing.

Zoey stopped when she wound our way to Mr. Wood who was conversing with several foreboding men. My heartbeat quickened at the sight of him. It was clear he held weight in this society. The men he was talking with seemed to hang on his every word as if he was solving all the world's problems (which maybe he was).

Zoey handed Mr. Wood my leash without a word before disappearing into the crowd. I wondered about her role in his house when the attention of the men shifted to me.

"Nice acquisition," one man said to Mr. Wood, causing me to blush. I wasn't used to being considered property yet. "Do you mind if I give her a spin?"

Mr. Wood smiled at him. "Be my guest."

"Kneel, slut," the man said to me.

I obeyed without hesitation, remembering Mr. Wood's instructions and wanting to please him. My heartbeat quickened as I sank to my knees, eyes lowered, and thought here we go.

The man walked in front of me and examined me as if I were fine porcelain. He stroked his hands over my arms, up to my shoulders, across my chest, taking a moment to consider each breast, measure them in his hands, before releasing them, watching as they bounced back into place. He walked around me, his hands wandering onto my back and then down to my hips. I was sitting on my legs, my sex tucked underneath me, out of reach. He didn't seem to mind.

He circled back around until he stood in front of me. He unzipped his dress slacks, allowing his engorged cock to pop out in front of my face.

"Suck."

I opened my mouth and allowed him to slip his hard cock inside. I widened my eyes, surprised by its saltiness as it pushed against the back of my throat. He didn't grab my hair and I didn't dare touch him. I kept my hands at my sides as he pumped his cock in and out.

He was bigger than I was used to and it took everything I had to open completely to him. All my focus went towards allowing his cock to penetrate me. I forgot about Mr. Wood and his other guests who I'm sure were enjoying the show. Instead, I focused on this cock, sucking it in, hoping I pleased it, as it found a steady rhythm.

I swirled my tongue around the shaft as I opened my throat to take the cock in deeper. I heard the men talking above me as I continued to focus on my task. The man soon picked up his rhythm, fucking my mouth with more urgency, until he stilled and spilled himself down my throat.

He pulled out without ceremony and without a word. The remnants of his semen dripped from my lips and I did nothing to stop them from dripping onto my dress.

The ballroom slowly came back into focus as I sat there, my first duty as an inferior female complete. I felt initiated, only here to please, and I wasn't sure how I felt about it. My mind felt overwhelmed. I wasn't aroused but I wasn't turned off either. I sat there stunned, as if I had just witnessed something that I couldn't quite get my mind around. I had never sucked off a stranger before.

The men continued talking as if it were nothing, as if I were nothing, but I wasn't listening. I knew they weren't directing any of their conversations towards me and it literally went over my head. I took this time to observe the rest of the party.

Most of the women were standing off to the side of their men, eyes lowered, waiting to be summoned. Some were nude with male hands absentmindedly roaming over their bodies, pinching their nipples, enjoying the squeeze of their breasts, sliding in between their legs. Others wore sheer gowns that skimmed their bodies, showing them off just the same. A few had leashes. I wondered if this was another thing I would advance out of—the need to be led everywhere. I wanted more than anything to please Mr. Wood and advance through the collars as soon as possible. I wondered if these men ever fell in love with their women or if that wasn't a consideration.

The night went on with me kneeling through most of it. I had thought Mr. Wood would have shown me off more but he seemed content to have me kneeling by his side. Part of me wondered if he had forgotten about me. Most of the men seemed oblivious to the gorgeous women surrounding them. Even though there was a band, no one danced. It was merely background music.

Women came around with cocktails, beer and wine every so often, delivering the drinks to the men. They wore corsets that synched their waists and pushed up their exposed breasts. Their long slim legs were covered with sheer black stockings, topped off with black lace garters, leaving their undersides exposed. They walked around as if it were nothing, not flinching or even noticing when someone pinched their nipples. They didn't wear collars which made me think they were brothel girls, available for free use and unclaimed. I prayed I never became one of those.

I noticed one man smack one of the waitress's ass before bending her over and fucking her from behind. She had a full tray that she balanced while he plowed into her. My nipples hardened at the sight and I was amazed that I was the only one that seemed to notice them. Everyone continued as they were, not bothering to glance over as the man fucked her, grunting from the effort. Once he finished, he pulled his limp cock into his pants and walked away. The waitress straightened as if it were nothing, semen leaking down her inner thigh. She didn't wipe it away as she continued with her duties. The whole scene made me wet.

Mr. Wood must have caught where my attention had wandered. He leaned down, stroked my hair and whispered into my ear, "Don't worry, my pet, you'll have your turn. Practice patience. You're here for us, not the other way around."

I didn't look up at him since he hadn't instructed me to and soon he was back talking with the other men. I let his words sink in. It was the first time I realized that it was no longer about me. It was about them. My wants no longer mattered. I loved it.

AFTER A WHILE, Mr. Wood had me stand so some of his friends could examine me more thoroughly. They ran their hands over my body, over my lips, over my breasts, between my legs and down my thighs as if they were examining a thoroughbred. They didn't speak to me and I kept my eyes lowered. My body hummed from the attention and I started to wish someone would bend me over and fuck me like the waitress but no one did.

One waitress brought me a tall glass of water which I drank down in a couple of gulps. I hadn't realized how thirsty I'd become. It also alerted my stomach that I hadn't eaten in a long time. I wondered how the food worked here. I assumed they'd feed me since the office woman went on about how they fed the brothel girls, how they didn't want anyone starving. I knew I couldn't ask, at least not now, so I sucked it up and attributed it to another skill I needed to learn.

I noted that Mr. Wood kept his hands off me the whole evening. I found this odd since he was the one who purchased me. It made me wonder why he had a house full of women and what he did with them.

I tried listening to the conversations throughout the evening but they discussed work stuff, import/export, investing and real estate holdings. They talked a bit about how to continue building the society on the island. They had more than enough men willing to be part of it but they only allowed men who had the financial means to support themselves and the women with business dealings that weren't dependent on the local economy.

I learned how to fade into the background, to become the ornamentation that I was there to be. Hands found their way on my skin as they absentmindedly tweaked a nipple or caressed my ass. I didn't lean into their touches or do anything to welcome them. I simply stood there and accepted it, my pussy aching, wanting something more.

I zoned out as I stood there, oblivious to the pain the platform heels were causing, growing oblivious to the groping. My mind quieted, becoming almost blank. I leaned into this feeling as the night stretched on. I witnessed more waitresses being fucked without ceremony, even a few of the collared women being bent over and taken, but for whatever reason, I seemed off-limits despite my black collar.

I watched as Zoey circulated, her long blonde hair flowing behind her. Since she wore a yellow collar, other men were only allowed to touch her, which they did as she passed. She didn't seem to notice or care. She wasn't a waitress but she seemed to be looking out for the needs of the other women. I wondered why she wasn't standing at Mr. Wood's side and why there weren't any other women with him. Were they left upstairs somewhere? My mind contemplated different possibilities. This society would take some getting used to.

After what felt like a long time, Mr. Wood turned to me. "How are you holding up?"

"I'm fine, Mr. Wood," I said, an automatic response as I kept my eyes lowered.

He chuckled. "Your feet must be killing you and I know you must be hungry. Don't lie to me. How are you feeling?"

"You're right, Mr. Wood, my feet are killing me and I am hungry."

"Please excuse us," he said to the men he had been talking to.

They nodded, said of course, before Mr. Wood led me away by the leash. He walked me through the ballroom, pausing to say hello to various men. Hands found me as I walked, stroking and pinching. I acted like it was nothing as my body hummed with excitement. It had been a whole evening of being aroused. I felt honored to be led by Mr. Wood. I had no idea where we were going and I didn't care.

We left the noisy ballroom, the massive oak doors closing behind us, leaving us in the hush of the foyer. The only sound was the clicking of my heels on the marble floor. Mr. Wood led me down a long hallway, passed closed doors, until we arrived at a grand kitchen. It was all white with gleaming marble countertops and an island in the middle.

"Sit," he commanded, nodding towards a stool at the counter.

I sat, my exposed underside sinking onto the plush fabric. My feet throbbed with relief. I longed to kick off the heels but didn't dare. I watched as Mr. Wood made his way to a hidden fridge and pulled out yogurt along with a carton of strawberries. My stomach grumbled at the sight of them. He set them in front of me with a spoon but didn't tell me to eat so I sat there doing nothing.

He smiled at my lack of action.

"Good," he said as he poured me a tall glass of water from the fridge. "You're waiting."

He put the glass of water in front of me. I longed to drink it, my throat parched.

"You did well today," he said as he stood across the island from me. "I'm pleased and it takes a lot to please me."

My heart fluttered at the complement. I longed to please him.

"You may look at me," he said.

I raised my eyes to him. He looked even more handsome and commanding in this stark kitchen with its overhead lighting. He was leaning on his hands, leaning towards me, his green eyes captivating. I hoped he liked what he saw. I rubbed my lips together, a nervous habit, as our eyes connected. I felt a stirring deep in my soul.

His smile lit up his face.

"You may always look at me directly when we are alone. I prefer it. However, if we're in the company of others, even other females, you must keep your eyes lowered. Do you understand?"

"Yes, Mr. Wood."

"Good. Now drink and eat the yogurt. I will feed you the strawberries."

My eyes went wide at the thought of this man feeding me but I didn't hesitate to gulp down the water and start in on the yogurt. It was strawberry and tasted like heaven.

He watched as I finished the yogurt off in no time, a smile lingering on his lips. I blushed under his scrutiny but I liked him being there. I liked having his full attention. I felt like a flower that had wilted but came alive under his gaze.

"Better?" he asked.

I nodded. "Yes, Mr. Wood. Thank you."

He smiled. "You're most welcome. As I told you earlier, I want you to be happy here."

Even though I had no reason to, I believed him. It warmed me and filled me with longing. I couldn't put my finger on what it was exactly but something inside me shifted.

He came around the counter to take a seat next to me. I kept my eyes on him as he moved, his movements fluid and confident. He flipped open the strawberry carton, took one out and brought it to my lips. I opened my mouth before biting into it. The berry's sweetness exploded in my mouth. I took another bite and then another before finishing it. Mr. Wood smiled as he reached in for another. He fed me like this until half the carton was gone. Strawberry juice dripped down my chin but I didn't care.

"Thank you, Mr. Wood," I said, meaning it. Maybe this would be less difficult than I thought.

He smiled and closed the carton.

"My pleasure, Annabelle." The sound of my name on his tongue was intoxicating.

He scooted closer to me, our knees touching, as he studied me. He ran his thumb across my bottom lip, opening my mouth slightly. I sucked in my breath as heat seeped through me. His thumb lingered on my lip, bringing it further down until my mouth was open, my tongue not sure what to do.

I watched him studying me with curiosity, like he wasn't sure what to make of me. I wasn't sure what to make of him either. My heart fluttered as he put his thumb in my mouth. I closed my mouth around it, sucking it in, swirling my tongue underneath it.

His lips curled into a half smile, his eyes intense on mine. I didn't look away as I continued to suck on his thumb, to worship it with my tongue. I felt like he was seeing straight through me, seeing all that I was. It was unnerving but amazing.

He gradually pulled out his thumb, leaving me feeling empty. He never lost eye contact with me as he leaned in and softly kissed my lips. The tenderness was so unexpected that I wanted to weep. He immediately deepened the kiss, snaking his hand through my hair, pulling me in closer, as our mouths melded together.

I let myself get lost in him, in his kiss, as his mouth devoured mine. His hands wandered lower, cupping my breasts, fingers brushing against my erect nipples. I was on fire. I couldn't get enough of him.

I didn't dare touch him but I ached to feel the muscles of his chest under my fingertips, to loosen his shirt and touch his skin. Instead, I kept my arms loose at my sides as his mouth devoured my neck, sucking in the tender skin, his fingers pulling on my nipples, sending electricity racing through me.

His mouth moved lower as he pushed my sheer dress off my shoulders, letting it drop to my lap, leaving my breasts bare for his hungry mouth. He took one nipple and then the other, sucking them in, biting gently, sending waves of arousal crashing through me. My entire body sparked under his demanding mouth, aching for more.

His hands found my ass, turning me towards him, my front facing his as his mouth fed on my aching nipples. I felt his hard cock against my inner thigh, straining against his tuxedo pants. I wanted to free it. I wanted it in my mouth, buried deep inside me, claiming me. I ached for this man, this man I just met, who had bought me at an auction, who had God knows how many women at his disposal but I didn't care. I was lost in this moment. Nothing else mattered.

He pulled my ass to the edge of the seat. My legs went around his as he entered the space between my thighs. My breathing got shallow as he unbuttoned his pants, allowing his glorious cock to spring free. I was surprised and pleased that he didn't wear undergarments as I took in his long, thick cock that pulsed with need.

He lifted my chin to bring my eyes back up to his.

"I've been wanting to do this all night," he said as he plowed into me, never losing eye contact.

I opened myself to him, wanting all of him and more, as a wave of euphoria washed over me. He watched me with intense eyes as he pushed even deeper, filling me completely, making me his. I wanted to cry out, to grab him, but I didn't dare. Instead, I gave in to the rush of emotions that threatened to overtake me, relishing his control over me, as he pulled out before slamming back into me.

His hands gripped my hips for leverage as he plowed into me again and again, his eyes never leaving mine, his expression dark and serious. I opened to him, enjoying the ease in which my body gave into his, sucking him in deeper, wanting more. I felt lost and found and never wanted it to end.

His mouth found mine, drinking me in, as his cock continued to take possession of me. His hands were on my face as if to steady me as his tongue explored my mouth, rough and sweet. I was delirious from it, intoxicated.

He increased his rhythm as the delicious sensation of his cock pumping into me sent me over the edge. I growled as an earth-shattering orgasm ripped through me. He mumbled "God yes" in my ear as he gripped my hips and plowed deeper into me. It didn't take long for him to still, pushed to the hilt, before he spilled himself inside me. I felt the warmth of him deep inside my pussy as I clamped my legs around him, wanting him to stay buried deep inside me. I wanted to claim him in my own way as he had claimed me.

"That was fucking incredible," he said in jagged breaths as he pulled out, his glorious cock limp and satiated. "I knew you'd be incredible. I knew from the moment I saw you. I may need to change your collar quicker than I intended. I can see myself being possessive of you."

My heart fluttered at his words. I wanted him to be possessive of me. I didn't believe in love—that was best left for fairy tales—but I believed in some sort of twisted monogamy. I knew this man would never be about one woman—I still had no idea how many women he housed and cared for—but I could dream that it was all about just me when we were alone. I prayed I'd be alone with him a lot during my stay.

He tucked himself back into his pants and zipped up as I remained sprawled out before him, catching my breath. He hadn't permitted me to speak so I said nothing, letting my eyes wander over his fine form, his broad chest and his handsome face.

He ran his hand down the side of my cheek as if he were admiring me.

"I want you in my bed tonight," he said. "Follow me."

FIVE

M r. Wood led me up the back stairs off the kitchen to his bedroom. I followed like a puppy as we passed the second floor and arrived on the third which opened up to an enormous foyer with white marble floors and a crystal chandelier. Mr. Wood pushed open the double oak doors to reveal his private chambers. I had to keep myself from gasping in awe.

A king-size bed with a white leather headboard dominated the space, hovering in the middle, as floor to ceiling windows looked out over a pool and the sea beyond. An impressive yacht bounced against the dock, lit up as if waiting for a party to start. A crystal chandelier hung from the middle of the ceiling, casting soft light everywhere.

Two white leather club chairs framed one wall with a tiny table between them while a sleek white dresser hugged the other wall. Two abstract paintings in cool blues and greens hung on the walls, lit by spotlights. Another door opened up into an opulent master bath with a white marble floor and God knows what else. I'm not sure what I was expecting but it wasn't this.

I stood in the middle of his room as I took it in, wondering how often he brought the other women here. I wanted to think I was special but I pushed that thought away. My only purpose here was to please, not worry about myself.

He slipped off his tuxedo jacket and laid it on one of the leather chairs before taking off his tie and unbuttoning his shirt. I watched his purposeful movements with awe and appreciation. He was a beautiful man who exuded a sense of power and authority without saying a word.

His intense green eyes flicked up to meet mine, sending a jolt of electricity through me. He discarded his shirt on the chair, leaving his muscles bare under the soft light. I wanted to run my hands over his chest, to touch his power, but I stood there waiting to be told what to do.

He slipped off his shoes before walking towards me. My dress had slipped off in the kitchen, leaving me bare before him. He drank me in as he approached, his eyes full of lust and something else.

"You're beautiful," he said as he stopped in front of me. He pushed a strand of hair off my face, tucking it behind my ear, his eyes never leaving mine. "While you're in this space, unless I tell you otherwise, I want you to speak freely and move freely. Do you understand?"

Adrenaline shot through me as I realized I'd be able to touch him as I wanted. I nodded. "Yes, Mr. Wood."

He smiled. "Good. Now that that's settled..."

Mr. Wood traced my bottom lip with his thumb, sending shivers through me. Even though he had permitted me to touch him, I found it difficult to do it. It was like an invisible binding kept me from reaching my hand up and brushing his stubble covered cheek. I stood still as his thumb opened my mouth slightly before slipping inside. I drank him in, surprised by the sweetness I found there mixed with remnants of myself.

He watched me intensely as he slipped his thumb in and out of my mouth. I sucked it in, twirling my tongue around it, sucking it in deeper as I met his gaze with a boldness I didn't know I possessed.

He seemed to enjoy watching me as I sucked his thumb, a small smile played on his lips, his eyes bright with curiosity. I wished I could read his thoughts. What was this about? What was this society about? I wanted to know more. I yearned to know more.

He smiled as he slipped his thumb out of my mouth and trailed it down my neck. He watched me as he trailed it lower, over my full breast until it brushed over one of my nipples, sending waves of pleasure through me.

Happy with my reaction, he pinched the nipple and pulled. I felt a rush of ecstasy. He laughed and pulled the other then both at once. I leaned into it, waves of sweet pleasure washing through me, my mouth slack, ready for this man to lead me wherever he wanted me to go.

"You will be a delight to train," he said as he released me.

My eyes went wide, not knowing what he meant.

Catching my reaction, he smiled. "I train all my acquisitions. It makes their transition to this lifestyle easier. It's nothing to be afraid of. In fact, you should be happy I've had the foresight to do it. I promise it won't be too horrible."

I swallowed, pushing the frightening possibilities of what that meant out of my mind. I'm here to obey and submit, I reminded myself. I don't need to concern myself with anything else. I wanted this.

"You'll learn and I think you'll like it here," he said. "You're a natural submissive and will find this lifestyle comes more naturally to you than you suspected. You've been brainwashed to be something you're not, to want something that's out of alignment with your truth. This is your opportunity to be true to yourself."

I took in his words, wondering if he was right. I had always felt out of place in my regular life, like something was missing. It had never occurred to me that it could be something like this.

"I'm not going to fuck you again tonight," he said. "We're both tired. But keep in mind that as long as you wear the black collar, you need to make yourself available to any man who wants you without question. Word will get back to me if you hesitate or, worse yet, deny anyone. This is part of your training so I expect you to fully comply. Do you understand?"

"Yes, Mr. Wood," I said as a shiver of fear ran through me. This was real. This is what I signed up for.

"Good. You'll sleep in here tonight but on the floor. Sleeping in my bed is a privilege that must be earned and you haven't been here long enough for that."

He gestured towards the plush white rug at the side of his bed. Although it looked thick and luxurious, I doubted it'd be much cushion against the slick white marble underneath.

I nodded. "Thank you, Mr. Wood. It would be my pleasure."

He smiled.

"While I want you to sleep just as you are, as a reminder of who you are, I want you to clean me with your tongue."

He unbuttoned and pushed off his tuxedo pants, leaving himself bare in front of me. His impressive cock hung to one side, semi-hard. I blinked at him, unsure what he wanted.

"On your knees," he said, offering me guidance.

I sank to my knees on the hard marble floor and took his cock in my mouth without using my hands even though I knew I could touch him. It didn't feel right so I didn't do it. Instead, I sucked his cock in, marveling at its heft in its semi-hard state and enjoyed cleaning him.

I didn't suck him in as deep as I would have normally but focused on lapping my tongue around him. I circled the bottom of his cock, ensuring I did a thorough job, before lapping at his length and finishing up at the tip. I had never given a man such a thorough cock washing with my tongue but I loved doing this for him. He didn't get hard again but he seemed to enjoy it which pleased me.

When I was done, I released him and sat back on my heels. I looked up at him because he said I could and blushed as he looked down at me with satisfaction.

"You may use the bathroom if you like. There's an extra toothbrush in the left drawer you can use. Other than that, I don't want you to clean yourself. I want you to sleep with me still on you."

I understood.

"Yes, Mr. Wood," I said before slipping into the bathroom.

THE FLOOR WAS as hard and uncomfortable as I predicted. I curled myself into a ball on the plush rug, using my arm as a pillow, but no matter what position I got in, I couldn't get comfortable. I usually slept on my side but that felt worse than anything. I ended up sleeping on my stomach, getting a few hours of sleep before the sun crept up over the horizon and blinded me. His bedroom didn't have curtains which allowed the sunlight to flood in unencumbered.

I pushed myself up and peeked over the edge of the bed. I was disappointed when I found it empty and already made. It couldn't be later than seven.

Unsure of what to do without instruction, I weighed my options. He had told me to move around freely while in this space, assuming no one else was here, but I wondered if that only applied to last night. I didn't want to displease him so soon. I never realized how challenging it would be to be fully under someone's control. When they weren't around, what was I expected to do?

Thankfully, I didn't have to wait long before Zoey pushed into the room. She wore a short sheer dress like the one I had on last night with nothing on underneath.

"Oh good, you're up," she said as she approached me. "Mr. Wood wants me to start your training today. This house works better when everyone knows what's expected of them."

She motioned for me to get up which I did slowly. I still had my shoes on since I hadn't thought to take them off, making me a few inches taller than her. She didn't seem to notice.

"We start each day with a shower and a complete shave but Mr. Wood gave explicit instructions for you to skip that today. We start each day at 7 AM despite how late you're kept up. Sometimes we have the luxury of napping during that day. That will depend on how your day goes. Our first and only priority is to be ready and available for Mr. Wood and his guests at all times. Follow me."

Zoey led me out of Mr. Wood's room and down two flights of stairs as she continued talking.

"Breakfast is on your own from eight until nine. Women always eat in the kitchen unless invited to dine in the dining room. It's self-serve but the fridge and pantry are always stocked. Josie is the house cook at the moment which means she cooks all Mr. Wood's meals. She's not your cook so don't even ask."

We arrived at the kitchen. A woman at the stove with long brown hair, a green collar and an apron was cooking an omelet as we walked in. She looked me over, clearly not happy to see me.

"This is Josie," Zoey said to me. "Josie, this is Annabelle, Mr. Wood's latest acquisition."

"Hi," I said as Josie gave me the once over.

"I'm starting her training today," Zoey said.

Zoey showed me around the kitchen while Josie cooked, showing me the pantry, the fridge and where all the plates and utensils were kept. I wasn't much of a cook—I never had the time—and was pleased to see cartons of yogurt, hard-boiled eggs and ready-made salads in the fridge along with a variety of fruits and vegetables. Zoey handed me a yogurt while she grabbed one for herself.

"We don't do coffee here but we have herbal and decaffeinated tea. Use the kettle to heat water, not the microwave. There's also no alcohol unless it's provided to you by a man. The men like to have the women alert and not under the influence of anything. With that said, there is absolutely no drug use tolerated outside of prescriptions. If you're found using drugs, they will ship you home without compensation."

I had never done drugs so this wasn't relevant to me but I was going to miss coffee.

We finished our yogurts while standing around the kitchen counter. Josie finished her omelet and scooped it onto a plate. She poured herself a glass of orange juice and sat down to eat while talking with Zoey about mundane house stuff, like who would run for groceries and when.

"We all have assigned house duties," Zoey explained, "although I'm not sure where you will fit in yet. Mr. Wood will make that decision and let us know once your training is complete. While you're training, you don't need to worry about it."

I wanted to ask so many questions but since Zoey had shut me down yesterday, I didn't bother. They had to know I was curious about how everything worked but resigned myself to learning via my training since that seemed to be the proper protocol.

It surprised me how comfortable I felt being naked in front of other people. I think it helped that both Zoey and Josie were also exposed. Josie wore an apron but with nothing underneath.

"We're going to the library," Zoey told Josie as she threw her yogurt in the trash and put the spoon in the dishwasher. I followed suit and followed her out.

Zoey led me through a contemporary living room with a white marble fireplace and a white pool table before leading me into the library. I had suspected that library was code for crazy bondage dungeon but it was a library lined with white bookcases filled with leather-bound books. A modern white desk sat in front of the window with a white leather swivel office chair. A sleek white laptop sat on top along with a crystal lamp and a crystal vase filled with red roses.

"Have a seat," Zoey said, indicating the floor next to one of the white leather club chairs.

I kneeled with my knees shut and my hands on my lap.

"Very good," Zoey said as she stood in front of me. "That was a trick command and you passed."

Zoey kneeled opposite me. I felt like two women about to share secrets and wished that were the case.

"You are to sit on the floor unless instructed otherwise. Mr. Wood may permit you to sit wherever you like at some point while in his house. He's done this with me and Josie which is why you saw Josie sit at the counter. However, when you're in public or at someone else's residence, you will resort back to sitting on the floor unless otherwise given permission. This rule helps us to remember our place and that we're only here to please.

"Mr. Wood will give you a position within this household but while you're in training, you won't have one. You will be expected to clean up after yourself and keep your room and bathroom clean. No one acts as a maid here—we're all responsible for the cleanliness of this house.

"You'll notice women in all sorts of attire or no attire at all. I know they went over this with you during your intake but I'm reiterating it so you understand our society. During your training, you will be kept naked with shoes only unless Mr. Wood wants you dressed differently. Again, this is to remind you of your place and also to allow easy access to your body from whoever wants it.

"As part of your first day of training, I'm going to take you for a walk through town and then out to lunch. You may be given an allowance—that's up to Mr. Wood—to spend as you want. There are several cafés and fine dining establishments on the island along with other shops tailored for women. Mr. Wood doesn't mind you spending your free time pursuing any interests you like as long as they're in line with what the island considers womanly pursuits. Think flower arranging, playing the piano, anything crafty, reading, mani/pedis, etcetera. He may also have you work but that'll be up to him."

SIX

Zoey and I left the house after our talk. She wore a short sheer dress while I had on nothing but platform heels. The warm breeze kissed my skin as we stepped outside. It thrilled me to be outside naked. The sun peeked out behind a cloud, drenching me with its warmth. I wanted to throw my head back and bask in it but needed to keep up with Zoey who was walking at a quick clip.

Mr. Wood's house wasn't too far from town. We walked along a wide sidewalk that was sandwiched between the expansive lawns of enormous homes and the narrow street. Majestic palm trees lined the sidewalk, reminding me of a tropical paradise. I spotted a few women outside gardening—some naked, others with short skirts and tops. They seemed carefree, something I longed to be.

As we got closer to town, mostly women crowded the sidewalks, carrying bags, running errands, oblivious to their states of undress. I only felt self-conscious for a moment as we joined the crowd, unused to being out in public with nothing on, but I quickly adapted, feeling more comfortable being surrounded by other undressed women.

Women of all shapes and sizes filled the streets, some slender, some curvier. None of that seemed to matter as they went about their day which I found refreshing. Very few men were out which made me wonder where they all were and what they did during the day. I had no idea what Mr. Wood was doing today. I wanted to ask Zoey but I knew she'd tell me that Mr. Wood would let me know when he felt it was appropriate. Zoey wasn't exactly Ms. Warm and Fuzzy. It made me wonder if I'd be able to make any women friends while I was here. I hoped so.

As I watched the other women mill about, it seemed like some of them were paired off or in trios, chatting away like women anywhere. Maybe that's why I didn't see any men—maybe this was a space allowed only for women so they could relax and talk without worrying about the men.

I shook my head as I took in that thought. I wasn't the most talkative person but it would take some getting used to not talking when a man was present. I assumed the restaurants and shops were staffed by women otherwise the women wouldn't be able to converse. Plus, I couldn't imagine a man serving women here. That would go against everything this society stood for.

Zoey glanced back at me as if to make sure I was following her. I found it odd she didn't want to walk side by side but maybe this was her way of establishing some sort of hierarchy over me. I didn't mind. It allowed me the chance to look around without worrying about her.

Zoey stopped when we reached a little grocery store. An array of fresh fruits and vegetables spilled out onto the sidewalk, tempting shoppers.

"This is the only grocery on the island," Zoey told me as she picked up a basket and led me inside. "Sometimes you'll be asked to fetch groceries for the household or you can come here to collect whatever it is you want with your allowance. As you probably noticed, only women work in the shops and restaurants, all of which are owned and operated by the men who live here. Occasionally you'll see a man in one of the shops but only if he's checking up on something, otherwise they're men-free zones."

The inside of the grocery store was just like any other small grocery store. A section of fruits and vegetables greeted us when we walked in, giving way to a small deli counter, bakery and further back a meat counter. The inside aisles contained all the basics while the dairy and frozen sections were off to the left. In the back was a cooler containing a variety of special import beers connected to a vast wine and liquor room.

Zoey gave me a tour of the store while she picked up a few things as we went along. Since I had no money, I couldn't buy anything despite my sudden craving for strawberries. No men were present so we could talk freely but Zoey didn't say much other than noting where everything was located. I wondered how long it'd take until this became second nature. I also wondered how difficult it would be to assimilate back to the real world once this experience was over.

Zoey checked out, chatting with the clerk who she seemed to know. It dawned on me that the island wasn't all that big and at some point I would probably know most everyone, too.

Back outside, the sun had disappeared behind some clouds. Zoey led me past several women's clothing stores before ducking into a bookstore. I loved to read so I was delighted to have a bookstore on the island. Zoey browsed the magazines while I explored the rest of the store. It was set up like any other bookstore with its rows of shelves but I quickly discovered that most of the books leaned toward subjects that were considered womanly, such as cookbooks, sewing books and bodice-ripping romance novels.

I enjoyed romances as much as the next woman so flipped through a few while I waited for Zoey to get whatever she needed. It didn't surprise me when the romances I picked up were about forceful alpha men who dominated and ruled over submissive women. It made sense that they'd want to keep this mentality going while the women were on the island. It made me wonder if Mr. Wood's library had books I'd be allowed to read.

Zoey found me browsing the romances with a couple of magazines tucked under her arm.

"Do you like to read?" she asked.

I nodded. "It's one of my favorite things."

She smiled, one of the first smiles I'd seen from her. "Mr. Wood will appreciate that about you. He likes intelligent women who are open to learning. I have a few novels back at the house if you want to borrow them."

"I'd love that," I said, surprised at her generosity. "Thank you."

"No problem," she said.

She paid for her magazines before we spilled back out onto the street.

We walked a bit before crossing over into what felt like a different section of town. We were suddenly out of what I considered the women's section and walked right into the men's section. The women went silent as the men's voices carried out onto the sidewalk.

Restaurants spilled onto the sidewalks with their crisp white umbrellas covering round wood tables and tan wicker chairs. Most of the women were standing or kneeling next to their men as the men ate, drank and conversed. I remembered not to make eye contact with anyone as Zoey led us down the street. I had a million questions but knew I couldn't voice them now. I tried to store them away for later.

I was more conscious of my nakedness as men watched us as we walked by. Zoey seemed oblivious but it was new to me. A blush crept up my chest as we walked further into the men's section, past bars with big-screen TVs and long oak bars.

I heard catcalls as we walked but was unsure who they were directed to. We weren't the only women out but the number of women had thinned once we reached this side of town. It looked like women were able to traverse freely around the island, something I appreciated, but it also seemed like the women kept more to the women's section and I could understand why.

I felt vulnerable traveling in this section without Mr. Wood's protection. At least Zoey wore a yellow collar. My black collar allowed anything and I had no idea what anything could entail.

A sense of unease crept up my back as we continued walking past various bars and restaurants on one side and the sparkling sea on the other. I spotted a harbor in the distance with massive yachts bobbing in the water. I wondered if Mr. Wood owned a boat and, if he did, would I get the chance to go out on it. I found being out on the water soothing but rarely had the chance to go out once I got older.

Zoey slipped into one of the bars at the far side of town, close to the harbor and across from the glistening sea. High tables and a long bar greeted us as we passed through the gate. Most of the bar was outside with only a small portion tucked inside towards the back. Palm trees jutted out in between tables, creating a maze effect along with a sense of privacy.

I kept my eyes lowered as we passed tables filled primarily with men. Hands found my ass, squeezing and slapping it as we passed, while a few grabbed at my tits. My nipples hardened at the attention while my mind shot between being mortified and turned on. I watch Zoey get her fair share of gropes. She took it in stride, not stopping and not reacting.

She stopped at a high table towards the back, nestled in near the bar and a hallway that escaped into the depths of the building. She didn't sit but stood at the table and I did the same. She grabbed a menu from behind a row of condiments and indicated for me to do the same. The menu consisted of the typical bar fare: burgers, sandwiches, a couple of steaks. I had no money but assumed Zoey was paying since she brought me here.

A waitress with long flowing brown hair with gold highlights and a green collar approached us. She had on a sheer frilly apron and nothing else except for Lucite heels. Her nipples were hard and pointed right at us as she descended on our table. I couldn't help but take in her ample breasts, flat stomach and bare mound.

She nodded at us, her pen poised. Zoey went first, pointing out what she wanted on the menu. The waitress nodded then turned to me. I pointed at the turkey club and a soda, finding it odd and slightly exciting not to be permitted to speak.

Once the waitress left, Zoey gave me a questioning look as if to ask what did I think about all this. I wasn't sure how to respond without talking so I shrugged. I had no idea. I was feeling overwhelmed and excited and interested to see how it would play out. I didn't want to become jaded but I looked forward to a time when I felt more comfortable being in town naked.

Our waitress returned with our drinks. We clinked glasses before taking a sip. I appreciated the coolness as it slipped down my throat. I hadn't realized how parched I was. Drinking and food were the last things on my mind since arriving. I understood how many of the women stayed so thin while being here. Food felt like an afterthought.

While we waited for our order, two men came by our table. They were older with greying temples and rounder bellies. They wore khakis and polo shirts as if they were taking a break from a round of golf. One man slipped behind Zoey, his hands finding their way to her nipples, while the other hovered behind me.

I sucked in my breath as cool hands came around my sides and pulled at my nipples. Both men pinched and pulled at our nipples, not saying a word, as if they were testing us out. The man behind me cupped both my breast as if weighing their heft, as if making an important decision about whether I was worth his effort.

It felt strange and exciting to be randomly groped in public. I lowered my eyes but could see Zoey's breasts being measured before her man's hands wandered lower.

The man behind me pulled at my nipples one more time, pinching them to the point of pain, before his hands found my ass. He caressed each cheek, massaging it, which I found pleasurable, before his fingers snaked their way into my wetness. His breath was hot on my neck as he pushed his fingers into me, bending me forward so my nipples grazed the table, my breasts dangling, giving him better access.

I forgot about Zoey and being in the back of a bar as the fingers worked against my clit, causing an ache deep inside me to blossom and overtake my senses.

"What a good bitch," he said into my neck before pulling his fingers out.

I snapped back to reality, flushed with embarrassment, as the man pushed my head down onto the table. I heard him unzip before he pushed his fat cock into me. I gasped at the invasion. He grabbed my hair as he pushed himself in, stilling when he reached my capacity.

My pussy expanded to accommodate him, spread wide. My breathing became shallow as he pumped in and out, taking me like I was nothing, using me like the slut I was there to be. Arousal swirled through me along with conflicting emotions as I was taken and used, fucked hard from behind. I heard him grunting with the effort as I panted, taking in all he offered, my body flooding with waves of pleasure.

"Fuck me," he grunted into my ear before pushing in one last time, spilling inside me.

He pulled out and slapped my ass.

"Thanks, cunt," he said before walking away.

I blinked into the wood table, unsure whether to straighten up yet. I felt ridiculous in my current position but was unsure how long I needed to wait before it was OK to move.

I waited a few minutes as my breathing returned to normal before easing myself up. I felt his semen leak down my inner thigh. I felt disgusting while also feeling whole. Zoey was studying me, her man gone as well. I knew the yellow collar meant she could only be groped so she hadn't been fucked, too. I wondered how much she watched.

Our food arrived a moment later. The waitress winked at us as she left. I wondered how many times she got fucked during a shift and if I were to be sent to work, how many times would that happen to me.

I didn't lose any time digging in. I was starving and had no idea how long I would have to eat before some other man came along to use me. The sandwich tasted amazing. I gulped down my soda and smiled when the waitress brought me more.

Zoey and I exchanged looks while we ate but I had no idea what any of them meant. It was weird not to talk during our meal but I also found it refreshing. I was never a big fan of small talk and was thankful I didn't need to attempt to keep the conversation going.

I was pleased when I was able to finish my sandwich without another interruption. I started to understand why Zoey sat us in the back corner. A few other women were sprinkled in among the men but most of them looked attached to someone which made them more off-limits than us.

Zoey paid when the waitress came around to collect our plates. I wanted to thank her but gave her a little smile instead, hoping she understood.

I followed Zoey out of the bar, conscious of the stickiness between my legs. More hands groped us as we walked out. One man pulled my hair, causing me to stop, while he slipped his fingers into my wet pussy. I gasped at the intrusion, embarrassed by my wetness. His hand released my hair while his fingers probed my pussy. He pulled on a nipple and laughed as my pussy clenched around his fingers.

Zoey stopped to wait for me, hands finding their way around her body, as the man played with my clit and tits. I kept my eyes lowered while I allowed him to use my body, reminding myself that I had asked for this experience as my body flooded with shame and arousal.

He pushed on my back, bending me over at the waist. I rested my hands on knees, my tits dangling, as he pulled out his fingers and replaced them with his cock. He wasn't as wide as the last guy but thin and long. He slid in easily, grabbing my hips for leverage. He fucked me quick and hard, letting out a groan as he came inside me.

"Fucking good, slut," he said as he pulled out, spilling his semen down my leg.

He slapped my ass which I took as a dismissal. Zoey gave me a slight nod as I unfolded myself as if to say I did well. I walked away from the man without looking back, surprised by how willing and receptive my body had been. Arousal cycled through me as we left the bar and wandered back up the street the way we came.

I received more ass slaps and nipple pinches as we walked. I knew I must look a mess with my hair wild and come running down my legs. I felt loose and relaxed as we walked, as if I had been properly oiled, which I supposed I had been. My mind buzzed with what had just happened, how easily I had given myself over to these men without question, without hesitation. I knew this what was expected of me but to have it happen and for me to so easily go along with it, that was something else. I felt christened, initiated. I had stepped into my role here and a big part of me loved it.

SEVEN

Back at the house, Zoey let me shower. She told me she had received a message from Mr. Wood that he wanted me showered and fresh for the evening. I showered in the my bathroom. The bathtub was calling me but I didn't want to get in trouble over something so trivial.

The warm water felt soothing against my skin. I was happy to wash away all the hands that touched and fondled me today along with the two men that had fucked me. I wasn't a prude but I had never fucked two men on the same day before and never a man I didn't at least have a drink with first.

Zoey didn't say much once we arrived back at the women's side of town. She asked how I was and I said fine. What else could I say? My mind wasn't fully comprehending all that happened and my body felt well used and loose. I had to agree with everyone who claimed that having sex increased a woman's libido—I felt horny as hell. It was no wonder since I hadn't come. I rarely came from penetration alone and the men who fucked me didn't attempt to get me off.

I wondered whether coming was permissible as I washed my body, enjoying the way the creamy soap felt against my smooth skin. I wanted to touch myself, to get myself off, but knew that probably wasn't allowed. It was another thing I wanted to ask Zoey about although I doubted she'd tell me.

Josie hadn't been around when we entered the back door off the kitchen. I was curious about her and what she did with her days. I also wondered if there were more women in the house. Zoey made it sound like I would be part of a harem.

I rinsed before shutting the water off and wrapping myself in a plush white towel. I could get used to this. I wasn't missing working for a crappy job I hated in an overcrowded town one bit.

Back in the bedroom, a long white sheer gown was draped across the bed along with sparkly silver platform heels. Happy to not have to decide what to wear, I slipped the dress on, enjoying the way it hugged my curves and showed off my form.

I returned to the bathroom to pull my long auburn hair into a loose topknot, leaving a few stray wisps around my face. I searched the drawers until I discovered a variety of high-end makeup. I sat at the vanity and applied a soft foundation, smoky eye shadow, subtle blush, black mascara and red matte lipstick.

I admired myself in the full-length mirror once I finished. My eyes sparkled as I took myself in. I wasn't this girl a week ago. I felt radiant and beautiful in a way I hadn't before.

The dress left nothing to the imagination. My erect nipples pushed against the sheer fabric as if demanding attention while my freshly waxed pussy looked ready for more action. I couldn't believe how aroused I felt. My body shimmered with it. I was excited to see Mr. Wood again. At least I hoped I'd be seeing him tonight.

Unsure what to do with myself, I kneeled on the plush white carpet in the bedroom and sat back on my heels with my hands open in my lap the way I was instructed. My heart hammered with excitement and nerves as I waited, my eyes lowered, facing the closed door. I wondered if Zoey would collect me or if Mr. Wood himself would do the honor.

About a half-hour later, Zoey opened the door. I felt disappointed it wasn't Mr. Wood but tried not to show it.

"Oh good," Zoey said as she approached me, "Mr. Wood will be pleased you waited in the kneeling position."

Since we were alone, I looked up at her, surprised she was carrying a little black bag. She wore an elegant sheer blue gown like mine, her hair pulled back, highlighting her slender neck.

"I brought you a few more things," Zoey said, indicating the bag. "Mr. Wood wants you to wear a few more things for tonight's event as part of your training. I already reported how compliant you were this afternoon with the men at the bar and Mr. Wood was extremely pleased. You should be happy about that."

My heart zinged with pleasure. It thrilled me to know that Mr. Wood had been thinking about me.

I watched as Zoey pulled out a funny-looking metal contraption with leather straps, a blindfold and a couple of leather cuffs. Nerves snaked through my stomach.

"Don't worry," Zoey said as she approached me. "None of this will hurt. The blindfold will enhance your experience. It's also another reminder that you're not the one in control."

Like I could forget.

She started by inserting the double circle metal contraption in my mouth, which held it open, and latched it around my head.

"This is an open mouth gag," she explained as she latched it. "It will allow anyone easy access to your mouth."

I felt ridiculous with my mouth pried open but knew I didn't have a choice. If this was how Mr. Wood wanted me, this was how I would be. My mouth started to feel dry within minutes as I breathed through my mouth, conscious of the saliva pooling under my tongue.

"Don't be surprised if you start to drool with this thing," she said. "It's part of the experience."

I blinked at her, not sure how I felt about that.

Before I could protest, she slipped the blindfold over my eyes, sending me into darkness.

"Stand," she said.

I pushed myself up, careful not to stumble on my new heels.

As soon as I straightened, she placed cuffs on my wrists and secured them behind my back. I felt like a kinky prisoner, arrested for a crime I didn't commit. I breathed in through my mouth and reminded myself that I wanted this. I wanted the experience of being submissive, to give myself over completely, and here I was.

Zoey led me by the elbow, talking me through each step. My mind focused on not falling as I walked. I was hyper-aware as the sound of voices grew louder. I felt nervous and excited, reduced to nothing more than an object to be admired and used. It felt freeing and scary all at once.

"Just go with whatever happens tonight," Zoey whispered in my ear. "This is part of your training and how Mr. Wood will decide whether to keep you."

I hadn't thought about Mr. Wood not keeping me. This increased the stakes for tonight. I needed to please him now more than ever. I had developed a fondness for Mr. Wood and didn't want to be at the mercy of anyone else. I needed time to adjust to this new way of life.

I heard doors open before the voices grew louder. People cheered and clapped. I felt myself reddened as I visualized a room full of strangers taking me in as we entered. Zoey kept her hands on my elbow, steering me through the crowd. No one touched me which surprised me until I realized that Mr. Wood must be present. It was proper etiquette for men to ask another man's permission before touching their women. The thought of Mr. Wood watching me made my heart flutter.

Zoey stopped, squeezed my elbow, and then abandoned me. I stood there, a million thoughts flooding my brain, as I wondered what I was supposed to do. Voices swirled around me, laughing, talking, but I couldn't pick up on any particular conversation.

My mouth had dried out from being forced open. I blinked behind the blindfold as if that would help me see. I focused on standing straight, tits out, as my nerves threatened to overtake me.

I took in a deep breath as I tried to clear my mind. Think nothing, I told myself. You are nothing. You are only here to please. Be blank. My mind is blank. I am blank.

The words helped me relax. I repeated them over and over, like a mantra, to keep my thoughts from flailing.

I was so lost in the mantra that I jumped when someone grazed my nipple then tweaked it. I heard a deep laugh as the hand went for the other one, grazing then tweaking. My nipples hardened as he continued to play with them, pulling and pinching, the pain radiating straight to my pussy as I felt myself become aroused.

"She's exquisite," a deep voice said as he continued to play with my sensitive nipples. "I wish I had been at that auction."

Mr. Wood laughed. "That would have been unfortunate for me. I'm happy you were otherwise detained."

"If I could stay on this island 24/7, you know I would," the deep voice said. "Unfortunately, some of us are needed on the mainland."

"Your last acquisition wasn't too shabby," Mr. Wood said. "I always enjoy seeing her around town."

The deep voice laughed. "She was a wonderful acquisition. She's been adjusting beautifully to life here. I'm hoping she decides to stay."

"When is her contract up?" Mr. Wood asked.

"Next month. I had offered to move her to a white collar—that's how serious I am—but she wanted to stay with the green. I think she likes the attention when in town."

"She's a natural submissive," Mr. Wood said. "That doesn't surprise me."

"What about this one?" the deep voice asked as he pulled hard on my nipples, causing me to gasp. "Think you'll be selling her anytime soon?"

I felt a hand on my ass, caressing it, almost being tender.

"We shall see," Mr. Wood said. "That will depend on her."

The hand on my ass roamed further down until it slipped between my legs. I widened my stance to accommodate it. A finger slid against my wetness a few times before dipping into my pussy. The finger probed before hooking me from behind. I stood there trying not to react as my body flushed with arousal.

The finger pulled out before Mr. Wood commanded, "Kneel."

I sank to my knees, feeling the hard, cool marble against my legs. I sat back on my heels, keeping my back straight, with my hands at my sides.

I heard a zipper before a cock slid into my open mouth. I tasted the pre-cum at once, finding it odd to have a cock in my mouth without being able to suck it. The metal cage in my mouth prevented it. I did my best to lick at the cock but it was hopeless. All I could do was sit there as the cock moved in and out of my mouth, trying to hit the back of my throat with each thrust.

A hand brushed the wisp of hair from my face while another pulled at my nipples. The cock continued to work itself in and out. I felt drool leak down my face, dripping on my breasts, making me feel like I was no longer in control of my body. The cock increased its pace while hands grabbed my head, pushing me deeper onto the cock. I felt it hitting the back of my throat, gagging me, but I controlled my gag reflex, opening my throat to the assault.

A couple more thrusts and the cock spilled itself down my open throat. The hands on my head kept me positioned so I couldn't back out, not that I would have. I accepted all of it as I imagined I would be accepting everything else in this world—without question. I wanted to experience this, to be open and available, to be nothing more than a receptacle for cocks.

Once the cock drained itself, it pulled out, dripping come down my chin and onto my breasts. I would have thanked him if I could have talked. Before I could react, another cock slipped into my open mouth. This happened again and again until I lost count. Cocks drained themselves in my mouth, spilling my drool along with their come down my front. I knew I was a mess and felt a mixture of shame and arousal as they used me again and again.

Conversations continued over my head as my mouth took in cock after cock but it didn't take long before the voices melded into a pleasant hum that I could no longer understand. My mind became almost brainless, empty. I had become the inconsequential female I had always wanted to be—open and receptive and not much else.

The cocks continued for some time. Men pinched and pulled at my nipples, grabbing my hair to thrust themselves in deeper, but none of them said a word to me outside of "suck it, slut" or "good girl" when they finished.

I lost Mr. Wood's voice in the hum of voices but I knew it didn't matter. This was what he wanted of me and that was all that mattered.

My mouth ached as they used me again and again. I felt myself slip into a trance, oblivious of time and the number of cocks depositing themselves down my throat. At some point, they slipped my dress off my shoulders. It pooled around my waist. My knees had gone numb on the hard marble and I knew it'd be impossible to stand. My nipples ached and throbbed from all the handling while my pussy dripped, aching for release and feeling neglected.

After a while, the cocks abandoned my mouth. I felt empty and blank, blissfully zoned out. It wasn't until someone touched my elbow to help me stand that I came out of my haze. My legs were stiff as I gradually straightened them. They had fallen asleep and tingled. I felt my dress fall to the floor as the hand at my elbow tugged at me to follow. I tried stepping out of my dress before following, my heels clicking against the marble until they fell on soft carpet.

"Step up," Zoey said in my ear. "We're taking steps."

I took step after step until she told me we were at the top. She led me a little more before stopping.

"Kneel," she said.

I sank onto the plush carpet, thankful for the added cushion.

I felt Zoey unhook the contraption around my mouth and pull it off. I swallowed, my mouth full of leftover come.

"Drink," Zoey said.

I opened my mouth and felt a straw. I drank the water, thinking nothing had ever tasted so good. She allowed me to drain the water which felt like a lot.

"Do you need to use the bathroom?" she asked.

I considered it a moment. It had been the furthest thing from my mind. I hadn't eaten or drank much today so I felt OK. I shook my head.

"Ok," she said. "Wait here."

Butterflies danced in my stomach as I heard her leave, closing the door behind her. I blinked behind the blindfold and took in a few deep breaths, calming my nerves. Even though I had already been through a lot today, I had no idea how much more I would be asked to endure.

My legs ached underneath me but I didn't dare move. I did my best to sit up straight, to look as pleasing as possible, while I waited.

"You did well today," Mr. Wood said from across the room. He had been in the room this whole time, probably watching me. "I'm very pleased."

It warmed my heart to hear him say those words. I beamed with pride.

I heard him get up and approach me. He traced his fingers along my cheek.

"You're a mess and I love seeing you this way," he said as his fingers tangled in my hair. "Perhaps I should keep you like this always —decorated with come."

I shivered at the thought.

"You have one last cock to suck tonight," he said as I heard him unzip. "Mine."

I opened my mouth and waited. I heard him chuckle.

"You are an eager one," he said. "I appreciate that."

He slid his thick cock in my mouth, filling me in the most delightful way. I opened my throat wide for him, wanting to accommodate as much of him as possible. He let out a soft groan as he gripped my head and pulled me in closer. I felt his cock tickle the back of my throat but I willed myself not to gag. I opened myself up for him as much as I could.

"Good girl," he said as he pumped himself in and out of my mouth. I tried sucking him in, keeping him there, but he was too strong and started fucking my throat at a clipped pace. I accepted it, accepted my place, as he ravished my mouth, happy to please him in this way.

I kept my hands at my sides even though I longed to touch him, to feel the muscles working in his thighs, but I didn't dare. He kept his hands on my head as he pumped into me, gaining momentum, fucking my mouth harder, rougher. My mouth ached as my tongue worked on him, giving him everything I had.

He let out another groan before spilling himself down my throat. I took it all, grateful for it, happy I could please him. He slowly pulled out, leaving me feeling empty once again.

"God, that was amazing," he said. "You have a gift."

He took off the blindfold. I blinked as my eyes adjusted to the brightness of the room. We were in his bedroom. I was on the rug where I had slept. I looked up into his intense green eyes. He smiled at me, sending a ripple of pleasure through me.

"Stand."

He held out his hand to help me. My legs had gone numb again and it took me a moment to balance myself. Once I was standing, he bent down to unbuckle my platform shoes before pulling them off. I felt short standing in front of him without the heels and had to look up even more to catch his gaze. He brushed his hand against my cheek in a caress before moving to retrieve something from his side table.

He came back with a small pink dildo with a wide flat base.

"Spread your feet apart."

I complied and watched as he positioned the dildo at my pussy and pushed it in. I was wet beyond belief so I gave no resistance and loved how it filled me. He clicked on something in his pocket and the dildo came to life, vibrating inside me. He moved through various speeds and rhythms until he came to one that made me squirm.

"You'll wear this tonight and maybe for a few days," he told me. "It will keep you on the edge of an orgasm. You have permission to orgasm as many times as you want but you'll find it's in your best interest to hold back as much as you can. This thing won't turn off just because you orgasm and I assure you it will become too much if you do."

My eyes went wide as my body hummed around the vibrator, the pressure already building deep in my abdomen, wanting so badly to release.

"This is part of your training," he said. "Fight the orgasm as much as you can. You will sleep in the guest room this evening, on the floor. Zoey will collect you in the morning for breakfast. You are not to shower until told to do so. Do you understand?"

"Yes, Mr. Wood," I said, my body feeling overwhelmed.

"You may go," he said, dismissing me.

EIGHT

The night was torture. I wanted to come so many times but I managed to hold back. I knew he was right that once I orgasmed, the vibration would be too much and I wasn't ready to experience what too much felt like. It was already challenging enough to sleep but I did, waking up every so often to toss and turn and wish the vibrations would stop.

Zoey woke me up in the morning. Bright sunshine poured in through the curtainless windows blinding me.

"Mr. Wood said you may shower and then to come down for breakfast," she said after I blinked at her a few times. "You can take the vibrator out to use the toilet but then you must put it back in."

"How long will this go on?" I asked as I pulled myself up.

Zoey smiled. "You know the answer to that—only Mr. Wood can tell you."

I groaned. I knew she'd say that.

After Zoey left, I used the toilet then took a cool shower, washing off the dried come that was caked over my breasts and stomach. I hadn't realized what a mess I was until I started washing it off. The water felt amazing. I probably stayed under the spray too long but I didn't care. I felt my cares and worries wash away with the water and it was exactly what I needed.

Last night, after the buzz of being used so thoroughly wore off, my mind flooded with questions. What the fuck was I doing here? Why had I agreed to come? I knew I was more than this, more than a body to be used. While the thought of being used excited me, I wanted more. I needed more. It was only day three and I wasn't sure I could last another week.

I pushed the vibrator back in after I showered. It pulsed at an erratic rhythm that kept me on edge. I felt horny and sore all over. I could have slept for a million years and still wanted more.

Unsure what to wear and since nothing was laid out like yesterday, I slipped on my platform heels with nothing else and headed to the kitchen. Josie was at the stove making eggs dressed in an apron with a short sheer dress underneath. Her hair was pulled up and she wore heels. She looked me over when I walked in. I was no longer embarrassed about being naked in front of people but I didn't appreciate her scrutiny.

"Vibrator day, right?" Josie asked as I went to the fridge for yogurt and fruit.

I nodded as I stood at the counter, digging into the yogurt.

"Don't worry. It gets easier. Mr. Wood likes to throw a lot at you at once but then it'll ease up and become somewhat normal."

"Are there other women in Mr. Wood's house?" I asked, hoping Josie would be more willing to talk than Zoey had been.

"Not at the moment," Josie said as she continued cooking. "There were a couple of other women here the week before you arrived but one was sold and the other went home."

"Is it common for Mr. Wood to sell women?" I asked, worried that he'd sell me, too.

"It's not common but it happens," Josie said as she plated her eggs and joined me at the island. "But this woman wanted to be sold. She couldn't tell Mr. Wood that but it was obvious she was better suited for one of his friends."

"That's a consideration?" I asked, surprised.

Josie laughed. "Of course it is. These men aren't animals. They want what's best for the women. They want this society to work and the only way it will is if the women are happy. The women come here voluntarily. There's no tolerance for anyone who doesn't want to be here. All a woman has to do to leave is report to the head office—that's where you were first brought in—and tell them she wants to leave and they'll put her on the first flight out. It's up to the men to determine what level of this lifestyle each woman can handle. That's why there's a collar system. It's an easy way for other men to know each woman's level."

"I thought the collar system was based on seniority or something, like you move up the levels the longer you're here."

Josie took a sip of tea. "That's not how it works. The collar system is based on individual needs and preferences, not seniority. For example, I've been here longer than Zoey yet she has a yellow collar and I have a green one. She has less tolerance for being fucked by anyone where I get off on it."

I stared at her, letting her words sink in.

"Why do I have a black collar then? I thought it was because I was new. Do they think I need to be at the lowest level?"

Josie laughed at the horrified expression on my face.

"Most women start with the black collar and get switched as their man learns more about their preferences—that's true—however some women will start at other collar levels because the intake professionals don't believe they could tolerate the lower levels well. You must have shown that you have a high tolerance for submission to be given a black collar."

I felt my cheeks redden. I thought everyone started with a black collar and worked their way up. But, no, they thought I wanted to be at the lowest level, that I would get off on it, and so far I had done nothing but prove them right. Was I really that depraved?

"Don't let it spook you," Josie said. "It's a good thing to have a high tolerance for this lifestyle. It will make you that much more valuable and that much more able to stick around."

"How long have you been here?" I asked as I finished up my yogurt.

"I've been on the island almost six months and in this house about four," Josie said. "I bounced around a little before landing here."

"Are you going to renew your contract?" I asked, unsure if I could make it another week.

"Hell yeah," she said. "This is the best thing to happen to me. I love it here. I'm able to cook as much as I want, I have the freedom to do just about whatever I want and, if I want to get fucked, all I have to do is wander over to the men's side of town."

She made it sound so simple.

"Don't overthink it," Josie said. "Just go with it. You must have signed up to be here for more than just the money. Let yourself give in to it. If nothing else, you'll have an interesting and fun experience to share with your friends back home when you return or, if you're lucky, you'll discover that this is where you're meant to be."

I took in her words. Was this where I was meant to be? I came here to try it out, to experience something I had only dreamed of experiencing, to let myself be someone new and to escape my life for a while. I always had every intention of returning to my previous life but now, who knew. Would I want to stay? I couldn't imagine it.

"What are you up to now?" Josie asked as I finished my yogurt.

I shrugged. "I don't know. I wasn't given any instructions except that it was OK to shower."

"Well, no news is freedom around here," Josie said with a smile. "Sounds like you have some time off. I could show you around more if you want. I'm sure Zoey showed you some things yesterday but there's so much more for you to see."

"Shouldn't I stay here and wait for Zoey or Mr. Wood to tell me what to do?" I asked. "I'm still in training. I'm sure they'll have something they want from me."

"I believe Zoey left for the day," Josie said, "and Mr. Wood is usually gone all day, too, leaving you and me free to explore. Come on, it'll be fun. Otherwise, what are you going to do? Sit in your room all day?"

I wanted to explore more of the island and Josie seemed like she'd be a lot more fun than Zoey. At least Josie was willing to answer my questions.

"OK, sure," I said. "Sounds fun."

JOSIE STRIPPED off the apron and her short sheer dress so we were both naked girls on the town. It felt liberating this time to be walking arm in arm with nothing on but heels. The vibrator hummed away in my pussy, a constant reminder of my sex and my purpose here. It caused me to walk with more sway as I tried to hit just the right spots with each step.

We walked through the women's side of town before crossing over into the men's. This time I took in the appreciative glances even as I kept my eyes lowered. Men catcalled. Some tweaked a nipple or slapped an ass. I was getting used to this random attention and even craved it. Each touch, pinch or slap was a reminder of my true purpose in this society and, for whatever reason, it made me crazy horny. The vibrator wasn't helping either.

Josie walked us out to the docks where enormous yachts bobbed in the calm water. A few men were acting as deckhands which surprised me but it made sense those roles would be too much for most women. The men were helping to secure one of the larger yachts to the dock, looping ropes around the cleats, yelling instructions to each other.

Since there were men present, I couldn't ask Josie questions although I was beyond curious to know why she had taken us here. A frisson of fear snaked through me as she took us out onto the wide dock, closer to the boats and the men securing the lines. This felt more dangerous than hanging out in one of the men-dominated bars since who knew where these yachts could take us. I imagined us being kidnapped and taken from this place, never to return.

I touched Josie's elbow. She turned to me and smiled. I'm sure she could see the fear in my eyes. She gave a little nod towards one of the yachts and a look that I guessed was supposed to reassure me. I felt anything but reassured but I followed her, the vibrator buzzing away, my body humming.

She turned at one of the planks leading out to a massive yacht. She walked down it as I trailed behind her, my heart hammering, my heels feeling impractical and the vibrator annoying. She grabbed my hand to make sure I stayed with her as she pulled me through sliding doors that opened automatically for use and into an elegant dining and living room combo. Two older men sat inside smoking cigars. They stopped talking when they saw us.

"Ah, Josie, I see you brought me a little plaything," one man said. I relaxed slightly when I realized she knew them but tensed again when his words registered in my brain.

"Yes, sir," she said as she walked closer to them, her hips swaying. "This is Annabelle, Mr. Wood's latest acquisition. I thought you'd enjoy meeting her."

It surprised me that she spoke but then I remembered that they must have given her prior permission because neither seemed upset by it. I, on the other hand, kept my eyes lowered as I inched towards them, right on Josie's heels, feeling uncertain and timid.

"Ah, I heard about her," the other one said. "She made quite the impression last night."

My face reddened as I wondered if these men were at the gathering last night. I probably had sucked both their cocks and didn't know it.

One got up and approached me. I kept my eyes lowered, my stance straight.

"Mr. Wood lucked out with this one," he said as he grazed my nipple with the back of his hand, causing it to harden. "So responsive."

"Mr. Wood has her on the vibrator today," Josie said. My face reddened more as the pulse of the vibrator continued to drive me insane. "I'm sure she's fully turned on."

The man circling me reached between my legs and gave the vibrator a little push deeper into my pussy, causing me to buck. I was so close to coming but I was doing everything in my power to hold back. I tried focusing on anything else as my pussy ached for release.

"Nice," the man said, his hand now wandering up my ass and squeezing it. "I'm guessing her cunt's off-limits for the moment. Isn't that how it works?"

"I'm not sure what Mr. Wood's plans are for her today," Josie said. "Zoey wasn't given any instructions and Mr. Wood didn't leave word. I won't tell if you don't."

"Naughty girl," the man said to Josie as his hands continued to roam over my body. My body hummed with arousal. "You know I can't claim what's not mine. Even though she's wearing a black collar, Mr. Wood obviously has her training for his own reasons. I can't interfere with that."

I relaxed at his words even though I ached to be fucked.

"I'm sure we can find some other ways to entertain ourselves," the man said as his fingers found their way to my ass. I tensed, having never had anyone go there before. He must have felt it because he chuckled. "Ass virgin?"

I nodded, too mortified to speak.

"Too bad," the man said, his fingers retreating. "I'm sure Mr. Wood will want to break you in himself. What shall we do with them, Bill?"

Bill got off the sofa and approached me. Josie was standing next to me, taking it all in, looking pleased by my obvious discomfort. Bill pinched my nipples before pulling them, watching my reaction. I let out a gasp as the pain shot through me. He pulled them more, causing me to arch into it, unsure what else to do as he didn't let up.

While Bill continued to pinch and pull at my nipples, the other man started playing with Josie, feeling her ass, bending her over. He unceremoniously pulled out his cock and jammed it in her. Josie gasped at the intrusion but didn't say anything. Bill watched with delight as the other man pounded into Josie. I didn't know which hole he was using but I could guess.

He grabbed her hair as he got rougher. Bill pulled out his cock and shoved it in Josie's mouth, leaving me abandoned. I wasn't sure where to look or what to do as Josie took in both cocks. I felt helpless and useless as the vibrator threatened to push me over the edge.

Josie's groans got louder as the men picked up their pace. The man behind her grabbed her hair, pulling her head up while Bill pulled at her nipples as he fucked her mouth.

"This is all you're good for," the other man said. "Three holes aching to be filled."

Josie gasped as the man plunged his fingers in her vacant hole, filling her completely. My pussy ached, wanting sweet release, but I held back as I clamped down on the vibrator. I wanted to touch my sore nipples, pull at them, create some sort of pain to distract me, but I knew better than to touch myself. I wasn't there for my pleasure but theirs.

"Oh fuck," the man behind her said before stilling and spilling into her, causing Bill to come at the same time. Both men pulled out, allowing their semen to drip down her chin and inner thighs.

The man behind her slapped her ass.

"Up," he said. Josie straightened. "Annabelle, on your knees. Clean us."

I knelt without hesitation as he slid his wet cock into my mouth. I tasted Josie mixed with semen and did the best I could to suck it clean. I kept lapping at it until he was satisfied, replacing his cock with Bill's. I sucked Bill's cock clean as he pulled on my aching nipples. My body flooded with pleasure as my mind went still. My thoughts centered on the cock in my mouth.

I lost track of time until Bill pulled out, satisfied. He patted my head and said, "Good girl. I hope we get to play again soon."

"Will that be all, sir?" Josie asked, her voice more demure than it was earlier.

"That's all for now, Josie," the other man said. "Let Mr. Wood know that we'll want to play with Annabelle as soon as she's finished with her training. Hopefully, it'll be sooner than later."

"Yes, sir," Josie said before helping me up and escorting me off the boat.

I wanted so badly to ask Josie how she knew those men but kept my mouth shut as we walked past the deckhands and back into the men's side of town. Hands reached out and groped us as we walked, something I was getting used to. It surprised me when we weren't stopped for another round but also grateful as the vibrator continued to hum away, leaving me exhausted. Josie quickened her pace and I struggled to keep up.

Once we crossed over to the women's side of town and there were no men in sight, I relaxed.

"How do you know those men?" I asked when I felt it was safe to talk.

"You'll get to know most of the men on this island by the time you're done," Josie said, "but I work for those two as their executive chef when they're entertaining."

"Do you ever get to go out to sea?" I asked, trying to imagine the parties that must go down on that boat.

"All the time," Josie said. "They never leave the island's jurisdiction or wander to any other islands so it's all good. Why? Would you like to join us next time? Ernie was smitten with you."

"You don't think Mr. Wood would mind?" I asked, not sure how I felt about it. They seemed OK but I'd much rather hang out with Mr. Wood and his crowd.

"Sure," Josie said. "Mr. Wood wants us to be happy here—I'm sure he's told you that—so he'll be open to you doing pretty much anything you want. Maybe not during your training—he's more strict during that time—but after. Think about it. It'd be fun to have you along."

"I will," I said, already knowing I'd never ask Mr. Wood. I could always tell Josie he said no or somehow weasel my way out of it. I was much more interested in getting to know Mr. Wood better and I didn't like the idea of being stuck on some boat unable to get off.

We walked back to the house in no time. It was well into the afternoon already. A part of me worried that my disappearance might upset Mr. Wood. I let out a sigh of relief when he didn't seem to be around.

"What time does Mr. Wood usually return?" I asked as we went into the kitchen. Josie grabbed an apple out of the fridge while I poured myself a glass of water.

"It varies. He doesn't keep regular hours."

"Does he go to an office?" I asked, figuring this may be my only chance to get answers to my questions.

Josie shrugged. "Probably. I never asked and he never said. I have no idea what the men do on this island when the women aren't around."

"They must have businesses or jobs or something," I said, although who knew. Maybe they were all independently wealthy.

"There's no real industry on the island outside of the shops and the bars which I think are owned jointly by all the men on the island. It's almost like a commune in that sense—the men support everything that happens here and all the money keeps getting recycled among them. I don't think they even pay for the amenities here since it goes back into their pockets anyway. I never thought much about it."

I was still burning with questions but decided not to ask Josie any more. She started to sound annoyed and that was the last thing I wanted to do.

Before I could say another word, Mr. Wood walked in looking murderous.

"Where have you been?" he asked.

I looked quickly to Josie, unsure who he was asking.

Josie piped up. "I took Annabelle for a walk to the docks. I wanted to show her around."

"It's not up to you to show her around," Mr. Wood said. "That is Zoey's job. I had left Zoey explicit instructions for the day and you derailed them."

Mr. Wood turned to me. "Even though you're new here, you should have known better. While you're in this house, you will do nothing unless I tell you it's OK or Zoey tells you I told you it's OK. Do you understand?"

"Yes, Mr. Wood," I said, my eyes lowered, afraid to look at him. Somewhere deep inside I knew I needed to stay here and I still left with Josie. I knew I was as much to blame as she was. "I'm sorry."

"That's a start," Mr. Wood said, "but to teach you a lesson, I will punish you both."

I dared not look at Josie as I let the words sink in. I had only been here for three days and already I was going to be punished. I had always considering myself a rule follower, one reason I thought coming to the island would be fun and interesting, it'd be in my nature, but I had let Josie sway me to break the rules. Maybe I wasn't as much of a rule follower as I had thought.

"I understand, Mr. Wood," Josie said. "I'm sorry I took Annabelle out. I was under the belief that no assignments meant we could do what we wanted."

Mr. Wood crossed over to her until he was only a foot in front of her. I thought he might slap her.

"Under normal circumstances that is the rule in this house however with trainees, the rules are different. They are under strict training and can't just go off because they haven't received their commands for the day yet. As someone who's been here for four months, I would have thought you'd know that by now."

"Yes, Mr. Wood," Josie said, "I must have forgotten."

"Well, you'll have plenty of time to think about it when I send both of you to the pillories for the night."

The blood drained from my face. I had no idea what the pillories were but it sounded severe.

Mr. Wood turned to me. "I didn't want to start your training this way, Annabelle, but the pillories will help you remember why you're here and what your place is in this society. I will have Zoey take you both in ten minutes. Use that time to use the bathroom. Annabelle, you may remove the vibrator. You won't be needing it."

With that, Mr. Wood strode out of the kitchen, leaving us gaping after him.

"What are the pillories?" I whispered to Josie.

"They're not good" is all she said.

NINE

Zoey led us through the men's side of town on leashes as if we were dogs. We were blindfolded, the leashes helping to guide us but also making me feel less than human. We were naked except for our platform heels that clicked on the concrete with every step.

Nerves shot through me as the anticipation built. I had no idea what I was in for. I knew enough to not ask Zoey as she led us out the door. Mr. Wood wasn't around, probably disgusted by the both of us. My heart hurt at the thought of disappointing him.

The men catcalled as we walked, grabbing us at every chance they got although Zoey never stopped long enough for them to do much more than grope us. Some spit on us which was new. I wondered if they knew where we were going and that was part of the experience.

After what felt like forever, Zoey stopped.

"Are these the girls?" a man said.

"Yes, Sir," Zoey said. "They're each to receive five hours. Mr. Wood would like someone to escort them back once they're done."

My stomach turned at five hours. That was a long time.

"OK," the man said. He must have taken hold of our leashes because he gave them a hard tug. "Follow."

I did my best to follow his quicker pace without tripping. He didn't walk far before stopping. I heard him unlatch our leashes before commanding us to bend forward. I bent until I felt my neck hit something hard. He pulled up my arms so they were at neck level but out at my sides before bringing down a wooden frame to secure my neck and hands.

I squirmed as I took in the severity of what was happening. I couldn't move. I couldn't escape. Up until now, I felt like I could flee from whatever was happening. This was different. There was nothing I could do but take whatever was coming. The thought frightened me but also thrilled me in some demented way. This was the absolute relinquishment of control. I was at the mercy of whatever they wanted to do to me.

I heard locks clicking, completing my captivity.

"You're all locked in," the man said, "for five hours as dictated by Mr. Wood. At the end of the five hours, we will release you back to Mr. Wood. During your punishment, you will be used and punished as the men see fit. Your collars are irrelevant in the pillories which means your green collar might as well be black.

"You are not to speak during this time or else we will prolong your time for each infraction. You may make noise such as moans or screams but they cannot form words or make sense. Consider yourself nothing more than playthings while you're here. I assure you it won't be pleasant but it will give you ample time to consider why you were sent here in the first place."

My heart hammered as I squirmed against the restraints. This was serious. I had no idea what I was in for and I had no way to see it coming which amplified my nerves. I didn't know if we were alone or if there were more women. I heard men talking in the distance along with the clinking of glasses which made me guess we were somewhere near the bar district. I had no way of knowing whether we were inside or outside. I couldn't feel the sun on my skin but it was late evening so we could be out of the sun's reach wherever we were.

I wanted to talk with Josie, to ask her what to expect, but I didn't dare. I had a feeling that we were being watched and didn't want to make things worse.

I jumped when the first hands touched me. The hands spread my ass cheeks before a cock jammed itself in my pussy. I was surprisingly wet and took it with ease, grateful he hadn't aimed higher. He slapped my ass as he plowed into me, pumping away in a quick and brutal pace. I knew better than to come but the rapid fucking wasn't arousing me. I simply took it, an open vessel to be filled.

I was contemplating this, thinking it wasn't so bad, when a cock pressed against my lips.

"Open," a gruff voice demanded.

I opened my mouth, allowing the thick cock to slide in. Just like the cock that continued to pound my pussy, this one pushed all the way back, almost causing me to gag. I had nowhere to go, no way to escape, so I opened my throat, taking the abuse as the cock pounded in and out of my mouth. I didn't lick or suck but kept myself open and available for it, not concerned with making it pleasurable for him.

"Good cunt," he said before spilling himself down my throat and pulling out.

Another cock replaced him as the cock in my pussy pushed hard into me and stilled, coating my insides with his semen. He slipped out, spilling himself down my legs, slapping my ass. He didn't bother saying anything to me.

This went on again and again, cocks in my mouth, cocks in my pussy, pounding away, until my mind went numb. I could hear Josie next to me getting equally pounded but I no longer cared. I had fully become what I had always wanted to be—nothing more than an inferior female whose only purpose was to be used by men. I felt something shift inside me, as something clicked over, as I allowed this to be my full existence. Nothing else mattered. This was who I was.

It wasn't until I felt a sharp slap on my ass that I was startled out of my comfortable trance. A cock was pounding into my pussy while someone kept striking my ass with their hand, causing it to sting and warm. I tried to squirm away from the slapping but with a cock in my mouth and a cock in my pussy, I was stuck. I tried taking in a deep breath through my nose, willing myself to accept the pain, telling myself that this was my punishment for leaving the house without explicit instruction.

The cock pulled out of my pussy before it came and lingered at my ass. I had never been fucked in my ass and I didn't want this to be my first time. I knew it would happen eventually, especially on the island, but this was not how I wanted it to be.

The spanking continued, leaving my ass on fire, as the cock pushed itself slowly into my virgin ass. I gasped on the cock in my mouth as the cock slipped in deeper in my ass until it pushed itself all the way in. I felt more impaled than I had ever felt before. The pain was intense but it brought another level to my submissiveness that my body leaned into. I felt completely at their mercy as the cock slowly pulled out before pushing back in even deeper.

I must have clasped onto the cock in my mouth because he grabbed my hair before spilling himself down my throat. He pulled out then slapped my face. It wasn't hard but it shocked me, leaving a lingering sting.

Another cock replaced the one in my mouth, fucking deep and steady, while the cock in my ass continued to torment me.

"You're so tight, cunt," the man in my ass said as he used my hips to push himself further into me. I tried to relax my ass muscles but all I could feel was a searing pain as my ass stretched to accommodate him. I felt full, like a stuffed pig, as he wiggled around inside me. My pussy went untouched. Semen ran down my legs.

I lost myself in the fullness, my ass stretched to its limit, the pain turning into arousal, reminding me of my purpose and place in this society. I accepted it as the cocks had their way with me.

The cock in my ass finally came, spilling itself inside me, before pulling out. He slapped my ass a few times, the sharp pain radiating through me.

"She's tight," I heard him say before another cock slipped into my now lubed ass.

I took this one easier but I was still raw and over-stretched. My ass burned as the cock fucked me and I did my best to ignore the pain. He pushed deep into me again and again as the cock in my mouth sped up its pace. This time instead of spilling itself down my throat like the rest, the cock in my mouth pulled out and sprayed itself over my face. Thankfully, I had the blindfold on so nothing got in my eyes but now I had semen all over my face, dripping down, and there was nothing I could do about it.

The cock in my ass must have liked that idea because he pulled out and came over the top of my ass. They started a new trend as cocks started spilling themselves over my ass or face, leaving me covered in come.

Cocks used my mouth, my ass and my pussy for hours. Some played with my tits, pulling on them, slapping them, pinching my sore nipples. Some slapped my ass, slapped my face and spit on me. All I could do was open my mouth and endure it, let myself be used as the minutes ticked by.

Finally, I heard the click of a lock and the pillories were opened.

"Stand," a man said, roughly helping me to straighten myself.

My legs felt weak and my back ached. Come dripped down my neck and legs as I straightened. I felt the leash being attached and a tug at my collar. I followed without a word, too afraid to speak, my head spaced out, my mind blank and numb. I walked with unsteady steps, happy to be led, happy to not have to think, happy to be done with the pillories.

We walked what felt like forever, winding through the men's side of town. I heard catcalls as we walked but not as many hands reached out and groped me this time. Being covered in come must have worked as a deterrent. I was exhausted and starving when we reached Mr. Wood's house. Our handler removed our blindfolds as he walked us up to the door and knocked. Zoey answered wearing a sheer yellow dress, looking fresh and vibrant. I'm sure we looked a mess.

"Deposit them in the kitchen," Zoey said, showing our handler the way.

He tugged on our leashes as if we didn't know which way to go as he led us into the bright kitchen. Mr. Wood stood behind the island, his face full of disapproval, as the handler unhooked our leashes and handed them to Zoey.

"Thank you, Todd, for escorting my women back," Mr. Wood said to the handler.

"No problem," Todd said before leaving.

Mr. Wood circled us while Zoey stood there, taking in our shame. I kept my eyes lowered, afraid to look anywhere.

"I am so disappointed in you, Annabelle," Mr. Wood said when he stopped in front of me. "Look at me."

I raised my eyes to meet his. I shrank when I saw the fury there.

"I hope you learned your lesson this evening," Mr. Wood said. "I'd prefer not to send you to the pillories again but I will do so if needed. Do you understand?"

I nodded. "Yes, Mr. Wood."

"Good. As for you, Josie," Mr. Wood moved to stand in front of Josie, "I expected much better of you. You have been in my household a while now and I thought you knew my rules. Since your infraction was bigger than Annabelle's, I'm taking away your green collar and replacing it with black until further notice."

Zoey was right beside him with a black collar. Mr. Wood unlocked and unhooked Josie's green collar, replacing it with the black one, locking it into place.

"You also won't be able to shower for two days," Mr. Wood said to Josie. "Annabelle, you won't be able to shower until tomorrow. I want you both to spend the night remembering exactly who you are here and that your purpose is to please me. Zoey, put Josie in the stable and, Annabelle, you're coming with me."

I followed Mr. Wood up the stairs, my head lowered in shame at displeasing him. Seeing his disappointment made his punishment feel justified.

He led me to a room I hadn't entered before. It was next to his master bedroom. For a moment I thought he might have me sleep in his room but my heart plummeted when he pushed open the door to the room next door. Inside everything was white and minimal with no bed and no furniture, not even a chair. Instead, a large white wooden cross was on one wall with an assortment of floggers and whips hanging on hooks on another. What scared me most was the white cage that sat in front of the windows.

Mr. Wood went straight for the cage and opened it.

"This will be your sleep quarters for the night," he said. "You may use the adjoining bathroom now but do not wash yourself."

I slipped into the bathroom and used the toilet before washing my hands. I looked at myself in the mirror and couldn't believe the woman staring back at me. My auburn hair was pulled up and off my face, coated with come. My nipples were raw. I looked a mess, like a total slut.

Not wanting to keep Mr. Wood waiting despite my trepidation of being kept in a cage, I returned to stand before him.

"Turn around and spread your legs," he said.

I did as he commanded. He pushed a dildo into my pussy and a plug into my ass, filling me. Next, he had me step into a contraption that locked them into place and cinched around my waist. He slipped a lock into it, locking me in. He directed me to get into the cage. It was low, about 3 1/2 feet tall, so I had to crawl into it. The bottom was metal and cold with nothing to cushion it. Thankfully, it was about eight feet long and four feet wide so I had some room to stretch.

He closed the cage behind me, locking it. A frisson of fear ran through me. I was trapped.

"You're on camera," he said, motioning to a webcam tucked into the wall, "so you'll be monitored. If you need anything, wave to the camera and someone will attend to you. Do you understand?"

"Yes, Mr. Wood."

"Good. Try to get some rest because I have a busy day planned for you tomorrow."

After Mr. Wood left, I tried to get comfortable. I felt more at ease knowing I could signal someone for help if things got too weird or if I needed to use the bathroom. I liked the idea of being monitored. I didn't feel as completely alone.

TEN

I slept better than I had in days which surprised me. I stretched out in my cage, feeling full with the dildo and butt plug wedged inside me. I felt more content than I had in a long time. I had nowhere I needed to go, nothing I needed to do—my life was outside of my control and it felt liberating. I was at Mr. Wood's mercy and I loved it. It felt like pulling on a cozy sweater after freezing out in the cold for far too long.

I startled when the door opened and Mr. Wood walked in.

"I saw that you were awake," he said. "How did you sleep?"

"Like a baby, Mr. Wood," I admitted. "Really well."

He smiled. "I'm happy to hear that. I'm sure yesterday's activities wore you out."

"It was intense."

"I hope you learned your lesson. You're not to leave the grounds without either me or Zoey telling you it's OK during your training. Do you understand?"

"Yes, Mr. Wood."

"At some point, you'll have more freedom but during your training, you have activities that you must go through and it's all very timed. Learning to obey me is part of your training. If you're unsure what to do, if no one has given you any instructions, then you are to sit in your room on your knees and wait. Do you understand?"

"Yes, Mr. Wood."

"Good."

He unlocked the cage and opened the door. I was desperate to get out but didn't dare move until he instructed me. I was learning, more slowly than I'd like, that every action I did was part of the training process. I didn't want to be punished again so quickly. I wanted to please Mr. Wood and for him to know that I could take direction well.

"You may exit," he said with a smile.

I crawled out and stayed on my knees in front of him, looking up into his unreadable eyes.

"You may stand."

I uncurled myself, my limbs stiff and awkward.

"I want you to shower and change into the outfit laid out for you on your bed. You will then come down to the kitchen for breakfast. You only have 30 minutes to complete these tasks so don't dawdle. I will take you into the office with me today."

My heart jumped at the thought of spending the day with him. I wasted no time scurrying to the my bathroom. I showered, scrubbing every inch of me, washing my hair twice. Not wanting to waste time, I pulled my hair up into a loose topknot and brushed on some mascara. I brushed my teeth, used the toilet and spritzed the perfume I had found in the bathroom along my neck.

I was pleased to see a long black sheer gown waiting for me on my bed. I pulled it on, grateful for the feel of it against my skin, covering me while also leaving me exposed. No undergarments were left which didn't surprise me. I slipped on my Lucite heels and made my way to the kitchen.

Josie wasn't in the kitchen which made me wonder where she was. I knew Mr. Wood was less pleased with her than he was with me so I imagined he had continued to punish her after the pillories as he had with me. I knew enough not to question it but I hoped she was OK. She was my only ally and confidant in this place and I didn't want to lose that.

I grabbed a yogurt out of the fridge and gulped it down along with a tall glass of water. Since I was feeling dehydrated after spending a day losing fluids, I gulped down a second glass as well. I felt sexy in my outfit and was excited to visit Mr. Wood's office. I still had no idea what he did.

I was careful not to sit while I waited. There were no clocks in the kitchen so I wasn't sure how much time had passed. I stood by the kitchen counter and waited, bursting with excitement for the day ahead.

Mr. Wood walked in some time later dressed in a dark tailored suit and looking as handsome as ever. He gave me the once over, taking in my curves under the sheer fabric, stopping at my erect nipples. I hoped he liked what he saw.

"Let's go," he said.

I followed him out the back door and onto the street. Mr. Woods walked in the opposite direction of the areas I knew towards the business side of town. He led me to a midsize office building with floor to ceiling mirrored windows. The entryway and lobby were unspectacular, like any office building I've been in.

He led me into the mirrored elevator, hitting floor four. We rode up without a word. I understood that I was there to observe and do whatever he wanted from me. Maybe he'd put me to work, test out my skills, to see how I could benefit him. I had never considered working to be part of my time here but I was open to doing something productive. I knew I'd get bored sitting in the house day after day, waiting to be told what to do.

The elevator opened into a modern office with white marble floors, a reception desk and a small waiting area with white leather chairs. A blonde woman with a white low-cut blouse that more than hinted at her ample cleavage and a yellow collar sat behind the reception desk. She was on the phone.

"This is Clare," Mr. Wood told me. "She's my receptionist. If all goes well, you'll be seeing a lot more of her."

We didn't stop to say hi but I smiled at her as we passed. She looked me over as if she'd seen it all before, which she probably had.

so I wasn't under any false impressions that we'd be friends anytime soon. I was probably one of the many that Mr. Wood paraded through his office—no one special.

We passed through a wide room lined with offices with floor to ceiling windows with desks parked in front. Cute secretaries sat at the desks in the hallway, most dressed in crisp white button-down shirts that were unbuttoned to varying degrees, showing off their braless cleavage. They wore different color collars but most were yellow or green. Inside the offices, men worked, on the phone or on the computer. In the last office, a man was fucking a woman over his desk, her black skirt pulled up over her ass. I tried not to stare.

"It's not always easy to get work done with all the distractions," Mr. Wood said as way of explanation. "We try to keep the women mostly covered inside the office but it's not always enough to discourage them from being fucked. This is a place where it's acceptable for a man to fuck his secretary."

Mr. Wood pushed open the door at the end of the hall, exposing a massive office with a large white desk and floor to ceiling windows overlooking the harbor. He walked over to the desk and settled behind it, leaving me standing as I took it all in. Two white leather chairs sat in front of his desk with a leather sofa against one wall and a small bar on the other. Mahogany paneling covered the walls, a sharp contrast against the white interior.

He clicked on his computer while he picked up the phone.

"Bring me the Burton files," he said then hung up.

A moment later Clare walked in with a thick file and placed it on his desk. She wore a short red skirt that barely covered her ass and high red heels.

"Anything else, Mr. Wood?" she asked.

"Yes, please show Annabelle around and get her settled into the desk outside my office. I want to see how she'd be working here."

"Yes, Mr. Wood," Clare said before indicating to me to follow.

A flash of anxiety rolled through me as I walked out the door with Clare. I wasn't afraid of working for Mr. Wood but Clare intimidated me. Although I knew she'd follow Mr. Wood's order without question,

I wasn't sure she'd make it a pleasant experience for me. I knew I'd have to do my best to get on her good side.

Once outside with Mr. Wood's door closed, Clare looked at me as if she were unimpressed.

"I heard Mr. Wood had made a new acquisition but I assumed he'd keep it out of the office," Clare said. "Do you have any skills besides sucking cock?"

I blinked at her horrified. She was talking while men were present. I didn't want to say a word.

"Oh, you can talk here," she said, aware of why I wasn't answering her. "Inside an office like this, it's OK as long as you're part of the office staff, which I'm guessing you are at the moment. We'll see how long that lasts. Otherwise, it'd be impossible to get any work done. Follow me."

I followed her to a break room complete with a coffeemaker, fridge and small dining table with chairs.

"This is the coffee room. As you can see, it's just like any other one you'd see on the mainland except," Clare opened the fridge, "this one has select beer and champagne for our guests as well as different outfits for the women in the cabinets."

Clare pulled open a couple of drawers showing sheer dresses and crisp white blouses.

"Most of the women are ordered to wear white blouses to keep things more professional but that doesn't keep them from being groped and fucked whenever the men please. Mr. Wood will probably want you to wear one as well while you're working here so change into these."

Clare handed me a white blouse and a black miniskirt. I assumed she wanted me to change right there which I guess didn't matter since the sheer gown showed everything anyway. I slipped the gown over my head and pulled on the miniskirt, which barely covered my ass, and the blouse, leaving a good amount of the buttons undone. I assumed none of the women in the office wore undergarments so I didn't ask. Instead, I handed the folded gown to her. She took it and shoved it in a drawer.

"Mr. Wood expects his secretary to have his coffee ready at his desk when he walks in. You'll never know when he's arriving unless, of course, you arrive together so he doesn't expect you to be a mind reader but once you see him step out of the elevator, get your ass in here and make it. We have a Keurig so you can brew one cup at a time. He prefers the Columbian dark roast black so that should be easy enough to remember."

"Should I get him one now?" I asked, feeling overwhelmed. I had never worked in an office. I went from college to waitressing to here.

Clare gave me a look. "Yes. Of course. Go give it to him then meet me back at reception when you're done."

Clare turned on her heels and left. I found the coffee and slipped it into the Keurig, hitting brew and watching it drain into a mug. While I waited, I snuck a peek into the other cabinets, curious to see what else was there. A few contained random office supplies like copy paper and pens while others held thick black rope, floggers and canes. I had a feeling I'd enjoy working here.

Once the coffee finished brewing, I took it to Mr. Wood's office, knocking and waiting for him to say come in before I entered. He looked powerful and commanding behind his desk, the phone to his ear as he talked to someone in a stern voice, telling them to get their shit together and do what he said.

I brought the coffee to his desk and set it down in front of him, bending at the waist to give him a good eyeful of cleavage. I had left enough buttons undone so it looked like my nipples might escape at any moment while keeping them hidden beneath the crisp white fabric.

I smiled inwardly as Mr. Wood's eyes went straight towards my chest while he talked on the phone. He reached out and undid another button, slipping his hand inside and pulling on a nipple. I stayed bent over as he pushed my blouse aside so my right breast sprang free. He continued to talk while he played with my nipple, pulling on it until I squirmed from the pain and pleasure. I wanted to moan but since he was on the phone, I held it in. He smiled at my discomfort and how much he was affecting me.

He pulled out my other nipple so both breasts were exposed, giving it attention while he continued to talk. I loved being manhandled in his office, another reminder of why I was here.

"Before you do that, get the hell in here," he said then hung up.

He pulled on both my nipples, smiling as I moaned into the pain, my pussy aroused and wet from his attention. A moment later his office door opened and a man's voice said, "Oh yea," behind me. Mr. Wood continued to pull on my nipples as the man lifted my skirt and ran his fingers through my wetness.

"She's dripping," the man said. "Can I indulge?"

"Be my guest," Mr. Wood said. "That's why I called you in here. I thought you'd be interested."

The man needed no more encouragement. I heard his zipper before his cock pressed against my pussy. With one thrust, he was inside me. I leaned against the desk for support as he pulled out slightly before giving me everything he had. Mr. Wood pulled and pinched my nipples as the man whose face I hadn't seen fucked me from behind. My pussy clamped down on him, threatening to come. Sensations rolled through me, the waves of pleasure building, until I thought I'd burst.

The man behind me grabbed my hips as he dove in deeper, driving into me with a steady relentlessness. Mr. Wood held my gaze, pinching and pulling at my nipples, watching me being fucked. My mind spiraled as I gave in to the sensations, losing myself in it, allowing myself to let go.

I screamed when I came, my body convulsing. The man behind me laughed as my pussy clamped down on his cock, willing it to stop, but he pushed through my orgasm, pumping in and out, causing my body to go along with it, accepting him fully.

"You have another one," Mr. Wood said. "I know you do. You've been holding out the past couple of days."

He was right. I was pent up.

I gripped the desk as the fucking continued, my pussy open, accepting, fulfilling its purpose. His thrusts became deeper, more urgent, as another orgasm threatened to roll through me. It was too much—too much sensation, too much pressure. I felt like I was about to explode again.

"Give it up," Mr. Wood commanded.

At his words, I came. I screamed out, convulsing around the cock. The man behind me grabbed my hips, thrust in one more time, and came inside me as my orgasm continued to roll through me. I was still coming down from it, waves washing over me, as the cock slid out, slapping itself on my inner thigh and leaking its afterglow down my leg.

"She's a good one," the man said, smacking my ass. "Thanks for the ride."

I felt liquid and floaty as I heard the man leave, closing the door behind him. I wanted to collapse on the desk, to give in to my exhaustion, wanting to do nothing more than lay there, but I held myself up, my hands planted on the desk, my eyes on Mr. Wood.

"You did well," Mr. Wood said, wiping a stray hair from my face. "Now if you can type, I'll be all set."

I smiled at him, knowing he was only partly joking.

I SPENT the rest of the day at the desk stationed in front of Mr. Wood's office trying to concentrate on the little bit of work he gave me. He wanted me to type some things from dictation but I kept fumbling over the keys. Usually, I was a good typer but today I couldn't think. My underside sat directly on the white leather office chair, making me fully aware of my wetness. Mr. Wood had me button up my blouse a bit before I left his office, tucking in my boobs but leaving ample cleavage.

I felt rung out and exhausted from being so thoroughly fucked and finally coming. Twice. I wanted to curl up into a ball and do nothing but sleep for the next ten hours. My mind was mush and I couldn't put a thought together.

A petite female who wore a short sheer black dress with a black collar delivered lunch. She carried a variety of sandwiches in a basket, going around to the offices and secretaries, letting them select what they wanted. I took a chicken salad sandwich, grateful to be having something of substance today.

I wandered into the office kitchen in search of something to drink before I got started. Two men and a woman stopped chatting to look at me when I walked in.

"You must be the new girl," one man said. "Lance told us he'd be bringing someone in."

It took me a minute to figure out he was talking about Mr. Wood.

"Yes, sir," I said as I opened the fridge for a soda. "I started today although I'm not sure I'm doing the best job."

The other man laughed. "The women aren't here to do a 'good job' but to relieve our stress. I'm sure you're doing fine in that department."

The woman giggled as the man ran his hand under her skirt.

I blushed, wondering if he was the man who fucked me earlier. I never got a look at him and couldn't remember the voice. I had been too overwhelmed by everything to fully take it in.

"What is it you do here?" I asked, not sure if I was allowed to ask but I figured I might not have another chance.

The man chuckled. "It's none of your concern but we're an investment firm—investing in various companies, startups and real estate holdings. Lance is the owner and our boss. You're lucky to be with him."

I wasn't actually with Mr. Wood but I knew better than to correct him.

"Thank you for sharing that with me," I said, meaning it. It made sense that Mr. Wood was the head of something powerful.

"How are you liking it so far on the island?" the other man asked. "You're new here, right?"

"Yea, it's only my fourth day," I said, although it felt much longer. "I like it. It's taking some getting used to and I'm still in training but it's been an interesting experience."

"Most women go running out of here by their second day," the man said. "If a woman makes it past that second day then she usually ends up sticking around."

I was only taking it day by day at this point but the thought of sticking around for the six months and possibly beyond thrilled me. I always had a high sex drive and being able to succumb to that daily, even multiple times a day, was something I wanted to continue experiencing.

"The concept of this place intrigued me," I admitted. "I wanted to see what it'd be like."

The man smiled as he inched himself closer to me.

"And what's it been like for you to be inferior to the men here?" he asked as he plunged a hand down my blouse and tweaked a nipple. "To know that we can do whatever we want whenever we want, especially with your black collar?"

The other man came up behind me and stuck his hand up my skirt, cupping my ass before sliding a finger into my wet pussy. I sucked in my breath, not sure if I should answer, while the man in front of me stared into my eyes. He unbuttoned my blouse until my breasts popped out. He tweaked my nipples as he watched me squirm against the waves of pain and pleasure.

"You're nothing but a fucktoy for every man here, in this office and on this island," he said as he pulled on my aching nipples. The man behind me slipped in a couple more fingers, filling my pussy, stretching it. "This will be your life every day here, to be at our whims, to be toyed with, fucked, spanked, whatever we want."

The woman watched as they taunted my body, creating a surge of euphoria. I wanted to give in to it, to cave, to give myself over to them completely. This is what I wanted deep in my soul—to fully surrender, to become the fucktoy I always wanted to be, to live up to my true purpose in life.

"Answer me, bitch," the man said before slapping me across the face. It stung, startling me. He grabbed my face with his hand. "Is this what you want?"

I nodded. It was.

"I need to hear you say it," he said. The fingers in my pussy pushed in deeper, causing me to lean forward, accommodating it as much as I could. "Tell me you want to be a fucktoy."

"I want to be a fucktoy," I got out, my voice small.

"Louder," he demanded. "I want the whole office to hear."

I swallowed, embarrassment rolling through me. It was one thing to say it to the people in this room but it was another to announce it to the whole office. I knew this must be common, to announce such things, but it filled me with shame.

"I want to be a fucktoy," I said louder.

He slapped me again across the face. "Not loud enough. When I tell you to do something, I expect you to do it. This is your last warning."

I swallowed before opening my mouth and bellowing into the office, "I want to be a fucktoy."

ELEVEN

Mr. Wood was too busy to take me home. He was meeting with someone for dinner and he didn't invite me along. I spent the rest of the afternoon with my boobs out and my pussy aching. They didn't fuck me in the kitchen like I thought they would. Instead, they worked me up to a frenzy and left me that way, saying that all proper bitches should be perpetually turned on and the best way to do that was to keep them from coming or having the satisfaction of being fucked. It worked. I craved cock for the rest of the day.

Mr. Wood had instructed me to go back to his place on my own. He drew a map to show me the way but it wasn't complicated.

I had no issues walking back. Men and women dressed in business attire were coming and going but no one bothered with me. It surprised me to discover that the lack of attention disappointed me. My pussy ached to be filled and walking with my boobs out turned me on even more, especially when most of the other women were covered up.

It surprised me to see Josie in the kitchen when I arrived back. She was nude with a couple of welt marks across her ass and her nipples looked raw.

"Are you OK?" I asked, feeling overdressed next to her.

"I've been better," she said. She was fixing dinner, something in a pot.

"Is there anything I can do to help?" I asked, meaning the cooking but also in general, although I doubted there was much I could do in general. She knew this place better than I did.

"You can chop some cucumbers for the salad," she said, nodding towards the fridge.

I found the cucumbers and brought them to the kitchen island so I was facing Josie as she cooked. She had dark circles under her eyes and I wondered if she slept at all last night. I was beginning to think I had gotten off easy while she had bared the brunt of it.

Josie handed me a cutting board and a chef's knife. I started chopping, happy to be helping her.

"I've never seen him that mad," Josie said after a minute. "He was even more furious when I told him where I took you."

I gave her a puzzled look. "Why would he care about that? It's not like we left the island."

"Let me clarify," she said, "it wasn't so much the where but the who. He didn't like that I introduced you to Bill and Ernie. They don't get along with Mr. Wood. You could consider them rivals."

"Oh God. Why did you take me to them if you knew Mr. Wood wouldn't like it? I remember asking you if Mr. Wood would mind."

Josie looked at me, a drained look on her face. "I honestly didn't think he'd mind that much. We're nothing more than playthings here, interchangeable. We're meant to be fucked and submit to all their whims. Thankfully, most of the women here get off on that, including you, so for some strange reason, I thought Mr. Wood would be pleased that I exposed you to more men. Boy, was I wrong."

She went back to stirring the pot while I finished chopping the cucumber. I pulled out the spinach for the salad and tossed it with a salad spinner that was sitting out.

"What else did he do to you?" I asked, not sure I wanted to know.

She pointed her ass towards me. The welts across her ass were red and raised.

"Just your basic caning," she said as if it were nothing, "while being restrained. He clamped my nipples for a time."

"Were you able to get some sleep?" I asked, mortified that caning was an option here.

"Not much," she said. "The pain was too intense to sleep. I took some ibuprofen and Mr. Wood put salve on the welts afterward but it wasn't enough to dull the pain."

"Does it still hurt?"

"Of course it does," she snapped. "It'll take a while to heal. It doesn't hurt as much as it did last night but it still throbs. Caning stays with you for a while."

I wanted to ask if this was her first time being caned but I didn't want to push her. She had been through enough.

"Is there anything else I can do to help?" I asked. I had the salad assembled.

"No. I'm done here. I made us a simple stew since I was feeling like having comfort food tonight. You're more than welcome to have some."

Josie served herself, throwing salad into a small bowl before eating at the counter standing up. I felt grateful for the food but guilty for all she had been through on my behalf. I served myself some stew and salad and joined her standing at the counter.

"Where's Zoey?" I asked, wondering if she'd like to eat with us.

"Probably out with Mr. Wood," Josie said with a hint of jealousy.

"Out to dinner with him?" It had never occurred to me she'd be going out with him like that. She always felt more like his assistant than someone he'd have an intimate relationship with.

Josie looked at me like I was a moron. "Of course out to dinner with him. Zoey is Mr. Wood's favorite. That's why she has a yellow collar. He probably would have gone white with her but she enjoys a little attention."

I took a bite of stew, surprised by the ball of jealousy settling in my stomach. It wasn't like I expected to have a romantic relationship here. The men didn't seem interested in that. They viewed women as nothing more than playthings, entertainment. But still, it bothered me.

"This is delicious." I said, wanting to change the subject.

"Thanks," Josie said. "Old family recipe."

We ate the rest in silence. I didn't know what else to say and I didn't know how to apologize for getting Josie into trouble. I knew it had been her idea to take me to the yacht but I could have said no. I could have waited in my room for Mr. Wood or Zoey to tell me what I needed to do. I hated someone else suffering for something I did. I wondered how I could make it up to her, if I could.

Once we finished, I gathered up our plates and silverware and told Josie I would clean up. It was the least I could do. She didn't protest and left me alone in the kitchen. I wondered what her room was like and if I would stay in my current room the whole time. Zoey had mentioned being moved but maybe that was after training. I knew we were the only women in the house but a new one could be brought in at any time. I didn't want to think about that. I was having enough trouble adjusting to being here.

I washed everything up and wiped down the counters, wanting the kitchen to be pristine for Josie in the morning and super sparkling for Mr. Wood. I knew I was dawdling, hoping to catch Mr. Wood and Zoey as they made their way home. There were no clocks in the kitchen so I had no idea what time it was. The sun was low on the horizon so it had to be getting late.

It was interesting having no sense of time. Usually, I'd be obsessed over it, wanting to fit in as much as I could into every hour, but here I had started to experience an unwinding around it. I forgot about it most of the time, happy to go along with whatever was happening at the moment. It was nice to not have to worry about being somewhere at a specific time, to let the day be dictated to me, to go along with whatever someone else wanted. It felt freeing.

I waited up as long as I could before it became obvious I'd been waiting up. I wasn't sure how Mr. Wood would take that. I wandered back to my room, tempted to peek into the other rooms but I didn't dare. I wouldn't be surprised if this place had cameras all over watching my every move. In a way, it was comforting but it could also get me into trouble if I dared to do anything I knew Mr. Wood wouldn't want me to do.

I was tempted to take a shower once I was in my room but since I wasn't told I could, I decided against it. Instead, I curled up on the rug next to the bed and closed my eyes, hoping for another solid night's sleep.

"MR. WOOD WANTS you in the office again," Zoey said as way of hello when she came into my room the next morning. The sun was streaming in, rousing me. "You're to wear the same attire as yesterday but a fresh set. I've laid it out on the bed for you. You're also to shower and pull your hair up. Try to look professional. Light makeup. Got it?"

I looked up at her. She wore a little sheer yellow dress with matching heels. She looked fresh and well-rested. I couldn't help wonder if Mr. Wood let her sleep with him. I knew she wouldn't tell me if I asked so I didn't bother.

"Yes, got it," I said, pushing myself up, happy for the chance to shower.

Zoey left. I took a quick shower, dried my hair and pulled it up, and dabbed on light makeup as instructed. The outfit was on the bed as promised. I slipped into it, leaving a good amount of buttons unbuttoned, wanting to give Mr. Wood a proper view.

I went into the kitchen to grab my usual yogurt. Josie wasn't there. I hoped she wasn't enduring even more punishment. Maybe Mr. Wood let her sleep in, giving her a rest after all she went through yesterday. I winced at the thought of the welts on her ass. I prayed I wouldn't have to experience the cane while I was here. It gave me a great incentive to do what I was told.

Zoey was nowhere to be found so I decided to head into the office as instructed alone. I hadn't needed an escort home so I figured I didn't need an escort there. I enjoyed having more autonomy. I couldn't wait until I got more into the rhythm of this place. Working for Mr. Wood would help keep me from getting bored and hopefully allow me to interact with more women. I liked that we could talk there. It made life easier and feel more normal.

The walk to the office was uneventful. I passed other women dressed similarly and men in suits. Everyone seemed too preoccupied to get where they were going to bother with me. Today I was grateful not to be noticed as I slipped into Mr. Wood's office building and went up to his floor. I didn't want to be late and I didn't want to be rumpled. I wanted to present myself fresh and ready to work.

The office was buzzing when I walked in. Most of the women were at their desks already. Some men were in their offices while others gathered in the hallway and the kitchen. No one was fucking anyone (that I could see) so I took that as a good sign. I wondered if a day would go by when I wasn't groped or fucked.

I knocked on Mr. Wood's closed door and waited.

After a few minutes, I heard his muffled come in.

He sat behind his desk working on his computer when I walked in. He waved me over. I went and stood in front of him, taken in by his expensive suit and dark green eyes. He gave me the once over.

"Where's my coffee?"

My heart dropped. Fuck. I had forgotten.

"I'll go get it for you now, Mr. Wood," I said, turning to leave.

He grabbed my wrist, stopping me.

"Not so fast," he said, pulling me to him. Before I could react, he pulled me so I was over his lap with my ass in the air. He pulled up the back of my skirt. "You deserve something for forgetting."

I jumped when his hand landed on my ass with a loud smack. My ass stung from the impact. Before I could digest it, his hand landed again, harder this time. He continued spanking me until my ass was on fire and I had tears in my eyes. I knew better than to try to stop him but not only did it hurt, I felt humiliated, like a little girl being reprimanded. He landed a few more before he stopped and pushed me up.

"I want you to keep your skirt up in the back so everyone will see that I spanked you," he said. "Your ass is a nice cherry red. Go get my coffee."

My face flamed red, too, as I turned and scurried out of his office, closing the door behind me. I had never felt more humiliated. At least when I was in the pillories I didn't have to witness anyone looking at me. Now, in this office environment, it felt shameful to be walking in front of everyone with my skirt hiked up and my ass red.

A few girls snickered as I passed. I kept my head down as I went into the kitchen. Two men were hanging out in there but I was careful not to meet their eyes. I went about my business preparing Mr. Wood's coffee as if this were all normal.

"Looks like someone got in trouble," one man said as he reached out to touch my hot ass. He gave it a little slap which made me jump. "You're the new girl, aren't you?"

I nodded, pressing brew on the Keurig.

He slid his hand between my ass. "You're expected to answer when a man asks you a question. A nod isn't enough. I should spank you more for that."

I winced. "Yes, I am. I'm new."

His fingers found their way to my pussy, sinking into my wetness. I tried not to react but was surprised by how good it felt.

"You're Lance's new piece," he said. "I heard about you. Sent to the pillories on your third day. Now your ass is cherry red. What a way to start."

I said nothing, anxious to get back to Mr. Wood with his coffee, but I couldn't move because he had his fingers lodged in my pussy, working them. He pushed them in deeper before abruptly pulling them out.

"Go deliver your coffee," he said. "I don't want to get you into more trouble."

I let out the breath I was holding and returned to Mr. Wood's office. I knocked and waited for him to say come in before opening the door. I was surprised to see Zoey standing next to Mr. Wood in an outfit similar to mine.

I brought Mr. Wood his coffee, setting it on the coaster on his desk. He didn't look at me or acknowledge me. Instead, he turned to Zoey.

"Show her what I need done today," Mr. Wood said to Zoey, "then take her to the Cotton Club for dinner. I'll be at my usual table."

"Yes, Mr. Wood," Zoey said before escorting me out of his office.

ZOEY SHOWED me some stuff on the computer that needed to be done, mostly answering emails, entering data, nothing too challenging. She reiterated how important it was for me to follow directions explicitly. She told me how Mr. Wood was a patient man but how I didn't want to push him. She confided that she doubted Josie would be staying on the island much longer or at least not in Mr. Wood's house.

"She's always been a problem," Zoey said. "She likes to do her own thing which, you can see, isn't tolerated."

"But she's been here almost six months," I said. "How does she not know that by now?"

"Oh, she knows but that doesn't mean she's always obedient. She used to be more docile when she first arrived but then again she was in someone else's house. Mr. Wood acquired her about two months in."

I was surprised by how much Zoey was telling me but I wasn't going to mention it. Instead, I took it in, yearning for more, wanting to understand this crazy society.

"Why do you think she's acting out?"

Zoey looked at me. "Why do you think? Attention. She's not getting the attention she wants from Mr. Wood but if she acts out, he has to give it to her. Bad attention is better than no attention for some people."

I wouldn't want that type of attention but maybe on some level, it was exactly what she wanted.

"Does Josie work out of the house?" I asked, wondering how much I could get out of talkative Zoey.

"She used to work at a bar but lately she's been a cook on a yacht. I'm not sure that's what Mr. Wood wants her to be doing but since he doesn't always have the time to entertain her, he figured it'd keep her busy and satisfied. Anyway—that's enough about her. You need to focus on you and your desire to be here. I know this lifestyle isn't for everyone but you need to at least give it a fair chance."

I nodded. "I want to be here," I said, a little surprised that it was true. "I promise to do better."

"That's good," Zoey said, "because Mr. Wood wouldn't allow for two troublemakers in his house, especially if he thought they were conspiring. That would go against everything this place stands for. It'd be in your best interest to distance yourself from Josie."

I couldn't help think maybe she was right.

TWELVE

The rest of the morning was uneventful. Zoey and I stopped for a quick lunch in the break room which was fully stocked. I let out a sigh of relief when no men were in there. I needed a break. A couple other women joined us which made me happy. One was newer like me but she had been around for almost a month. She was loving living the lifestyle and said how she felt right at home. She also had a huge crush on her owner which I was learning was not uncommon.

"How many women are in your household?" I asked her.

"It's only me at the moment," she said with a huge smile, "but I've been warned by other women that he'll probably add a few more. He's new to the island, too, so he hasn't had the chance to build his household like some of the men. But he's super nice and has a wicked sense of humor. I wish these guys fell in love because I'd be all over it."

"Has any man fallen in love with his woman here?" I asked.

Zoey piped in. "It's highly unusual. Most of these men are here because they're tired of conventional women and they believe, on some level at least, that women are meant to be submissive to men. They're not looking for a partnership but to dominate someone. Love is rarely on the table although I've known quite a few women that have fallen in love with their owners but it's never reciprocated."

I hadn't thought about falling in love here—I knew that's not what this place was about—but I could see where it could happen, at least for the woman.

"Well, at least you're lucky to be with someone you're into," I said. "I can't imagine being with someone that you're not."

The other woman spoke up. "You're right, it's great to be with a man you're into but it can also be hotter to be with one you're not. I've been here for about eight months and spent some time with a guy I couldn't stand. Submitting to him even though he repulsed me made me hot. And there was no fear of falling in love with him which was a bonus. It makes me shudder to even think about it."

"How did you get out of that?" I asked.

"Oh sweetie," she said, putting her hand on my arm, "I didn't get out of it. I had to do what he said. He got tired of me and sold me off to one of his friends. Usually, the not so great ones have a shorter attention span but it's still up to them. I'd still be with him if that was his choice and I would have accepted it. That's what this lifestyle is all about—acceptance and surrender. You'll learn that once you're here longer."

I couldn't imagine being with someone I didn't like and felt grateful that I wasn't repulsed by Mr. Wood. He seemed like a nice enough man and, besides sending me to the pillories, had done nothing to me I wouldn't have done willingly. I knew I had a lot to learn and hoped to make a couple of female friends in the process to help make being here easier.

We wrapped up lunch quickly, not taking more time than necessary away from our desks. I was learning that the men didn't mind the women sometimes doing their own thing as long as it didn't interfere with what the men wanted them to do. At work, our job was to be at our desks working so they expected us not to take a long time with our lunch break.

I thanked the women for their insights and told them I hoped we could talk more. They both smiled at me in a way that had me wondering if I'd have the chance to talk with them like that again.

The rest of the afternoon went by in a blur. Mr. Wood called Zoey into his office at one point, closing the door behind them. Jealousy snaked up my spine as I imagined what they were doing in there. I knew enough not to ask her when she emerged smelling like sex and looking satisfied.

Mr. Wood left for the day earlier than us, wanting us to finish some correspondence that needed to get out that evening. We worked as quickly as we could while also ensuring that we weren't making mistakes. I liked the rhythm this job provided. I hoped Mr. Wood would keep me on as his secretary and wondered if there was anything I could do to help make that happen.

Zoey and I walked home together so we could freshen up for dinner. The thought of going out with Mr. Wood excited me. I knew Zoey would take me there as ordered by Mr. Wood but I wondered if she'd be staying. Part of me hoped to have Mr. Wood to myself for the evening.

Zoey told me to shower and wear the outfit she laid out on the bed for me. I liked not having to worry about my wardrobe as I emerged from the shower and slipped into a long sheer green gown with a sweeping v neck and little green crystals all over it. There were matching shoes encrusted with crystals and a delicate silver chain with a medallion on the end that read "fucktoy."

I put them on, feeling sophisticated. I pulled my hair up and smoothed on a slash of red lipstick. I looked myself over in the bathroom mirror to ensure I looked presentable and loved how the outfit sparkled.

I met Zoey in the kitchen. She slipped a white ribbon around my collar.

"Mr. Wood doesn't want anyone touching you until he sees you," she told me. "The men will see this white ribbon and will honor not touching you during our walk over."

I wondered if she'd be afforded the same luxury but I didn't ask.

The walk through the men's side of town was uneventful. With my white ribbon and Zoey's yellow collar, we got catcalls and they groped Zoey a few times but that was it. It was different not to be touched by anyone. I almost missed it.

The Cotton Club was a ritzy club that sat directly on the water with a grand open deck and a bar in the middle. We had to squeeze through a crowd of people as we entered. The hostess nodded to Zoey before escorting us to Mr. Wood's table that sat overlooking the water. Several men and women sat around the huge circular table. Mr. Wood stood when he saw us.

"Thank you for escorting her, Zoey," Mr. Wood said. "You may have the night to do with as you please."

Zoey smiled at Mr. Wood and said, "Yes, Mr. Wood," before disappearing the way we came. I let out the breath I had been holding, delighted that Zoey had been dismissed.

Mr. Wood touched my elbow.

"You look radiant, Annabelle," he said, causing me to blush. "This is your reward for going through your punishment without resistance. I'm proud of you."

He pulled out a chair for me and I sat, bursting with happiness that I made him proud. The women wore gowns similar to mine in a variety of colors, some with necklaces in addition to their collars. The men wore suits with ties. Everyone was sitting on chairs at our table but I noticed women at other tables sitting on their knees on the cool marble floor. Even though I could sit at the table, I kept my eyes lowered, careful not to look at any of the men.

The waitress came around and the men ordered for the women, including glasses of wine. Mr. Wood ordered me a petite filet with green beans and mushrooms while he ordered himself a regular filet with asparagus and a baked potato. I couldn't wait to eat a proper meal. It felt like forever. My stomach had adjusted to the less frequent meals and I hoped I wouldn't be starting from square one after eating tonight.

The men talked business while the women remained silent. The men seemed to work for Mr. Wood and I wondered if I had encountered some of these men in the office. A blush crept up my chest at the thought. Not that it mattered. These men probably had their way with all the women at the office and couldn't remember who was who. It was part of their life and my life now, too.

The entrees arrived quickly, looking and smelling amazing. I couldn't wait to dig in. I looked to Mr. Wood before starting, unsure whether I needed his approval. He gave me a slight nod. I didn't waste any time, appreciating the salty goodness of the steak blended with the mellowness of the red wine. Nothing had ever tasted so good.

I ate swiftly, enjoying each morsel, as the conversation continued around me. The men didn't include the women and that was fine with me. I didn't think I had much to contribute. I didn't fully understand Mr. Wood's business.

Mr. Wood kept his hand on my upper thigh, circling his thumb over my delicate skin which was driving me mad. He didn't touch me in any other way even though my body yearned for it. He ate and talked with the men, commanding the conversation, which made me feel even prouder to be the woman sitting next to him, like somehow this was a reflection on me.

I willed his hand to creep higher, to do something other than press into my thigh, but he didn't budge. I wondered if he was purposely tormenting me or simply liked having his hand on me.

"I heard there's another shipment on the way," one man said to Mr. Wood. "Do you think you'll acquire any more?"

Mr. Wood thought for a moment before saying, "I'm OK at the moment but my brother should look into it."

My ears perked at the word brother. I carefully looked across the circular table to a younger, more handsome version of Mr. Wood. He had the same broad shoulders and dark green eyes but with shaggier brown hair and a playful smirk. I pressed my lips together as I tried to take him in while not meeting his eyes. He must have felt me looking because he looked directly at me. I diverted my eyes, my heart hammering. I felt a blush bloom across my chest.

"I'll take a look at the new shipment," Mr. Wood's brother said. "I have the one but my brother tells me I need more."

Mr. Wood laughed. "It's the only way to get the full experience of this place otherwise it'll feel like a one-on-one relationship."

Another man laughed. "You don't want that. I've found four is a comfortable amount. It's not too many to manage but enough that you don't get bored with any of them."

I kept my eyes lowered, finishing my meal, getting aroused by the way they were talking about women as if we were nothing more than property to be exchanged. Mr. Wood only had three of us so I wondered if that meant he'd be adding to our household soon.

"God forbid I get bored here," the brother said, his eyes landing on me. "But what if I want a woman that's already here?"

I blushed, wondering if he was talking about me.

"That can sometimes be arranged," Mr. Wood said. "You'd need to discuss it with the woman's owner to see if he'd be willing to sell her to you. It's not uncommon for women to have various owners during their stay. Of course, there are always the brothel girls. Anyone can take them."

"Ah, the brothel girls," one man said, "always good for a quick fuck but not anything you'd want to take home and train. They're the rejects who didn't get picked up at auction or the girls who got kicked out of their house because they weren't being obedient enough. You don't want to deal with them. Wait for the fresh shipments. I think this one's coming in tomorrow evening."

"I'll go with you," Mr. Wood said to his brother. "I'll help you select one. You'll want to go with a girl who's had some training so you won't need to start from scratch. Those are easier. I don't think you're equipped to break anyone in."

"I think I can handle breaking a woman in," the brother said with a smirk. "At least the kind of woman I'd want. It could be fun."

I felt his eyes on me but I didn't dare look up again. Instead, I finished my wine and tried to look demure and not at all affected by his words even though my mind went straight to what it would be like to have him break me in.

"If you're determined to do it," Mr. Wood said, "at least let me help. Women can be complicated. Join us after dinner while I take Annabelle to the docks."

A frisson of fear and excitement spiked through me.

"It'd be my pleasure, brother."

ONCE EVERYONE FINISHED dinner and the plates cleared, Mr. Wood escorted me out of the restaurant with his brother at our heels. I still had on the white ribbon so no one touched me although I doubted they would have with Mr. Wood next to me. I was learning it was common courtesy for men to ask permission when the woman's owner was present.

I tried to walk as elegantly as I could while keeping my eyes lowered. I had no idea what Mr. Wood had planned for me but the idea of breaking me in didn't sound good. I couldn't imagine what else he could do to me that hadn't already been done. I doubted he'd deliberately hurt me unless I was being punished and after tonight's dinner, I felt like he had forgiven me for my previous disobedience.

We walked along the water out on the docks, passing enormous yachts. Most were lit up with parties. Music drifted down to us along with the loud murmur of conversations and the occasional moan or scream. A few women were bound on the back decks, their hands tied up over their heads, their bodies left for the pleasure of the men on board. I tried not to look but it was challenging not to. Their cries and moans made me curious about what was happening.

Mr. Wood turned at one of the larger yachts and boarded. Soft lighting illuminated light wood floors and elegant white surfaces. Smooth jazz drifted out to greet us. A woman wearing a short white skirt, a green collar and nothing else welcomed us with a tray of champagne and a smile. Mr. Wood took a glass for himself and handed another to me. His brother took a glass, smiling at the woman.

"Luke, let me introduce you to Sara, my chief steward," Mr. Wood said. "She will be more than happy to get you anything you need. Sara, this is my brother Luke. He's new to the island."

I watched Luke smile at Sara out of the corner of my eye.

"Sara, this is my latest acquisition, Annabelle. Please bring me my black case. We'll be on the sundeck."

"Yes, Mr. Wood," Sara said before disappearing into the boat.

I wondered how many other people were on board as Mr. Wood

escorted us up a flight of narrow stairs to the upper deck. It was a beautiful open space with a hot tub, a few lounge chairs and a wet bar. An overhang covered the bar area but otherwise the space was open to the evening sky. Since we had yachts on both sides, it wasn't private but offered an amazing view of the surrounding sea.

I was taking this in when Sara returned with a big black case and set it off to the side.

"Anything else, Mr. Wood?" she asked.

Mr. Wood eyed her. "Lose the skirt."

She instantly unzipped the skirt and stepped out of it. She had nothing on underneath.

"Bring us a couple of brandies in about 30 minutes. Otherwise, you're free to go."

"Yes, Mr. Wood," Sara said before disappearing down the stairs.

"You need to tell them what you want," Mr. Wood told his brother. "It's that simple. Sometimes it's about having them do things you know they don't want to do. We don't strive to hurt the women here but we do need to show them who's in control. You need to remind them of their place or else they'll become restless and want to return to their old way of life."

I stood there, eyes lowered, as I listened. My heart pounded as I wondered what he'd have me do that I wouldn't like.

"Disrobe, Annabelle," Mr. Wood said.

I dropped the gown off my body without hesitation, allowing it to pool at my feet. My nipples hardened in the cool evening air. I felt Luke's eyes on me, drinking me in. I shivered as if he had caressed me.

"Tonight we will play with restraints," Mr. Wood said as he flipped open the black case. He pulled out two leather cuffs and attached them to my wrists, buckling them closed and then locking them with tiny silver locks. Next, he put cuffs on my ankles, locking them into place. Last, he took off the white ribbon. "This will allow us to have our way with Annabelle without her having control over what's happening. She has been good at obeying but restraining a woman adds a level of control that not being restrained can't accomplish. When not restrained, she could be thinking in the back of her mind that she can always move, that she has a choice, where with the restraints, she doesn't."

I swallowed at the thought of having no choice. I wanted this but it also scared me. It felt like the ultimate test. Even though I had endured the pillories, this felt different, more intimate. At the pillories, it was random men and I was blindfolded, shielded from what was happening. Here nothing was standing between me and these two powerful men.

Mr. Wood guided me towards the edge of the overhang where he clipped my wrists over my head and my ankles out to the side so my feet were spread far apart. I felt stretched and immobilized, naked and exposed like the women I saw. My heartbeat quickened as I felt vulnerable and realized they could do anything to me.

Mr. Wood smiled at me.

"I want you to keep your eyes lowered this evening," Mr. Wood instructed. "You are not to look us in the eye or address us unless asked a question. Do you understand?"

"Yes, Mr. Wood," I said, my eyes lowered.

"Very good," Mr. Wood said as his hand reached out and grazed a nipple, sending a wave of arousal through me. "Tonight you will be our plaything, our entertainment, and your wants and desires will not be considered. This is part of your training, to see how well you can obey and be subservient. You may use the safe word if it becomes too much but know that will send you immediately off this island and cut of this society. I won't do anything that will scar or hurt you but it may be uncomfortable at times. I am very experienced and know what I'm doing. Do you trust me?"

"Yes, Mr. Wood," I said, meaning it.

Fear ran through me at the thought of what he planned to do. It must be something more than I've yet to experience for him to be making a point of telling me all this. I knew I wanted to take whatever he had to give me, to pass his test, because I wasn't ready to go home, but I knew it wouldn't be easy.

"Very well," Mr. Wood said. "Let's get started."

Mr. Wood disappeared behind me where the black case was,

leaving his brother in front of me. His brother didn't touch me but stood there looking at me which increased my anticipation, making me feel edgy. I wondered if Mr. Wood had planned this with his brother or if it had happened spontaneously. It surprised me that Luke hadn't been with a woman at dinner. He had mentioned having one but why wasn't she here?

My thoughts wandered, wondering about Luke, when I felt the first smack on my ass. I jumped at the sting, pulling against the restraints, when another one landed on my ass. I didn't make a sound but bit my bottom lip as heat spread across my ass. Another whack was followed by another one, each one resounding through me.

Luke watched as the whacks continued, each one hard and absolute, pushing me forward against the restraints, sending heat and pain across my ass. I closed my eyes against the pain, willing myself to take it, as Mr. Wood continued until I lost count.

I sank into a space within myself, my body on fire, my mind floating. I barely noticed when the whacking stopped. I felt strung out, my body humming, my pussy aching.

Mr. Wood said some words to his brother but I couldn't decipher them.

I felt a hand go between my legs and a couple of fingers slid easily into my wet pussy.

Mr. Wood said more words that I didn't hear. All my focus was on the fingers in my pussy and the pain radiating through my backside. The fingers teased and coaxed, pushing in and then spreading my vaginal walls, tickling my G-spot. I felt open and exposed in a way I had never experienced but I was beyond feeling embarrassed. It was more like being resolved that this was my life, understanding it didn't matter what I wanted, that it wasn't about me anymore. My mind eased at the thought and discovered a sense of freedom there as the fingers toyed with me.

Hands found my breasts, pulling on the aching nipples. I opened my eyes briefly to take in Luke's broad chest and his tapered waist. I caught his fresh woodsy scent as he moved closer, taking a nipple in his mouth. I thought I would die from ecstasy as pleasure flooded me. He teased one nipple with his tongue and teeth while massaging and pulling on the other one, working me up into a frenzy.

The fingers in my pussy abandoned me but I hardly noticed as all my attention was on Luke and the way he took each nipple into his fiery mouth while coaxing and pulling on the other one. Mr. Wood said more words but I didn't comprehend them, my mind too gone as the sensations rolled through me.

"She's delicious," I heard Luke say before pulling away, leaving me aching and strung out.

Mr. Wood said something from behind me I didn't catch.

"You're one lucky man," Luke said, causing a fluttering deep inside me. I radiated with pride, happy to have pleased him, happy to be right there in the moment with them. Something deep inside me felt complete, like this was right, like I needed to experience this.

I opened my eyes, still lowered, to see two sets of dress shoes in front of me. I dared not look up and closed my eyes to keep myself from looking at them. I knew everything Mr. Wood had done up until this point was more about pushing my limits than punishing me but I didn't want to give him any reason to punish me. I'm not sure I could have taken it and I wasn't ready to leave.

Someone pinched one nipple then pulled it before a clamp crushed down on it. A searing pain shot through me. Before I had time to adjust, my other nipple was pulled and clamped, the pain now shooting through both nipples. I squirmed at my new predicament and felt a tug that pulled on both nipples, increasing the pain.

"You don't want to keep these on too long," Mr. Wood said, "but it's a pleasant way to teach your woman that her body is for your enjoyment, not hers. See the delightful way she squirms? I guarantee you this is turning her on despite the pain. A woman's body is stimulated by pain as well as pleasure."

I squirmed as my nipples were tugged again and heard Mr. Wood chuckle. I bit my bottom lip to keep from crying out. I knew he was right about this turning me on. I felt helpless and vulnerable and wildly aroused. They could have done anything with me and I wouldn't have minded. My body ached to be taken, to be touched, to be used. I felt on fire, beyond ready.

I heard the men walk away and then a couple more male voices joined the mix. I wondered if they were men from dinner or different men, not that it mattered. I kept my eyes closed, blindfolding myself, because otherwise it would have been too much. Even with my eyes lowered, I could have seen them taking me in, witnessing my humiliation and use, and I didn't want to know how that felt.

I heard them move closer. Someone tugged on my nipple clamps, sending a fresh wave of pain through me.

"How delightful," an unfamiliar voice said. "Thanks for the invite."

"My pleasure," Mr. Wood said. "Sara, please get these gentlemen a drink."

I heard Sara take drink orders, feeling a rush of shame knowing she was witnessing me strung out like this. I'm sure she had seen women used in this way before—it seemed to be the thing to do on these yachts—but it felt more personal to me, more vulnerable. It's one thing to have men seeing me like this but quite another to have a woman who's not in a similar situation see me this way.

Conflicting emotions bombarded me as I stood there, legs spread, arms above my head, without being able to do anything about it. I felt my brain click into the fact that I was only a plaything, nothing more than a body to be used and enjoyed. The thought calmed and frightened me.

Fingers slid into me. I didn't know whose and I didn't want to look. They pushed in fully, at least three, before adding a fourth. I was wet, my body aroused and on fire, and I felt the stretching and the attention soothing.

He played with my clit, rubbing it with a thumb. I pulled on my restraints against the pressure, unsure if I wanted to pull away or sink into it. It felt too much. He increased the pressure and rhythm. Words were said, floating over my head, not fitting into my brain, as the pressure was building deep inside me, a deep ache longing to be released.

The torment continued until I cried out and came with a fierceness that shocked me and wrung me out. The fingers pulled out as I heard the men laughing, talking about what a sweet piece of ass I was and how lucky Mr. Wood was to have found me. I let myself hang from the restraints, grateful for their support, as my mind spun. Someone unclipped the nipple clamps, leaving my nipples raw and aching. One of them slapped one of my breasts, not hard but enough to sting I kept my eyes shut.

I heard Sara return as men thanked her and grabbed their drinks.

"What does Sara think of our little display?" one man asked. I felt myself go crimson. "Does she want to be next?"

"I am here only to please," she said.

"Then get on your knees and suck my cock."

I heard the zipper open and Sara fall to her knees. Part of me wished it was me instead of her on my knees. At least then I would feel like I was doing something more active than hanging there.

I dared a peek and saw Sara on her knees sucking one of the new men's cock. Hands found her breasts and tugged at her nipples as she worked, the man's hands tangled in her hair, pulling her mouth onto his cock. The scene aroused me and made my body tingle and ache, demanding attention.

The men talked over her head, about work, about their plans for the next few days, as she worked at the cock. The man quickened his pace, fucking her throat, before pushing himself deep into her and releasing himself. She took it, lapping it up, until he finished and pulled out. He petted her on the head before one of the other men took his place and stuck his hard cock in her mouth.

Mr. Wood talked with his brother about business and the island dynamics as if nothing unusual was going on. They sipped their drinks as they stood around the sundeck. The sun was slipping towards the horizon, casting long golden shadows. My arms ached from being stretched above my head. My ass and nipples had calmed down but the lingering pain made me aware of them.

Mr. Wood came up to me and stroked my ass before giving it a good smack, causing it to sting.

"The trick is to keep them unhinged," Mr. Wood said as he went back to stroking my ass. "Never let them get complacent and fall into a routine. It's easier to deal with stuff when you know what's coming. If it becomes routine, they check out. You don't want your women to check out. Instead, you want them on their toes, ready and willing to serve, wanting to keep you happy."

I felt his hand slide in between my ass cheeks, spreading them, before he pushed a well-lubed butt plug into my ass. It didn't hurt but filled me, stretching me.

"You need to keep it interesting," Mr. Wood said. "Remind them why they're here. Remember, the women come here voluntarily. They want to experience this lifestyle so it's up to you to ensure they do. It's a win/win for everyone. We fulfill a need for them while they fulfill a need for us."

Mr. Wood slipped a couple of fingers in my wet pussy from behind, stroking me, gently at first then with more urgency. I ached for his cock but knew better than to express that. Instead, I took what he offered, grateful to be receiving his attention, happy to not be forgotten.

Everything he said resonated with me. I chose this even though I was still figuring out why. Being used in this way, seen in this way, stirred something deep inside me, filled a deep longing to be of service, to be true to my submissive nature. I wasn't sure if I could go back to leading a normal life after this, dating men who'd take me out, open doors and expect nothing more than a kiss at the end of the night. I needed someone more forceful, someone who would put me in my place, command me, put me on my knees, use me as I yearned to be used.

Mr. Wood played with my pussy, teasing me, while Luke stood in front of me. They continued to talk about the best ways to use women and how to keep them in their place. Luke pinched and pulled on my nipples as they talked. They both dallied with me as if they were playing with a toy. I was only there for their amusement.

I kept my eyes lowered but opened. The other guy finished up with Sara, pulling out and spraying all over her face. She thanked him then sat there, waiting to be dismissed. He ordered her to get him and the other guy another drink then turned to Mr. Wood to see if they wanted anything.

"Yes, another round," Mr. Wood said, "plus some nibbles. Fix up a few of my favorites. And don't clean yourself off. I want you like this for the rest of the night."

"Yes, Mr. Wood," Sara said before standing and disappearing downstairs.

The other men joined Mr. Wood and Luke, their hands roaming over my body, slapping my ass, pulling on my nipples, playing with my clit, as they talked, commending Mr. Wood on having such a subservient steward and for inviting them for such a fun evening.

"The women seem to be getting more scarce around here," one of them said. "And the ones that do come don't tend to stay long. How do you keep your women from leaving?"

Mr. Wood chuckled. "I treat them like the playthings they are and show them their place, something they crave. I keep them busy enough to feel useful while not too busy that they can't be of service. And I never give them any tasks that would tax their brain too much and I always remind them of their place."

The men continued to talk as they fondled me. Even though my body ached and I wanted nothing more than for a cock to plunge into me, I felt a sense of freedom in not having to be anything more than a body to these men. I didn't need to impress them or be something that I wasn't. I simply needed to be and I found that liberating.

Sara returned with the drinks and nibbles, the come still on her face and in her hair. The men thanked her by slapping her ass.

Mr. Wood unhooked my hands and allowed me to shake them out. He kept the cuffs on and when he felt I had enough time to adjust, bent me over and cuffed my wrists to my ankles. With my ass and pussy now on display, a wave of humiliation washed over me. Mr. Wood tapped on the butt plug and swirled it around a couple of times before teasing my clit with his thumb.

"Be my guest, dear brother," Mr. Wood said. "She's aroused and wanting it."

Heat spread through my chest at the thought of Luke fucking me.

There was something about him that intrigued me. He seemed different from the other men here, not fully buying into this society while also being intrigued by it.

"If you insist," Luke said with a laugh before adjusting himself behind me. He pushed a few fingers into me and I squirmed at the intrusion. "You're right, she's sopping."

I heard a zipper before he pushed his thick cock into me, filling me perfectly as he gripped my hips for leverage. He groaned as he started fucking me, plunging in deeper with each stroke. My body hummed with need as he filled me, his cock stretching me, making me feel complete and as if I was made for this.

It didn't take long before he increased his rhythm, fucking me with everything he had. My pussy gripped him, wanting more, which caused a moan to escape him which was almost my undoing.

Pressure built low in my abdomen as he continued to pump in and out. Blood rushed to my head in this inverted position but I didn't care. All I cared about was the cock filling me, threatening to push me over the edge.

"Oh my God," Luke called out as he pushed into me and stilled, emptying himself into me. I took it all, squeezing myself around him, wanting more but accepting what he had to give. A part of me was disappointed I hadn't come but knew better than to expect that. That wasn't my role. My only purpose was to be a hole to be filled, to please these men, and that thought pleased me.

"That was amazing," Luke said as he pulled out. "Thanks, brother. I'm thinking I'll need to use this one again."

Mr. Wood laughed. "We'll see about that."

THIRTEEN

Mr. Wood unclasped my restraints soon after but kept the cuffs on, saying he enjoyed seeing me in them. He hand-fed me some nibbles and let me use the bathroom, instructing me not to clean myself except to wash my hands.

I couldn't believe the reflection I saw in the mirror. My red lipstick was gone and my hair had come undone, random strands falling around my face. I looked a mess. My mascara smeared under my eyes. My face was red from being inverted for so long. I longed to wash my face, to splash cold water on it, but didn't dare. I knew Mr. Wood liked me looking a mess, a reminder of my place, and in a way I liked it, too. I liked not having to be perfectly put together all the time.

I sat at Mr. Wood's knee for the rest of the night as the men drank, talked and ate. I liked feeling invisible after they finished with me, resting on my knees, allowing my thoughts to drift. I felt pleasingly calm and restful, my mind still. I had nothing to worry about and nothing to think about, allowing my mind to drift. I felt empty and blissful, truly content.

Luke fondled my breasts before he left, pulling each nipple, sending waves of pleasure through me. I kept my eyes lowered, thrilled by his attention.

"Thanks again, brother," Luke said. "You've inspired me."

"Glad to help," Mr. Wood said. "Don't forget to check out the new shipment. I'll help you train anyone you acquire."

"I'll let you know," Luke said and then he was off.

The other two men left shortly after, leaving me and Sara alone with Mr. Wood. Sara had been kneeling on Mr. Wood's other side this whole time, obedient and quiet.

"Time for bed," Mr. Wood said to us. "Shower and then join me in the master cabin. Annabelle, you can take the cuffs off."

Taking that as my cue to leave, I uncurled myself, taking a moment to find my footing on numb legs. I followed Sara down the stairs and deeper into the ship. We went down three flights of stairs to the lower deck that housed multiple cabins with adjoining bathrooms.

"We'll be sharing this room," Sara told me as she guided me into a compact room with two twin beds that reminded me of a luxury hotel room. There was an adjoining bath with a big open shower. "It'll be quicker if we shower together."

I was surprised but tried not to show it. I slipped off my shoes and undid the cuffs as Sara started the water and slipped in. I slipped in behind her. She showered first, washing her hair, sudsing up and rinsing, before allowing me to go under the stream. The water felt amazing, warm and soothing. I washed my hair and soaped myself before rinsing. Sara reached over and switched off the water before handing me a thick white towel.

"How long have you been with Mr. Wood?" I asked.

"About three months," she said. "I started my journey on another yacht—that's how I came to be here. He was my Dom until he sold me to Mr. Wood who was looking for an experienced steward. I've always worked on boats so I'm used to being ordered around."

"Have you ever thought about leaving?" I asked as I toweled myself off.

"God no," Sara said with a laugh. "This is heaven to me. I get to be on the boat all the time, which I love, and be of service both sexually and domestically. What's not to love? I hope I never have to leave."

Her response didn't surprise me and I was learning more about how much a lot of women craved and needed this lifestyle. Maybe the men were right in creating it—a space where both men and women could be free to pursue their true natures. I knew it wasn't a lifestyle for everyone but for the ones who needed it, I could see where this place was heaven to them. My only issue was I wasn't sure where I fit into all this yet.

"Don't overthink it," Sara said, sensing my hesitancy. "Just enjoy it. Even if you end up leaving at some point, consider this a chance of a lifetime. I know Mr. Wood was rough on you tonight but that was his way of pushing you to see how much you could take. He's not into pain so the paddling won't be a usual occurrence, that is unless you piss him off then watch out. He's not one for insubordination."

"I'm learning that," I said, remembering my time in the pillory. I felt reassured that Mr. Wood wasn't into pain because I didn't think I was into it either but I enjoyed giving up control.

"We better get moving," Sara said. "We don't want to leave Mr. Wood waiting."

Sara led us up one flight of stairs to the main deck which opened up to a massive living space with a dining room and the master cabin at the front. Mr. Wood greeted us as we entered the master cabin A luxurious king-size bed dominated the room with a desk and chair to one side and an L-shape leather sofa on the other. Lights lit up behind and beside the bed, giving the space a warm glow.

Mr. Wood had taken off his jacket, unbuttoned his dress shirt and slipped off his shoes. He looked more relaxed than I'd seen him with a brandy in his hand.

"You'll both be sleeping with me tonight on the bed," Mr. Wood said, "one on each side. I'm pleased with how you both handled your-selves this evening so this is your reward. I probably won't be using you further tonight since I'm tired but, other than using the bath-room, don't leave the bed in the morning."

"Yes, Mr. Wood," we both said before turning down the covers and climbing into bed.

I SLEPT LIKE A ROCK, cuddled on my side with Mr. Wood's weight behind me. It had been a while since I slept on a bed and I basked in its softness. I must have fallen asleep the moment I laid down because the next thing I knew it was daylight and I felt Mr. Wood's hard cock against my ass.

Without words he reached a hand around to fondle my breast, caressing the nipple which awakened the fire in me. It had never dissipated last night after not coming and was easily stirred up.

He pinched my nipple and pulled as he moved closer to my back. I felt the heat of him and wondered if Sara was awake yet. I felt honored to be receiving his attention when there was another woman in the bed.

He pinched my nipple hard, causing me to squirm.

"That's it, girl," he whispered in my ear. "I want to see your reaction."

His hand pinched my nipple one more time before disappearing behind me. I felt it on my ass and then moving between my legs until his fingers found my pussy and slid in. I knew I was wet and spread my legs for him, allowing easier access, resting my calf on his legs.

"Good slut," he said as his fingers plunged in deeper. "I love that you're wet for me."

He pulled out his fingers before replacing them with his cock, pushing into me with one thrust, almost sending me off the bed. I gasped at the sudden intrusion, my pussy opening to him, enjoying being filled. He pumped in and out, his hand on my hip pulling me in tighter.

I heard Sara stir on his other side while Mr. Wood fucked me hard with almost a desperateness to it. I assumed he hadn't come either last night and was just as pent up as I was.

I opened myself to him, loving the way his cock thrust in and out of me as if claiming me. Arousal spread through me, blossoming low in my abdomen, causing my head to spin and my mind to go blank. I loved this feeling of bliss that enveloped me as Mr. Wood pumped into me.

He grasped my hair, pulling my head back, as his pace quickened.

He slurred something in my ear but I was too far gone to comprehend it. All my focus was on the cock sliding in and out of my pussy, allowing the heat to envelop me.

I squeezed down on his cock as he plunged into me again and again, allowing myself to fall over the edge. I came with such an intensity that I thought I might blackout. He gushed deep inside me, emptying himself, as I welcomed him.

He released my hair and fell back into the bed, taking his cock with him.

"That was amazing," he said.

I stayed on my side, too spent to move. He patted my ass.

"Sara, clean me off," he said.

"Yes, Mr. Wood," Sara said. I had forgotten she was in the bed.

FOURTEEN

The next few weeks blended together as I continued to work for Mr. Wood at his office, doing menial office work but grateful to be busy. The office men took advantage of me every once in a while, mostly when I was on a break in the kitchen, forcing me to suck their cocks or fucking me from behind, pulling out to squirt over my ass, happy to have marked me, demanding me not to clean myself until Mr. Wood directed me to.

Mr. Wood never did anything more than grope me while at work, probably too busy with other women to be bothered with me. I never saw Josie again. I wondered if Mr. Wood sold her or if she left. I knew better than to ask. Zoey gave nothing away, happy to have slipped back into Mr. Wood's favorite position. I didn't mind as much as I thought I would. I had no substantial connection with Mr. Wood outside of sex and work. He was nice enough most of the time, happy to put me in my place and direct me, but he mostly left me alone, telling me my overall duties, like keeping the house clean and coming to his office, but otherwise, my time was my own.

I saw his brother Luke a few times at the office since Luke worked for Mr. Wood. He always winked at me which made me feel special although he never touched or used me again. I hadn't seen him using other women in the office either and wondered if he had acquired more women as his brother had suggested.

A flush of jealousy washed over me as I imagined Luke being pleased by his women, setting up his household, and fucking them whenever he wanted. Maybe he didn't need the office girls because he was satisfied at home.

I made some loose friendships in the office with the other women. We had coffee breaks together and lunched. Once in a while, one of them accompanied me to the shops on the women's side of town. Zoey must have done the grocery shopping for Mr. Wood because he never asked me to do it. Instead, I browsed the bookstores where all the titles reflected keeping a woman in her place. The thought still gave me a little thrill even though I'd been living the lifestyle a couple of months now. I still didn't know if I wanted to stay another six months but knew I had time to figure it out.

It surprised me the simple lifestyle didn't bore me but never knowing when I'd be used kept me on my toes. I had gotten used to walking around in almost nothing but going into the office covered up kept bringing me back to a more normal mindset and kept the revealing outfits that much more alluring for me.

The men never seemed to tire of using the women which amazed me. They groped, catcalled and demanded things if I wandered into the men's side of town which wasn't often. I still wore a black collar which left me open for anything. I wondered when Mr. Wood would switch it and sometimes wondered if he had forgotten about it or if I was still being trained. I never said no to anything or scoffed as I've seen some women do. That usually landed them in the pillories for a few hours and I didn't want to go back there.

I had fallen into a nice routine when Mr. Wood summoned me into his office one day.

"I appreciate the work you've been doing," he said as I stood in front of his desk, "and you've been an integral part of my household. As you may have noticed, Josie is gone. I couldn't continue to tolerate her indiscretions so I sold her to one of the yacht owners. You probably won't see her around town. I believe they have restricted her to the boat.

"I'm planning to acquire a few more women in the next couple of days. There's a new shipment coming in and I've heard good things about the women who will be arriving. I will need extra time to train them so I am sending you to live with my brother for the next month while I'm busy with these women."

I blinked at him, surprised, but said nothing.

"You are to obey Luke as you've obeyed me. He's newer to the lifestyle and only has one woman in his household so he may not be as strict as me. I want you to continue to follow the rules I've laid out for you or I will get word back and you will be punished accordingly."

I swallowed, unsure of what to think.

"Yes, Mr. Wood," I said, knowing no other response would do.

My head swam with the reality of being sent to Luke's household. It thrilled part of me—Luke seemed to have a more personal touch—while another part of me didn't want to learn someone new. I had just gotten comfortable in Mr. Wood's household.

"You will go to his house after your shift today. I'll give you directions. He's not far from here and is expecting you. You'll continue to work here under me a few days a week and my brother will dictate the rest of your time. Do you understand?"

I nodded. "Yes, Mr. Wood."

"Good. You may return to work."

I left with my head spinning. Was Mr. Wood not pleased with me? Was I being sold? I knew Mr. Wood said this was temporary but I couldn't help feel it may be permanent. I wasn't sure how I felt about that. I felt adrift, unmoored, as I tried to rationalize what had just happened. It didn't bother me that Mr. Wood was looking to acquire new women—although it made me wonder if I wasn't satisfying him. He had spent less time with me these past few weeks but I hadn't thought to question what that meant.

I wanted to ask my friends about it at lunch but felt too embarrassed to bring it up. I felt ashamed to be sent to someone else's household, like I wasn't doing something right. But as much as it was bothering me, I had to get their opinions.

"Have either of you been sent temporarily to someone else's household?" I asked over salads. There were no men in the break room so I felt more relaxed asking.

Kayla's eyes widened. She was a 23-year-old highlighted blonde who had been on the island for a few months. "I haven't. Is that happening to you?"

I looked down as I felt myself blush.

Kayla put her hand over mine.

"Oh sweetie, I'm sure it happens. There aren't any rules here except the ones the men give us. I'm sure it'll be all right. Is he sending you to someone awful?"

I shook my head. "No. He's sending me to his brother who I feel a bit of a connection with. What's bothering me is why he's sending me away. Is he tired of me already?"

The other woman laughed.

"Oh dear, whether or not he's tired of you, it doesn't matter. That's not your concern. You need to stop worrying about what these men think of you. The sooner you do that, the happier you'll be. Sometimes there's no good reason for what they do. They do it because they want to and that's good enough for them. It needs to be good enough for you, too."

I looked into her deep brown eyes. She had been here a month longer than me and already seemed to have it all figured out. I was envious. I still felt lost.

"Your only concern needs to be following orders and being pleasing. That's it. Everything else doesn't matter. We're all interchangeable—you must have realized that by now. The only reason we're valuable is because we're here voluntarily and they're not into having women here who don't want to be here. That's it. Allow yourself to give in to your role here and you'll be much happier. Find a way to enjoy it."

I let her words sink in. I had forgotten that what I wanted didn't matter here and that my only purpose was to please these men, any of the men, and to not worry about where I ended up. At least I felt like Luke wouldn't be cruel or abusive—something I feared when coming here. I wasn't into pain although Mr. Wood had shown me how to appreciate it and give myself over to it. I had to remind myself yet again that I chose this and I was free to leave at any time. Although the moment I left, I could never come back. I needed to be sure about making the choice to leave. I wasn't there yet but it was nice having that option.

"Thanks, Jade," I said, meaning it. "You're right—I have the wrong mindset. I haven't given myself over to this lifestyle yet."

"It's now or never," she joked. "You'll get the hang of it."

MR. WOOD LEFT directions to his brother's house on my desk. Nerves invaded my stomach as I made my way towards it with the rest of the after-work crowd. A few hands found their way under my skirt to my ass as I walked but I ignored them, no longer affected by them as I once was. Being groped had become a non-issue. I didn't feel honored or repulsed by it. It simply was.

As promised, Luke's place wasn't far from the office. Instead of a house like Mr. Wood's, Luke had a townhouse sandwiched in between other townhouses in a neat row overlooking a park edged with palm trees around an in-ground pool. I hadn't been in the water since I arrived and wondered if Luke would allow me to go for a swim. I wasn't sure how I would ask him since I wasn't supposed to ask the men questions but maybe he wouldn't mind me doing it on my downtime. Hopefully, I had downtime.

I wasn't sure whether to knock or to let myself in but decided knocking was the polite thing to do. I knocked a couple of times before lowering my eyes and waiting. It only took a few minutes before the door swung open and a short girl with a pixie cut stood in front of me. She wore nothing but a black collar and a wide, welcoming smile.

"You must be Annabelle," she said. "Come in. Luke is so excited to have you here and so am I."

I walked into a small foyer as the girl closed the door behind me. The space felt cramped and charmless. It reminded me of corporate housing—lacking personality.

"I'm Riley," the girl said, sticking out her hand for a quick shake. "I'm new here, too. Only two months. Luke acquired me first thing so I've only been with him. He hasn't taken me out much so I'm dying to explore the island. I heard things get wild here."

That was an understatement, I wanted to say but didn't. She seemed wide-eyed and innocent and I felt it only fitting that she discovers this place on her own. I didn't want to squash her enthusiasm or offer my own experiences. I learned that each woman needed to digest this place at her own pace and figure out what it meant to her.

"I'm happy to be here," I said instead, meaning it. My nerves were settled by Riley's warmth and from not having to see Luke first thing. "Welcome to the island. I hope you love it."

"I hope so, too," she said. "I know Luke's new, too, so I'm sure my experience has been a bit muted because of that but I'm not complaining. Let me show you to your room."

I followed Riley up the stairs off the foyer to a small room with a twin-sized bed, desk and chair. It didn't have an adjoining bathroom like I had at Mr. Wood's place but that didn't bother me.

"My room's next door," Riley said as she ushered me to it. It was set up like mine except with a few postcards on the wall and books stacked on the desk. "Luke's fine with me writing to my friends and family back home so I'm sure you'll be able to do that, too, if you want. He understands that six months is a long time."

I hadn't thought of writing to anyone. The one friend who knew I was here wasn't expecting anything from me but it was reassuring to know I could access the outside world if I wanted. I hadn't thought it was a possibility.

"What brought you here?" I asked, feeling bold as I took in her room.

"Oh, you know, I always wanted to be dominated by a guy. None of the guys I dated back home got it and I felt ridiculous trying to explain it to them. I had this inner need to be dominated. I know there are other ways to explore this lifestyle but none that pay like this."

I laughed. That was true. I had forgotten about the money.

"I thought I'd give it a go," Riley said. "I still can't believe I'm here. I have to keep pinching myself. I never considered myself an exhibitionist but now that I've spent the past two months wearing practically nothing, I'm not sure I can go back to being clothed. Don't you feel restricted in that getup?"

I looked down at my work outfit—the crisp white blouse and the black pencil skirt. It had become my uniform most days and I no longer thought much of it.

"It's whatever," I said. "Mr. Wood likes the office girls to be more covered so the men can get some work done. I like how it lends itself to a feeling of normalcy. It makes me forget where I am sometimes except in my real life back home I wouldn't go to work like this without undergarments."

Riley laughed. "Yea, I guess that's true. Luke likes to keep me nude, at least for now. He didn't tell me how he wants you so I guess you can decide until he tells you. Maybe he'll like this outfit."

Riley showed me the bathroom across the hall from our rooms before taking me back downstairs to show me the small kitchen, sitting room, downstairs bathroom and Luke's office. She chatted the whole time, telling me about herself and how much she was enjoying her time with Luke.

"Help yourself to anything in the fridge or pantry," Riley said. "I don't cook but I'm learning. Luke mostly eats out so no need to worry about him. Sometimes he brings me back leftovers since he knows I'm not the best cook."

I was hungry but didn't feel like eating. What I wanted was to see Luke so I'd have a better understanding of what he expected of me while I was here. I didn't think asking Riley was appropriate or that she'd know.

"What do you do with yourself during the day?" I asked, thinking that was a safe topic.

"I mostly clean," Riley said, "not that there's much to it, or read. Luke has a computer in his office but I'm not allowed on it. I write postcards to my family and friends that Luke brings back to me from the shops. Luke has the groceries delivered so I don't do that. In a way, it's nice—all this freedom. It's nice not to have to worry about all that much. Back home, I'm the oldest of six so I always had to worry about other people. Here I just need to worry about Luke."

"Aren't you going stir crazy?" I asked. The place was so small. "Do you know why Luke hasn't taken you out or let you out more?"

Riley laughed. "I think Luke is taking it slow with me. He told me some of the things that happen to the women when they're out on their own and he's not sure that would be good for me right now."

"But he gave you a black collar," I said, stating the obvious. "It allows any man to do just about anything to you. If he wanted to keep you untouched, he could have gone with a white collar."

Riley smiled. "Yes, that's true, but his brother, you know Mr. Wood, insisted that Luke starts with the black collar to help break me in. Mr. Wood told Luke that he believes women need to be broken in right from the start or else they won't thrive here. Luke went along with it because, seriously, what else was he going to say, but I don't think that's Luke's style. He's more one on one."

I wondered why he wanted me here then. But then I remembered it was Mr. Wood who had sent me here, not Luke. My heart plummeted at the thought. Maybe Luke didn't want me here. Maybe that's why he wasn't here to greet me.

Riley must have sensed my confusion because she said, "I'm sure he'll be happy to have you here. You came highly recommended by Mr. Wood."

"That's nice to hear," I said, not believing it while wondering how much Riley knew. Did Luke tell her everything or was she eavesdropping? I didn't want to ask because I didn't want to know.

"I think I will unwind a bit in my room until Luke returns," I said. "Do you have any idea when that'll be?"

"Probably after dinner. His schedule varies but he's usually not out too late. I think he had something important to do this evening or I'm sure he would have been here to welcome you himself. He's considerate like that."

I smiled at her before escaping to my barren room.

FIFTEEN

I must have fallen asleep on the floor. Not wanting to use the bed, I had curled up next to it, letting my thoughts wander. The next thing I knew, I was being gently shaken awake. I blinked into the darkness. A crack of light came under the door. A large figure loomed over me. My heart pounded as fear spiked through me. It took me a moment to realize where I was and who was standing over me.

"Sorry to wake you," Luke said, his voice soft, "but I wanted you to know that you're more than welcome to sleep on the bed. I know my brother makes his women sleep on the floor but sleeping on the bed is permitted in my house."

I blinked at him. I couldn't see his face. The light from the door was behind him, making him an inky silhouette. He offered his hand to help me up which I took. It felt warm and firm in mine and I was reluctant to let it go once I was standing.

"Thank you," I said. "What would you like me to call you?"

He laughed. "Luke is fine. I'm not formal, as you probably guessed during our limited interaction with each other. My brother wants me to be more strict, more like him, but that's not my style. Honestly, I only came to the island to please him. As you know, he can be a force."

I cracked a slight smile.

"I'm sorry I wasn't here to welcome but I had business to attend to that couldn't wait," he said, "otherwise I would have been here."

"No worries," I said. "Riley showed me around."

"She's great, isn't she?" Luke asked, sending a small spike of jealousy through me. "She's been easy to work with. She's a natural submissive."

As am I, I thought but didn't say. He must know that already or I wouldn't be here.

"Anyway, feel free to use the bed," he said, "and anything else in the house except my computer. Since you're familiar with the island, even more than me, you can come and go as you want unless I request otherwise. I know you'll continue your job at my brother's office and that's fine. I keep Riley nude because she enjoys being told what to do but you can wear, or not wear, whatever you want. I'll make sure you have some dresses or you can go out and buy them."

He peeled off a couple of hundred bucks from his pocket and handed them to me.

"If you wouldn't mind taking over the grocery shopping, too, that'd be great. I've been having it delivered but it'd be better if you get what you want. Riley's not much of a cook so she won't be able to help you but you can keep it simple. I mostly eat out or pick something up—I'm not the greatest cook, either—so unless you love to cook, don't worry about me."

I let his words sink in. I felt like a guest more than a submissive woman and part of me liked it.

"I'm not the greatest cook, either," I said, "but I'd be more than happy to make dinner or any other meals for you. I know a little and am willing to learn more."

I felt him smile at me. "That'd be nice, Annabelle. It's nice to have you here."

I OPENED my eyes and stretched. I had the best night's sleep that I've had in a while. I snuggled into the warm bed, pulling the pillow up under my nose, inhaling its clean fresh scent. Sunlight streamed in through the window. No blinds protected me from its glare, only sheer white curtains that hung loose and looked they were waiting to be flung open.

My heart tickled at the brief conversation with Luke last night. Staying with him sounded like it would be easier, more normal, that staying with Mr. Wood. I already wanted to please him more than anything.

Not knowing what to wear, I slipped back into my work outfit. I didn't have to go to work today but I liked the coverage.

My stomach growled, urging me to the kitchen. The lights were on but no one was around. The townhouse was quiet. I assumed they were both out but found it odd that Riley would be out, too. She told me last night she rarely left the house.

I went for the fridge, grateful to find yogurt and fresh berries. I pulled them out before opening and closing drawers until I found a spoon. I sat down at the counter, figuring Luke wouldn't mind since he had let me use the bed, and dove into the yogurt and berries. It wasn't until I finished and was cleaning up that I found a note for me by the sink.

Annabelle—

I know it's your day off from work today but please use the day to buy outfits for yourself along with whatever groceries you want. I left additional money in case you need it. I'll be back after dinner. Feel free to take Riley with you but don't feel obligated. I will understand if you need alone time.

Best,
*   Luke*

My heart blossomed at the note, happy to have a day to myself. Although Riley seemed like a nice enough girl, it had been a while since I went out on my own and liked the idea of shopping solo.

I folded the note and stuck it into the pocket of my skirt before going back upstairs to freshen up. I took a quick shower, pulling my hair up into a loose topknot. There was no makeup or much else in the joint bathroom so I figured I'd need to pick some up while I was out. I was never big on makeup but I liked to use some to enhance my natural beauty and hide the dark circles under my eyes.

I heard Riley stirring downstairs when I emerged fresh and ready to head out. Part of me wanted to avoid her so I wouldn't feel guilty leaving without her. I assumed she had slept in or maybe spent the morning reading or doing something in her room. Or maybe she had spent the night with Luke and he had kept her up late. I didn't like that possibility so I pushed it out of my mind as I descended the stairs.

Riley was all smiles when she saw me which only made me feel more guilty for wanting to go shopping without her.

"Hi, Annabelle," she said as she cooked something on the stove. "Sleep well?"

I stepped into the kitchen. "Yes, very well. And you?"

She laughed. "Oh, I always sleep well. I stayed up too late reading a novel Luke brought me but since I knew he'd be gone today and I could sleep in."

"I've yet to crack into any of them. Are they good?"

"Oh yes, they're good and very informative. The novels reinforce the theme that men are meant to dominate women so it's all very BDSM. I know Luke isn't that into it but he knows I'm submissive so he tries. There are some informative how-to type books, too, like how to best serve a man, stuff like that. I'm finding those helpful since this is all new to me."

I smiled at her enthusiasm. Maybe Luke was lucky to have her.

"I'm new to this, too," I said. "I hadn't been exposed to any of this before I got here."

Riley let out a little giggle. "That's reassuring. You look so relaxed and confident."

I laughed. "You will be, too, soon enough. I've been here longer than you. It takes time to adjust."

She finished cooking her eggs before turning her attention to me. I wanted to slip out the door, telling her to have a great day, and not looking back while something tugged at me to invite her along. I'd be giving up my alone time, something I craved, but it'd be nice to be the one showing the newbie around for a change.

"I'm heading out to the shops and the grocery," I heard myself say. "Want to join me?"

Her eyes sparkled. "Really? Are you sure?"

I thought for a moment and I was sure. "Yes. I'd love it."

SIXTEEN

Riley slipped into a sheer dress before we headed out. I felt it was better than wearing nothing even though it didn't conceal anything. The men were used to getting their way regardless of what the women wore but I didn't want Riley to be an easy target. We'd be going through the business district which was more professional and not that crowded on the weekends before pushing through to the women's side of town. She wore a black collar so Luke was cool sharing her so I didn't need to worry about that. I felt protective of her, like she was my charge during our time out together. It stressed me a little as we slipped out the door.

We didn't talk as we passed by men dressed in suits in the business district. A few men glanced our way but they left us alone. It wasn't until we hit the women's section that I let out the breath I'd been holding.

"Have you been over here before?" I asked as I took in the shops as we walked, wondering what I wanted to buy in terms of clothes.

"No," Riley said. "I've only been out to a few dinners on the men's side of town and I was with Luke both times. He's been busier lately so he's left me on my own a lot more but I don't mind."

I wanted to ask more about Luke but didn't want her to know I was interested. Instead, I popped into one of the boutique clothing shops with Riley behind me.

A rainbow of sheer dresses hung on one wall while the middle had various blouses and skirts, more colorful than the basic white and black I'd been wearing. Towards the back were rows of heels and sandals along with handbags. I didn't know where to start and wondered what Mr. Wood would think of me buying new clothes.

"Oh, this is cute," Riley squealed, holding up a sheer forest green blouse with long billowing sleeves. "This would look stunning on you."

I felt the sheer fabric, surprised by its weightlessness.

"You can pair it with this," Riley said, holding up a short plaid skirt that flared. "It'd be like a naughty schoolgirl but more sophisticated. Try it on."

I took the garments from her, intrigued, and turned to look for the changing rooms when I realized there weren't any. We were expected to change out in the open as if it were no big deal.

I slipped out of my white blouse, draping it over a chair by the mirror, before sliding into the forest green blouse. I loved the feel of it against my skin. I took off my skirt, putting it over my white blouse, before slipping on the plaid skirt. I studied myself in the mirror and was surprised by the woman looking back at me. She had a hint of naughty schoolgirl but something more. The sophistication was there, which I loved, but I felt more together, more sure of myself. Like I had arrived. Like I knew who I was.

Out of the corner of my eye, I spotted a necklace on one of the counters and slipped it around my neck. It was a simple silver chain with a teardrop pearl. It completed the look.

"You look beyond amazing," Riley said. "You have to get this."

I agreed. I needed this in my life.

I paid for the outfit and the necklace after asking Riley if she wanted anything. I figured she didn't have any money and I felt bad buying things without at least offering. She shook her head, telling me she was happy with the outfits she had and how she was kept nude most of the time which was fine with her.

From there we wandered into a makeup and lotion shop where two women fawned over us the moment we stepped through the doors. They wanted to give us makeovers which Riley accepted on our behalf. She explained to the women how she wanted to update her look so she'd be more desirable for the men. I hadn't thought of it that way. I was doing all this to please myself.

I let one woman direct me to the best makeup for my skin type and for achieving the more natural look I liked. She cooed about how men appreciate the natural look over the more made-up look and wasn't it nice that different men had different tastes. She convinced me to try the smoky eyeshadows, telling me how they were wonderful for evening adventures.

"You'd be surprised how much different makeup will make you feel differently about yourself," the shopgirl explained to me. "Try different looks for different occasions and to feel differently. The smoky eye will help you feel more alluring while the more natural look will help you feel, well, more natural."

I couldn't disagree so I nodded. I had never been much of a makeup girl but felt now was probably the best time to start. I let her direct me to other looks she thought I'd like, showing me how to apply each one for maximum effect. I appreciated how thorough she was and her wealth of knowledge amazed me.

This time, Riley wasn't shy about letting me buy her purchases which I did so gladly.

"I think Luke will love all that we bought today," Riley said once we were back out on the street, "especially your new outfit."

I felt a little frisson of something bloom in my abdomen.

"Maybe you should look at getting an evening dress, too," Riley said. "Each time Luke's taken me out, he's had me wear a long gown. Unless you brought some with you."

I hadn't brought anything with me and Mr. Wood hadn't sent anything over. I hadn't thought to ask to bring anything.

"That's not a bad idea," I said as I scanned the street for a dress shop.

After another hour of shopping, I had purchased two long gowns, a couple pairs of sparkly heels, and more jewelry to go with the gowns. Riley refused to let me buy her anything else, claiming she was just happy to be out shopping with me. We stopped for lunch at one of the little cafes on the women's side of town. No men were around so we were able to talk during our meal.

Riley filled me in on her childhood, telling me about her younger sisters and brothers, and how she was hoping to make enough money on the island to help send them to college. She hadn't gone but knew they all wanted to go but they wouldn't be able to go without going into debt, something she wanted to prevent if possible.

"We've never had a lot of money—it was just my mom and us kids after our dad died—so I want to do this for them. They're all so smart and ambitious that it would be a shame if they weren't able to go after their dreams."

My heart swelled at Riley's selfishness but she assured me she got as much pleasure out of giving as they would from receiving. It was her nature which was why being on the island was a natural fit for her.

I shared a bit about my background, how I graduated from college without knowing what I wanted to do with my life, how I figured this would help give me a jump start. It'd pad my pockets, allowing me more time to figure things out and possibly secure the best job for me once I returned home. I told her how my parents were older and retired, traveling the world, and how I didn't want to bug them for anything. They had raised me to be self-sufficient so I strived to make it on my own.

Riley smiled and nodded, asking me follow-up questions, like have I ever been in love or did I have boyfriends.

"I don't think I've ever been in love," I admitted, not realizing until that moment that I hadn't. "I thought I was once but I don't think it was actual love, more like a girlish crush on a guy who was never fully mine. He flirted with me but he never asked me out, never did more than kiss me a few times while we were all out at the club. I've chalked it up to being a college thing. People tend to hook up in college for no good reason. No relationship necessary."

"Kind of like here," Riley said. "They told me not to expect any kind of relationship with the men here. It's just not done."

I finished my salad. "Yea, I guess you're right. This is kind of like college except the men have the upper hand and the women just have to go along with it."

"Except we've agreed to go along with it," Riley said. "I think college girls sometimes want more."

I couldn't argue with that. I had wanted more but the guy I thought I was in love with just wanted random hookups, stolen kisses and nothing more. I didn't know what happened to him after we graduated. I wasn't significant enough for him to keep in touch.

I paid for lunch, thanking our waitress for everything. She smiled, said how she was happy to serve us. I wasn't ready to head back to the townhouse yet and it was such a gorgeous day, I asked Riley if she wanted to wander out to the beach. I had heard from the girls at the office that there was a gorgeous beach not too far from the woman's side of town where we could frolic in the water and relax.

Riley jumped at the opportunity to do a little sunbathing. We slipped into the drugstore and bought sunscreen along with two towels before heading to the beach. We skirted the men's side of town to avoid walking past the marina. I didn't want to chance walking past the boats.

Men catcalled us from their perches at the outdoor bars as we passed. A few groped us, fondling our asses and tweaking our nipples. It had been a while since I'd been groped on the street since I had spent most of my time in the office where I only gave the occasional blow job and sometimes got fucked over a desk. The lewdness of it stirred up something inside me.

I glanced at Riley who was soaking it all in. She walked with her head held high and giggled whenever anyone touched her.

The beach was crowded—men and women everywhere. White deck chairs faced the water, occupied only by men. Women sat on towels at their sides or off on their own.

We found a spot not too far from everyone but far enough that we had some space. I wanted a chance to swim and didn't want to make it obvious that we were available to be used.

Riley seemed to make a show of stripping off her sheer dress and folding it neatly on her towel. She knew enough not to say anything to me with the men present. I was sad that our conversation had to stop. I was enjoying our time together.

I slipped out of my blouse and skirt, sticking them into my shopping bag. I squirted sunscreen in my hand before handing it over to Riley. We lotioned up, helping each other get our backs. There was nothing sexual with our interaction but I couldn't help feeling we were part of some cheesy porn. After all, we were naked on the beach with a bunch of men watching. I felt their eyes on us, enjoying the show.

We made it into the ocean with no one approaching us. I welcomed the feel of the warm salt water against my skin, luxurious and relaxing. Riley splashed around not that far from me while I dove into the waves, allowing the water to wash over me, cleansing me, allowing me to let go of my negative thoughts, feelings and apprehensions.

I realized again that being here was my choice and one I could walk away from. I might as well enjoy being here and make the most of it. Once I left the island, I'd have to decide what I wanted to do with my life. Until then, I didn't need to worry about it.

We swam for a while, splashing around, laughing, sharing inside jokes with our eyes. A few others swam, too, but not close enough for us to hear them.

Back on the beach, we laid out on our towels, letting the sun dry us. I felt a sense of freedom as we laid there nude with no cares in the world. I wanted to continue talking with Riley—I liked her—but I also loved the silence, not having to talk, not having to do or be anything more than who I was.

None of the men paid us any attention which I was happy about. I wasn't in the mood to satisfy some random man's craving. That I could do without. I was starting to identify parts of this lifestyle I enjoyed and parts I didn't. I wasn't sure I would renew my time here but I was happy that I came.

We didn't stay much longer. Neither one of us wanted to burn. We wrapped up and walked back to Luke's, slipping on our clothes just to have something on as we walked through town. It didn't cover much but I liked the added layer it provided. It wasn't until we were back in the women's section that we could talk again. Riley expressed her surprise that we weren't used while I expressed my relief at being left alone.

"I honestly haven't had sex with that many guys," Riley told me as we walked into Luke's place. "I was hoping being here would broaden my horizons but it's only been Luke and me and sometimes his brother."

My ears perked up. "You know Mr. Wood, Luke's brother?"

I'm not sure why this surprised me but it did. Of course Mr. Wood got around.

Riley smiled. "He's your owner, right?"

I nodded.

"We've been out to Mr. Wood's yacht a few times and out to dinner. I think there's a protocol when you're out with your owner where the other men can't just come and take you. They need to ask permission. I think Mr. Wood being around intimated the other guys from asking Luke. I've felt untouchable despite my black collar. Honestly, I was hoping for more."

We settled into the living room after grabbing some water out of the fridge. We left our bags in the kitchen. Luke wasn't home and I was happy to get in some serious girl talk.

"What has your experience been?" she asked.

I explained as best as I could, giving her a rundown of life with Mr. Wood, how I was punished for taking off with Josie when I should have stayed in, life at the office and my time on the yacht. She remained silent while I talked, her mouth gaping. I tried not to feel embarrassed as I went on. I didn't get into all the details but enough that she got a solid idea of what I'd been through. I told her it'd been quiet lately and how Mr. Wood was acquiring new women which was why he sent me to Luke.

"How many women do you think Mr. Wood wants?" Riley asked.

"I have no idea," I said, "and it's none of my business. I've learned that our wants are irrelevant. They want to keep us happy so we won't leave but it's all about them. That's what we signed up for."

Riley's eyes went wide as she took it in. I hope I hadn't startled her but I felt it was better she found out sooner than later what she was in for on this island in case Luke let her out more. Some random guy on the street hadn't even taken her since she'd always been with Luke. Part of her seemed like she wanted it while the other part was apprehensive. I could relate. I still didn't know where I stood with it. My six months were coming up and I needed to decide whether I wanted to stay.

"Why do you think Mr. Wood sent you here instead of keeping you with him?" Riley asked. "I would think you'd be helpful showing the new girls around."

The question stung. It had been sitting in the back of my mind.

I tried to shake it away. "Mr. Wood has this girl Zoey who's more than capable of showing any new girls around. She's the one who showed me around when I first arrived and fills that capacity for Mr. Wood. She's very good at it. Other than that, I have no idea why Mr. Wood wanted me here. Maybe he thought Luke should have more than one girl in his house to keep it from becoming like a normal relationship. Who knows."

Riley smiled. "I fantasized about Luke and I falling in love and running away together. He's hot and so nice but I don't think he sees me that way. He's fucked me here and there but it always felt forced—like that's what he was expected to do. I've let go of the fantasy."

"That's probably wise," I said, curious why Luke had been reluctant to fuck Riley. She was a cute girl. Likable, too. My mind whirled with the possibilities. "Fantasies can be dangerous here unless they're of the purely sexual kind. They warned me about that from the beginning. The men here aren't looking for love."

"They warned me at intake, too," she said with a wistful look in her eye, "but I felt like maybe I'd be the exception. I'm sure sometimes it happens."

I let out a sigh. "I'm sure sometimes it does but I wouldn't hold my breath."

SEVENTEEN

Luke arrived sometime later, looking excited and energized. Riley and I were still curled up in the living room talking. I felt a tinge of guilt when he walked in, like I should be scrubbing floors or at the very least sitting on my knees waiting for him like a proper submissive, but he didn't seem to mind. He smiled when he saw us.

"I see you went shopping," he said. "I'm thrilled. Get some nice things?"

"Yes, very nice," I said. "Thank you. Riley got a few things, too."

"That's awesome," Luke said. "I hope you had fun."

"Lots of fun," I said, meaning it. Riley piped in, agreeing.

"That's great because I want you girls to get dressed in your fanciest outfit because I'm taking you out to dinner at one of the nicest restaurants on the island. Be ready in about 30 minutes."

We jumped up, grabbed our bags from the kitchen and hurried upstairs. I wanted to shower before going out and after a quick discussion with Riley, she agreed to let me hop in first. I washed as quickly as I could, conscious that Riley needed to get in, too. I pulled my hair up so there was no need for blowing it dry, not that I had a blow dryer.

I wandered back to my room and took my time putting on the new makeup I had purchased. I wanted to look amazing for Luke and for Mr. Wood if we saw him. I knew Mr. Wood and Luke socialized so there was a good chance I'd see him. Part of me wanted Mr. Wood to be sorry that he sent me to Luke—to see what he was missing—while another part of me felt I'd be happier hanging out with Luke and Riley a while longer. Luke had a laid back style that put me at ease. I needed this break.

Back downstairs, Luke waited in a tailored suit that hugged his broad shoulders and made me want to feel the muscles underneath. For a moment I let myself imagine that Luke and I were heading out for an actual date but I quickly reminded myself that was dangerous thinking and would only lead to heartache.

Luke whistled when he saw me, making me blush. I wore a long, silky emerald green gown that hugged my curves and had a dramatic v neckline that hinted at showing my hard nipples. I felt sexier than when I was naked. The silver heels completed the look, making me feel glamorous.

"You look beautiful," Luke said as I descended the stairs. "I'm happy my brother sent you to me."

I blushed and lowered my eyes, unsure how to respond. My heart blossomed.

"We'll have fun tonight," Luke said as he took my hand. It felt warm and comforting, the gentleness of it surprising me. I dared a look into his dark green eyes. He smiled. "I'm happy you're here."

Riley chose that moment to come down the stairs, all smiles, wearing a short white semi-sheer dress that flared out at her shapely thighs. Her nipples showed through the thin material but the scoop neck of the dress hinted at an innocence.

"There's my other girl," Luke said, extending his other hand to her. I felt a moment of jealousy as Riley accepted his hand but quickly shook it away. I liked Riley and she was here first. "I'm a very lucky man to have two beautiful women on my arms tonight."

Riley smiled and I couldn't help but smile, too, hoping this would be a fun night. It had been a while since I'd been taken out like this.

Luke walked us through the streets to the man's side of the island.

We got lots of looks and a few catcalls but the men kept their hands to themselves. The walk wasn't long but longer than I was expecting and my feet throbbed by the time we arrived at the restaurant. It was one I hadn't been to and sat right on the ocean.

Candles flickered on every table with low lit chandeliers everywhere, creating a romantic atmosphere. The place was packed. Most of the women sat on chairs around the tables but some were at the feet of their men. Some wore elegant gowns while others were nude.

A woman in an elegant floor-length semi-sheer gown greeted us as we walked in, recognizing Luke with a sexy smile and escorting us immediately to a table overlooking the beach. She handed a menu to Luke. The table was empty but set for four. I tried not to worry about who the fourth person might be.

Luke pulled out chairs for us which answered my question about where he wanted us to sit. I enjoyed being treated like a lady for once and not just a sex object. I made a point of smiling at Luke as he sat across from me. I wanted to ask who was joining us but knew better to initiate conversation in public.

A waitress showed up almost immediately in a long black apron and nothing else. She wore a white collar. She waited for Luke to talk before asking him what he wanted. Luke ordered a bottle of red wine along with several entrees. She scooped away the fourth place setting after asking Luke if anyone else would be joining us and he said no. I let out the breath I hadn't realized I'd been holding.

"I want it to just be us tonight," Luke said. "I want to celebrate Annabelle coming to stay with us and show you both that this island doesn't need to be all about the men taking advantage of the women here. I know you both signed up to be here for your own reasons and knew somewhat what to expect but I want you to know that some men want more than sex out of the women they're with."

The waitress returned with the bottle of wine, uncorking it for Luke and pouring him a taste before she poured out the other glasses. She told him the entrees would be out in a few minutes.

Luke raised his glass to us. "To two of the most beautiful women on the island. I hope you find what you want here."

I raised my glass to that, smiling, as I took a healthy sip, enjoying the deep berry flavor and the way the wine danced on my tongue. I felt like I was on a date but with Riley there as well. I think I could be OK being with a man who had more than one woman as long as it was something like this. This I could do and having someone like Riley around would be a joy.

A few men stopped by the table to chat with Luke, their eyes lingering on us, drinking us in as they talked business. One complimented him on his women and asked Luke if we were available to play.

"Not tonight, I'm afraid," Luke said. "Maybe some other time."

"Let's make that happen," the man said. "Sooner than later."

Luke gave him a smile. "I'll let you know."

The men moved on as the waitress returned with our entrees. She looked to Luke for guidance to what went where and he directed her. He had a steak with potatoes and asparagus, had her place a salmon with mixed veggies in front of me and something that looked like chicken in a white cream sauce over noodles in front of Riley.

"Eat up, ladies," Luke said, "before it gets cold."

I dug in, amazed by the complex flavors. I savored every bite, happy that Luke had sent the men away and allowed us to eat in peace. It wasn't unusual for men not to want to share but since both Riley and I wore black collars, most men would have assumed Luke would have been more than willing to share us.

Luke made light conversation during the meal, asking me more about myself and sharing a bit about his upbringing. He didn't mention Mr. Wood too much, focusing mainly on himself and how he went into law to make the world a better place. I was dying to ask him how he felt about the island and if he intended to stay. From what Mr. Wood had said, it sounded like Luke only came because his brother wanted him to and he wasn't convinced this was the lifestyle for him.

"Would you like any dessert, ladies?" Luke asked when we finished.

I was full to the point of bursting and shook my head no while I said, "No thank you, Luke."

Riley, on the other hand, beamed at Luke and enthusiastically nodded.

"The double chocolate cake, I assume?" Luke asked, a little twinkle in his eye.

Rile smiled and nodded again. "Yes, please."

Luke smiled back. "You've got it."

When the waitress came back, Luke placed the cake order along with a cordial for all of us. The waitress nodded as she cleared the plates, dipping lower than necessary when she was facing Luke's direction. Luke was an exceptionally attractive man, all broad shoulders and dark green eyes, but it surprised me that the waitress was being so obvious about it, especially with her white collar.

Luke gave her an appreciative look and met her eyes with a smile, letting her know that he liked what he saw. I felt a spring of jealousy that I quickly pushed down. I had no claim to this man and I couldn't get territorial with him.

The waitress gave Luke an exaggerated ass wiggle as she left to collect the cake and cordials. I couldn't help wonder what that was about. She clearly was a taken woman and not available for outside play unless, and the thought hit me like a brick, she was Luke's woman. The thought settled in the pit of my stomach like I swallowed a bowl of cement. It couldn't be, could it? Riley had said she was the only woman in Luke's household unless Luke had acquired this other woman and this was his way of letting us know.

I sat on my hands as we waited for her to return, my head swimming. Riley looked unaware and smiled at Luke as he chatted with her about something inane.

The waitress returned and set the chocolate cake in front of Luke with three forks. Again she leaned lower than necessary, keeping her eyes lowered as her apron gaped open. He looked at what she offered and smiled as she placed a honey-colored cordial in front of each of us. He thanked her before she turned and walked away.

Luke dug into the cake without a word, scooping up a forkful of chocolate goodness before feeding it to Riley. Riley opened her mouth wide and squealed with delight as she took it in. Luke looked pleased as he fed her bite after bite.

I took a tiny sip of the cordial, pleased by its warmth and almond flavor, as I tried not to let jealousy overtake me. They looked like an adorable couple with him feeding her and her licking her lips with appreciation. I felt forgotten. Maybe it hadn't been a great idea for Mr. Wood to leave me with his brother. I probably would have been better off getting acquainted with Mr. Wood's new acquisitions and helping them to settle in. At least then I wouldn't be jealous.

When it got down to the last few bites, Luke looked at me with the fork poised over the crisp white tablecloth.

"Care for a bite?" he asked, his eyes hopeful.

I opened my mouth, unable to resist, even though chocolate wasn't my favorite. Luke artfully slid the cake onto my tongue, letting me take it in, before he pulled out. He watched as I savored it, surprised by its richness and depth. A small smile curled on his lips as he saw my surprise that it wasn't an overly sweet chocolate thing but instead a deep rich complex mix of flavors.

"Another?" he asked, holding up the last piece.

I nodded, eager to have him feed me, wanting to experience that richness again. I also enjoyed having his attention.

I finished the last bite, licking my lips in what I hoped was an enticing way. Luke's gaze lingered on my lips which I took as a hopeful sign. The men weren't much for kissing the women on the island I had noticed. Mr. Wood had kissed me, taken my breath away a time or two, but most of the men were more about the sex with very little intimacy. We were mostly interchangeable and although that hadn't bothered me until now, with Luke it would have.

Luke escorted us out of the restaurant once he settled the bill, his arm around each of us as we walked at his side. He made small comments about the night as the warm breeze caressed my skin. I thought he might take us to another bar but instead, he led us back to his place. I felt slightly disappointed to have not had more of a night of it but knew it wasn't my place to say anything. I resigned myself to crawling into bed and having a peaceful sleep.

Once we were inside the house, Luke pushed the thin straps of my gown off my shoulders and watched as it fell to the floor. His eyes worked their way up my body, pausing as he took in my freshly waxed mound and my hard nipples. I felt raw and exposed even though he had seen me naked before. Riley hung back, probably not sure what to do, taking in the sight.

A blush crawled up my neck as I kept my head lowered, suddenly overcome with submissive urges. The air felt heavy as we all seemed to hold our breaths.

Luke grazed my nipples with the back of his hand. It was a gentle touch that sent shivers through me. I sucked in my breath as he captured one my of nipples with his fingers and pulled. He chuckled at my reaction before doing the same to the other one and then both at once. He had me on fire and he had barely touched me.

He glanced at Riley and nodded. This must have been her command to disrobe because she dropped her dress to the floor without question and stepped out of it. Her nipples were hard and pink as she stepped closer until she was next to me. Luke reached out and grazed her nipples before pulling on each one. She gasped at the pain, my nipples reacting as if they had been pulled.

Luke switched between us, pulling on my nipples before pulling on hers until mine were screaming. He seemed to delight in our discomfort which surprised me. I tried not to squirm or react to his pulling but it was difficult. I sensed Riley squirming next to me.

Once he was pleased with our red nipples, he lowered his mouth to mine and lapped at them before pulling them into the heat of his mouth. He sucked on the raw peak, pulling it deep into his mouth, which caused me to arch my back into it. It felt painful and exquisite. I was on fire.

He moved his mouth from one nipple to the other, sucking each in, playing with it on his tongue, while he reached over to pull on Riley's nipples as if not wanting to leave her out. We both stood there while he toyed with us, his attention more on me than her, which I tried not let go to my head. I knew it didn't matter—that we were both there solely for his enjoyment.

"Kneel," he instructed.

We both fell to our knees.

He looked down at us as if admiring his merchandise, his eyes warm but distant, like we were new to him. He pulled out his stiff cock and approached Riley first. She already had her mouth open, her tongue out, as Luke easily slid his cock into her mouth. I felt a swell of jealousy as she sucked on his cock, enthusiastic in her work. Luke seemed to enjoy it as he leaned into it, pulling her head in closer.

He didn't let her suck him long before he pulled out and turned his attention to me, his cock bobbing before my face. I opened my mouth and took him in, impressed by his length. He pushed himself in fully and I opened my throat to accommodate him, wanting to take it all without gagging. He pulled my head to help guide himself in, slow and steady, until my lips reached his base.

He slowly pumped in and out a few times as my mouth felt impaled by his cock. I relished taking him all the way in and wondered if Riley had been as successful. I knew we weren't in competition but I couldn't help think Luke must be comparing us.

I closed my eyes and savored the feel of him in my mouth. He tasted musky and clean. I inhaled deeply, losing myself in the task, enjoying the feel of him on my tongue. I ached to please him in ways I didn't understand. It was different with Luke than with Mr. Wood. Simpler, somehow.

He pulled out, leaving me feeling vacant. I blinked up at him as he smiled at me. He reached out his hand and caressed my cheek before doing the same to Riley.

"My girls," he said. "How did I get so lucky? I want you both in my room immediately."

I popped up and rushed to the stairs, letting Riley lead since she knew where she was going. I followed her up the stairs and down the hall to the last door on the right. She pushed it open to reveal a simple room with a king-size bed that dominated the middle with a four-poster wood frame. A soft white comforter covered the bed with four pillows propped up at the head. Luke was right behind us so I didn't have time to take it all in. I turned to face him, waiting for instruction, wanting more than anything to please him.

He looked us over as we stood there waiting. He took his time taking us in. This was a man who knew how to savor the moment.

He pulled Riley in first and kissed her, his mouth on hers, drinking her in, as he wrapped an arm around her, pulling her in tight against him. She giggled at the swift movement before quickly giving in to him as I stood there observing, jealousy dripping off me.

Luke deepened the kiss, his powerful arms around her, holding her tight, keeping her pressed to him. It was erotic to watch and I would have enjoyed it more if I wasn't feeling left out. I wanted to be part of it, become part of them, but I wasn't sure how to do it so I did nothing.

I watched as he caressed her ass, pulling one leg up against his hip, opening her to him, before his cock disappeared into her folds. He pumped in and out as he continued to kiss her, his other hand in her hair, pulling her in. She groaned into his mouth, losing herself in him, as I stood there watching. Her eyes were closed, head thrown back, as he moved in and out.

He turned his gaze to me as he fucked her, his green eyes intense and focused. I felt that look throughout my body, turning me instantly to liquid, making it difficult to stand. He continued to hold my gaze as he increased his tempo, fucking her harder, until she started panting, her breathing shallow, her groans louder. He wanted her to come—I could tell—and he wanted to break me at the same time. I saw the fire and determination in his eyes, like it wasn't about the body in his arms but it was about me and him. Something stirred underneath everything that I couldn't quite comprehend.

He slammed into her, determined, wanting to push her over the edge. She was almost there. I could hear it in her ragged breathing and the way she clung to him, lost. His eyes didn't leave mine as his cock ravished her, claimed her, used her completely.

He closed his eyes for a moment, breaking contact with me, as he gave one last push and came. She gasped at his eruption, taking it all, before he slowly pulled himself out. She looked limp and satiated as he held her up, her eyes closed, her head bobbing. Without a word, he scooped her up in his arms and carried her out of his room and down the hallway. I remained standing there, having not been dismissed and not wanting to ruin the moment, as I watched them go.

I heard a door open and a low murmur of words. I tried to tame the jealousy that spiraled through me as I waited, not sure he would return. For all I knew, he was tucking himself up next to her and falling asleep with her in his arms. He could leave me standing there all night—something that didn't thrill me but something I knew I would do for him.

I stood there waiting, counting my breaths as I slowly breathed in and out, calming myself, telling myself I could be waiting a long time, reminding myself that I needed to get OK with it, that this was all part of my journey.

I stood there breathing for I don't know how long. I lost track of time, allowing my mind to float away, as I stood perfectly still. I no longer noticed the ache in my feet or the jealousy that had wanted to overtake me. I was still. Silent. Patient.

I had fallen into a light trance when Luke returned, closing the door behind him.

He smiled at me, a wicked lopsided smile that made my knees go weak.

"You waited," he said as he approached. "Good girl. My brother will be proud of your obedience. He wanted me to continue with your training, to ensure that you'd give yourself over as easily to me as you have to him."

I met his eyes as he moved closer, standing only a few inches from me but not touching me, his lips dangerously close to mine. I breathed in, inhaling his woodsy scent. I felt the power of him, the pulsing of him, the air thick with it, like something major had shifted.

He was looking at me, taking me in, as if trying to interpret me, like he wasn't sure exactly what he was seeing before him. I didn't want to talk and ruin the moment, not that I had anything to say. My mind was blank, my thoughts muddled, as I looked back at him, this gorgeous man with full control over me.

His lips found mine, lightly at first, mere whispers that had me thinking I was imagining it, before they came crashing down, drinking me in, demanding everything. I melted into him, finding comfort as his arms came around me, pulling me to him. My breasts crushed against his solid chest as his tongue explored my mouth. I lost my breath and my mind as he ravished my mouth, leaving it crushed and aching for more.

He pulled back and stared at me, his eyes wild, his hands on my shoulders, as if he wasn't sure what he was looking at.

"Are you real, Annabelle?" he asked, my name rolling off his tongue, a sweet caress. "Are you fucking real?"

He captured my mouth again before I could think, his tongue exploring, lapping me up. I gave myself over completely to it, to him, loving the way my body exploded under his touch, how my heart hammered in my chest, threatening to burst. I felt explosive and alive and totally open, ready and willing for anything and everything this man had to give. I would have walked over hot coals for him at that moment, anything, to keep his hands and mouth on me.

His hand found its way into my hair, pulling my head even closer, controlling me, while the other one found my ass and squeezed. I wanted to squeal with pleasure but didn't want to break our kiss. He was plunging into me like a thirsty man in the desert and I was lapping it up, not wanting it to end.

He broke the kiss and spun me around before I could react.

"Hands on the bed," he said.

I complied, bending at the waist to put my hands on the bed shoulder-width apart. I heard his heavy breathing behind me, the weight of him even though he wasn't touching me. I had the feeling that he was admiring the view, taking me in, enjoying me being displayed for him, my ass in the air, my pussy free and wanting.

"God, you're gorgeous," he said, his voice low and heavy. "The things I want to do to you."

My heart skipped as I tried to stay still. It took everything I had not to wiggle my ass at him. Even though I knew he'd appreciate it and maybe even laugh, I didn't want to do anything without his explicit instruction. I wanted to obey him completely, to be exactly what he wanted, to please him.

I startled when he slipped his fingers through my wetness, fondling and playing before dipping inside. I bit my lip as he toyed with me, his fingers slipping in and out, playing with my aroused clit, rubbing it with his thumb, sending waves of arousal through me. I felt like I could come at any second but I held back, wanting to extend the experience, wanting to be as aroused as I could get for him.

His fingers left and were replaced by his tongue, lapping at my clit, making me delirious. The man knew how to work it as I felt myself falling further and further through the cracks of lust with him. I closed my eyes and luxuriated in his enjoyment of me. I knew I was beyond soaking, dripping for him, ready and willing to take whatever he gave.

He grabbed my hips as he worked, his tongue diving deep into my slit, causing me to lose my breath. My whole body was on fire for him, threatening to burst, but I managed to hold on, to hold back, as he worked his magic.

He mumbled some words I didn't understand as my head slipped into a delightful fog, oblivious to anything but his mouth on my pussy, his tongue in my slit, and how this all felt right. I gripped the bed as he continued to work his magic, my body delirious, my mind blank. I was nothing but pure sensation. I had become so good at holding back from coming that it was no longer a concern while my body convulsed under his assault.

I gasped when his tongue left me, leaving me feeling cold and abandoned. But I didn't have to wait long before his hard cock slipped easily between my folds and filled me. I bit my lip as he gripped my hips and pushed as deep as he could go. I thought I was going to come. He felt heavenly, filling me completely as I opened to him. He pumped in and out, slowly at first, almost agonizing, until he picked up the pace.

I panted as he plowed into me again and again, happy to be used, to be pleasing him any way I could.

He pulled at my hair, yanking my head back.

"God, Annabelle," he said, his voice ragged. "You feel incredible."

My heart swelled at his words.

He pulled my head back as he rammed into me, quickening his pace, swearing under his breath, until he unloaded himself into me. I felt the heat of him inside me which made me all kinds of happy. I wanted more of him, I wanted everything, but I knew I needed to be patient.

He stayed inside me a moment longer, his hands on my hips, before he pulled out. His semen dripped out of me, making me wish for a moment that I hadn't been given that powerful birth control. Somewhere deep inside me longed to be his in a more permanent way, to be his forever.

He gave my ass a light slap as he exited.

"God, that was incredible," he said from behind me.

I kept myself propped up until told otherwise, my pussy leaking his fresh juices.

EIGHTEEN

Luke let me share his bed that night. In fact, he demanded it. I curled up in his arms as he absentmindedly fondled my breasts as we fell asleep. I was in heaven. I had been thoroughly fucked and adored and it felt amazing. I wanted to stay curled up in Luke's arms forever. I wouldn't have minded if Riley had joined us. I could get used to our little threesome and didn't think I'd always be jealous.

The morning came too quickly, the sun streaming in through the open blinds. I curled into the pillow next to me only to find Luke gone. I knew it was ridiculous to expect him to be there in the morning, ready to take me again, but I felt a little abandoned. Last night had felt like more than just fucking. It had felt real. Something had opened up inside me, had cracked a little, and I wanted more of that.

I smelled eggs and bacon wafting up the stairs. I wondered if Luke had taken Riley instead this morning, using her to work out his morning wood. Jealousy clawed at me as I lifted myself and slipped on my heels. I felt sore between my legs and hadn't cleaned myself up after I used the bathroom last night. I had wanted to keep as much of Luke on me as I could.

Riley greeted me with a smile as she slid the eggs and bacon onto a plate.

"Wow—wasn't last night amazing?" Riley asked, her eyes wide, as she brought the plate to the counter. "Luke never fucked me like that before. I thought I was going to break in two. Want some?"

Riley offered her plate but I shook my head. I wasn't hungry all of a sudden. I went to the cabinet and grabbed a glass and filled it with water.

"Where is Luke?" I asked after I gulped down a full glass of water. I refilled the glass, not wanting to look at Riley, as I waited for her response.

"I'm not sure. He was gone when I got up and he didn't leave a note."

I scrunched up my nose, feeling disappointed.

I joined Riley at the counter. She was almost done with her food, a mug of something hot next to her. The food made me a bit nauseous, not hungry, which I found odd. I took a sip of water, my head swimming, not sure how to take in everything that I'd been through the past couple of weeks. Just when I felt like I had found my footing here, I felt disoriented again.

"What do you do when Luke's not around?" I asked, remembering how I was not to leave the house without explicit permission from Mr. Wood. I assumed the same rules applied here but I was interested to hear how Riley would respond.

"I stick around here," Riley said, finishing up her breakfast. "I clean and keep the house tidy and any other chores Luke thinks to tell me to do but he rarely does. Or I read. The main thing is for me to be ready when Luke returns."

I blinked at her. The thought of doing nothing all day felt overwhelming. It was Sunday so I wasn't expected in the office. I didn't know what I'd do with myself besides go mad.

I didn't have any books but knew Riley would lend me one if I asked. The problem was I didn't feel like reading. I wasn't sure what I wanted to do but I felt pent up and restless, like I needed to go for a run or a swim to release the built-up tension. I couldn't remember the last time I came, having become an expert at holding back. I was horny, still wanting, and a small part of me wanted to walk through the men's side of town to get fucked. But I knew leaving the house wasn't the best idea. I didn't want to be punished again.

I went to my room, conscious that I had spent little time there. My purchases from yesterday were spread out on the bed and dresser. I had been so excited to dress for Luke that I hadn't thought about the rest of what I bought. Not that it mattered. I'm sure I wouldn't be taking any of this stuff with me when I left the island, not that I'd be able to wear sheer dresses anywhere else. I realized how difficult it was going to be to acclimate back to regular life.

I took a shower, taking my time to wash my hair and clean every part of me. I wanted to be fresh and available for when Luke returned, hoping he'd take me again and curl me back into his bed. Fresh out of the shower, I piled my auburn hair on top of my head and secured it in a loose knot. I padded into my room and slipped on the naughty schoolgirl outfit, loving the way it clung to my curves and accentuated my breasts.

I took great care in applying my makeup, going a little heavier than usual, wanting to be alluring and sophisticated, someone worthy of being taken out on the town again and shown off. I was determined to be pleasing in every way for Luke, to show my devotion to him, to hope that he'd want to keep me around.

I sat on my knees in my room, hands on my lap, eyes closed, for a very long time. I fell into a deep meditative state as I allowed my mind to go blank. Thoughts wandered through my mind at first. I thought about my stay on the island, about what I had hoped to gain by being here and about what I wanted now that I had been here a while. I knew my wants and desires were irrelevant here but they mattered to me. I hadn't lost myself completely and wasn't sure I could.

Soon my mind quieted and I became empty and still. Peaceful. I knew I was here for a reason and I needed to continue to trust that. I had answered the ad, said yes to being here, and I wanted to see it through. I wanted to see what was here for me, why I had been drawn to it.

I STARTLED when I felt a light brush against my cheek. I opened my eyes to see a smiling Luke standing over me dressed in a dark suit that hugged his well-defined muscles.

"You're beautiful like that," he said, his words a warm caress. "So obedient. Have you been like this all day?"

I blinked at him, taking a minute for the words to process. I had fallen so deep into a mindless trance that it was like climbing out of a deep hole. I wasn't sure how much I wanted to return but my body reacted to him being near me, wanting to be with him.

"What time is it?" I asked, my eyes drifting to the window. It was still light out but muted.

"It's after six," he said. A subtle smile played on his lips as his hand lowered to graze my erect nipples showing through my blouse.

Arousal washed over me as I blinked at him again and nodded.

"Yes, Luke. I've been here all day."

His smile widened, his eyes crinkled, as his fingers continued to graze my nipples, almost absentmindedly. I didn't mind. I loved his hands on me. I craved his attention which I knew could be dangerous. I licked my lips as that thought sank deeper into my mind, the little inkling about what it would be like if I were truly his.

"Stand," he said. "I want to see all of you."

I slowly uncurled myself. My legs had fallen asleep, making it challenging to stand but I did my best. He must have sensed my unsteadiness because he held out a hand for me to balance on. I accepted it until I felt like I could handle standing on my own.

I had on the naughty schoolgirl outfit, having wanted to show it off for him. The sheer green blouse gaped at my breasts, showing my erect nipples that pointed straight at him. The short plaid skirt did nothing to hide my ass or my pussy. I blushed at the thought of having dressed for him, wondering if he knew.

He smiled at the sight of me, looking pleased. He circled me slowly as I stood still, trying not to blush under his scrutiny.

He cupped my ass, his fingers sliding underneath until they hit my wetness. His fingers dipped in. I gasped at his touch, welcoming it. I spread my legs to accommodate him, wanting this and so much more.

He gave one deep push, almost sending me over the edge, my body humming, before he pulled out. My body yearned for him, to be used by him, and I wished I had a way to communicate that to him that wouldn't sound ridiculous. This man could easily possess me and a part of me loved that.

He came around me, his dark green eyes finding mine. They were intense and determined but with a hint of a smile. He pulled at my nipples again, pleased as a groaned into the sharp pain.

"My brother wants me to continue your training," he said, his voice low and soothing. "He doesn't want you to get complacent. I assured him I'd do what I could to train you so he wouldn't request you back right away. I know he has his hands full with his new acquisitions and would rather not be bothered with you right now."

I knew I should have been insulted but I wasn't. I wanted to be with Luke. I hoped Mr. Wood's new acquisitions kept him busy for a long time.

Luke pulled open the blouse and tugged it off me, letting it fall to the floor. He pinched my nipples and then pulled. I bit my lip.

"I'm undecided whether to take you out or do your training here," Luke said, his fingers working my nipples, pulling and pinching, making me squirm.

"Whatever pleases you, Luke," I said in my most submissive tone even though I wanted more than anything to stay here. I didn't know where Riley was or if she'd be involved in my training but I preferred having Luke to myself.

Luke squeezed each breast, as if checking their firmness, as he watched me. I wanted to ask about Riley, where she was at this moment, but I knew better. It was none of my concern. He pinched and pulled both nipples until I gasped.

"My brother will be pleased that you take pain well," Luke said. "I'm not into whips and floggers but you can expect to be spanked by me from time to time, especially if you disobey and sometimes just because I want to."

I felt my cheeks redden.

Luke reached around and cupped my ass, his chest flat against my erect nipples. I inhaled his scent. He smacked my ass, causing me to jump. He smacked the other cheek and then again, warming my ass. He had his arms around me as he smacked each cheek, almost hugging me. I concentrated on remaining as still as I could as I took in each slap. His body crushed against mine, bracing me, and I wondered if this was part of his plan. I never questioned if Luke knew what he was doing but I had believed Luke wasn't as dominant as his brother. Maybe I was wrong.

Luke continued to work my ass, slapping one cheek then the other, smacking in different areas, working the entire surface, until my skin screamed. I wanted to squirm away from his hands but there was nowhere to go. I was trapped in his arms. Not that I would have left anyway. I knew this was part of my training, part of breaking me, so I needed to take it. I needed to prove to Luke and myself that I could take it. I no longer cared what Mr. Wood thought—it was all about Luke.

The smacks continued, my ass on fire, as my mind slipped into a fog. I was no longer my body. I was somewhere else. Lost but found.

"Good girl," Luke purred into my ear, sending ripples of pleasure through me. The spanking had stopped. My ass was on fire and my pussy ached for release. I couldn't believe how turned on I had become accepting all that Luke had to give me. Knowing I could accept it thrilled me. My heart felt like it would burst I was so happy.

His mouth found one nipple and sucked it in. I arched my back in ecstasy. He twirled his tongue around my nipple, teasing it, before nibbling it and sucking it in more. I closed my eyes and gave myself over to the sweet sensations. This man knew how to make my body come alive.

His hands were on my shoulders as he moved to the other nipple, sucking and tasting it, driving me insane. I wanted to beg for more, to help me come undone, but I knew this needed to be at his pace. Maybe this was his sweet torture.

Luke took his time, savoring each nipple, moving from one to the other until they were aching and sore, wanting more of him. He must have known what he was doing to me. The man was no fool. He was taking his time, driving me mad and making me more than willing to do anything for him.

When he pulled back, I was startled at first, wondering if I did anything wrong. My eyes opened and met his. His gaze was intense and unreadable, sending a shiver right through me, like he was really seeing me, seeing all of me, the broken parts, the ugly parts, all of it. I wanted to break his gaze, to look down, to escape it somehow, but he wouldn't let me. His gaze held me, captivated me.

"My God, Annabelle," he said, his voice rough. "What am I going to do with you?"

I blinked at him, unsure whether he was looking for a response or simply stating how he felt.

He held my gaze a moment longer before his mouth crashed down on mine.

I sank into him as his powerful arms wrapped around me and pulled me in tight against him. He deepened the kiss, drinking me in, exploring me, savoring. I let myself get lost in him, lost in the moment, as my heart soared and threatened to burst.

He tasted of scotch and something else, something very him. I let my body go loose in his embrace as he devoured my mouth, kissing me with everything he had. My bones felt liquid as my head spun. I had yet to be kissed like this here, maybe anywhere. It lit a fire inside me.

I pushed the thoughts aside as I gave in to the kiss, gave in to him. His hands were in my hair, on my back, on my ass, pulling me in closer. I felt his hard cock against my stomach. My mouth watered at the thought of it in my mouth, wanting to please him, to have him.

He broke the kiss and looked at me, his eyes wild. A moment later, he scooped me up in his arms. I burrowed into his neck, clinging to him, as he carried me out the door and down the hall to his room. He kicked the door closed behind us, making me think Riley was somewhere in the house, before he deposited me on the bed.

I stared up at him, my legs open and inviting, while he discarded his clothes in a heap on the floor. His magnificent cock sprung free, hard and majestic, as he pulled off his boxers. I licked my lips at the sight of it, of the sight of him, grateful for this moment to have him to myself.

He approached me like a wild cat, all muscles and smooth swagger with eyes on his prey. I felt captured with nowhere to run and I wouldn't have had it any other way.

He descended on me with a fluid movement, his hands on both sides of my head while his cock slid easily into me, filling me completely. He held my gaze the whole time, his eyes intense and hooded, as he slowly fucked me, plunging in deep then pulling out, again and again.

All of it overwhelmed me. After the spanking and the kiss, my body burned for him. I felt like my head might explode. It was too much and everything I had ever wanted at once. My mind couldn't comprehend it. It screamed at me for answers I didn't have. I blocked all that out and allowed myself to be fully present, to be fully available, to be nothing more than this moment of pure ecstasy.

I wanted to throw my head back as he fucked me, his cock filling me, to take it all in, but he wouldn't let me break his gaze. He watched me as he plowed into me as if reading me, as if seeing right through me, knowing all of me. My entire body shuttered and burst around him. It was too much. I clung to the bedsheets as I came hard, my body convulsing under him, my eyes locked on him.

He smiled as he quickened his pace, not giving me a moment to recover, not giving anything to me but his glorious cock, pushing in deeper. I squeezed myself around it, wanting more, wanting everything, as another orgasm started to build. This man was relentless and amazing. He was everything. I couldn't believe that I had made it to this place, to have this man buried deep inside me, claiming me, fucking me.

I screamed when I came the second time, clamping down on him, squeezing my eyes shut. He let out a groan as he pushed into me one more time and released himself inside me. I squeezed around his cock, not wanting to let him go, to keep him buried inside me. He felt right there, like he belonged.

He must have sensed my reluctance to let him go because he

stayed inside me a few minutes, his eyes finding mine as I slowly opened them. My heart swelled at the sight of him, all serious and determined. He brought his mouth down on mine, capturing me in a delicious kiss, both gentle and demanding. It was all the words that needed to be said.

I let myself sink into his kiss, savoring it, not wanting it to end. I let my hands find their way into his thick hair and over his broad shoulders. His muscles flexed beneath my hand as he deepened the kiss, sinking deeper into me, his cock still inside me.

NINETEEN

I woke up with his body curled around me, tucking me into the safety of his chest. I blinked against the blinding sunlight seeping in through the blinds. I had slept better than I had since coming to the island. I felt warm, cozy and completely satiated. Luke had taken me again in the middle of the night, waking me with lazy kisses across my face and then lower on each breast, sucking in my tender nipples, arousing me once more. I had come easily, letting myself go, letting myself be consumed by him. He chuckled in my ear when I came and murmured something I didn't understand. I feel asleep a happy woman.

My body felt loose and limber this morning, my mind peaceful. I loved that he was still wrapped around me, that he had slept deeply, too, had been just as consumed as me. I wished we could lay like this all day, all week, and not let the reality of the outside world in.

My mind wandered to Riley, wondering what she was doing, if she was wondering where Luke was, where I was. Was she picturing us together? Did she know we had spent the night together?

I knew it didn't matter—Riley's place wasn't to care what we did— but I wondered if she was jealous. I knew I would be if Riley had been in my place.

Luke squeezed me to him, his nose in my hair, his breath warm on my neck.

"How'd you sleep?" he asked in my ear, his arms around me.

I smiled. "It was the best night's sleep. I'm happy you're still here."

He chuckled. I couldn't believe I said that.

"I'm happy I'm still here, too," he said, his voice low and husky. "Thank you for an incredible night. How's your ass?"

I laughed. It still stung but felt mostly warm and cozy.

"A bit warm. I couldn't believe how much it turned me on."

I felt his smile.

"Me too."

His hand found my breast, his thumb grazing my erect nipple. Arousal shot through me from his simple touch. He pinched it as I squirmed against his hardening cock. His warm breath caressed my ear as he pulled on my nipple until it hurt. I sucked in my breath.

"You're so responsive," he said, releasing my nipple before going for the other one. "I love the sounds you make."

My heart swelled at his compliment while he pulled on the other nipple. I bit my lip as the pain aroused me. I never thought I'd be one to get aroused by pain but this entire experience was proving me wrong. It was a delightful surprise.

He released my nipple and kissed my shoulder. His cock pressed against my ass. I opened my legs for him. He slipped easily into my wetness. His hands cupped my breasts as he pushed into me from behind, his cock filling me, hitting my g spot as it slid in. I let out a gasp as his balls nestled against my ass. He pinched both nipples and pulled as he began fucking me slowly. I closed my eyes as I savored each sensation, letting the arousal wash over me.

He picked up the pace, plunging into me, taking me, and I was more than happy to take him in. I squeezed his cock as he fucked me, wanting all of him, wanting to please him, wanting to be the best fuck of his life. I wanted to claim him like he was claiming me and the only way I knew how was to be everything for him.

He pounded harder into me, pinching and pulling my nipples, as he lost control, coming inside me with a fierceness I've never experienced.

"God, Annabelle," he said into my ear after he came. I squeezed around his cock. "That was incredible."

I smiled. My heart warmed. I knew at that moment that I would do anything for this man. I felt full, complete, wanted and appreciated I prayed he felt the same.

"Lance wants me to return you to him but I'm not sure I want to let you go," Luke said, his breath hot against my ear. "Do you want to stay with me?"

The question burned through me. Of course, I wanted to stay with him. There was no question. But I knew I belonged to Mr. Wood and didn't want to do anything to upset him. I wasn't sure how to respond.

Luke pulled out of me, his semen dripping down my legs. He smacked my ass before pushing me over to my side so he could look at me. His green eyes were fierce and serious.

"Annabelle, do you want to be with me?"

My heart swelled then plummeted. I didn't know what to say.

He must have registered my uncertainty because he said, "I'm going to ask my brother if I can buy you from him. I know he's acquired a few new women so maybe he'd be willing to let you go. He's always telling me I need more than one woman so maybe he'll see this as my chance to broaden my household."

I blinked at him as I let the words register. I had no idea how Mr. Wood would respond to such a request but I loved the idea of being tethered to Luke.

"Would you like it if I bought you?" Luke asked, his voice soft, like a caress.

I nodded. My body quivered at my admission.

His face broke out in an enormous smile before he brought his mouth over mine. He kissed me with a fierceness, bringing his body over mine, crushing me to the bed. His hands wound their way in my hair, pulling me closer to him, demanding my full attention. My mind melted into his kiss, wanting nothing more than to be in his arms always. I could even deal with Riley and whoever else Luke brought into the equation as long as I could have him. The whole thing felt like a dream I didn't want to wake up from.

When he broke the kiss, he looked at me with eyes I couldn't read.

"Lance wants you in the office today," Luke said. "Shower, look nice and put on the typical office outfit. Don't mention my wanting to acquire you. Even if he brings it up or hints at it, act like you don't know what he's talking about. You can be truthful if he asks you if you want to stay with me but don't let him know I talked with you about it. That would go against what this place is about. I shouldn't have asked you what you thought but it was important to me."

He kissed me once more before pushing himself up and off the bed. He gave me one more look before disappearing into his shower.

I WISHED I could have stayed in Luke's bed forever but I knew Mr. Wood was expecting me at the office and didn't want to give him any reason to punish me. I pushed myself up and made my way to the bathroom in the hall. I hoped I'd run into Riley but she wasn't upstairs as far as I could tell.

I took a quick shower, piling my hair on top of my head and applying office-appropriate makeup, including red lips. I had been thoroughly fucked, came more times than I could count and wanted that somehow reflected in my appearance. I slipped into my work outfit, leaving most of the buttons undone on the blouse to offer an appealing view. I felt loose and relaxed even though I had no idea what the day had in store for me.

I grabbed a quick breakfast in the kitchen, surprised Riley wasn't there. I felt a little worried since Riley had told me Luke didn't let her venture out on her own. I hadn't thought to check on her while I was upstairs and hadn't noticed whether her door was open. I told myself she was fine as I went out the door.

I walked like a woman with a purpose to the office and only had a few hands squeeze my ass. It surprised me how I barely noticed.

Inside the office was a flurry of activity. I gave Clare a nod before going to the break room for Mr. Wood's coffee. The break room was empty, allowing me to make his coffee in peace and without delay.

Mr. Wood called me in as soon as I knocked. He waved me in as he was on the phone. I set his coffee on the coaster on his desk, thinking I'd leave and get to work, but he caught my wrist before I could turn to go. I stayed that way, with him holding my wrist like he was afraid I would run away until he finished his call five minutes later.

"Kneel," he said as he released me.

I sank to my knees in front of his desk. Mr. Wood came around so he stood in front of me. I expected him to pull out his cock but he simply stood there, looking down at me as if assessing me. I knew my blouse gaped open, showing an expanse of cleavage. I had no idea who the new women were that he acquired and I couldn't help wonder how I stacked up.

"How have things been over at my brother's?"

My heart hammered as heat rushed into my face. I swallowed, unsure of how to answer. I decided simple was better. "Good. Really good."

"Has he shared you with anyone?"

I felt like I might betray Luke but I couldn't lie. "No. Not intentionally."

"What do you mean by that?"

"I was groped a few times when Luke wasn't around, while out shopping but Luke hasn't shared me."

Mr. Wood considered this. I wondered if he had told his brother that part of my training was ensuring I was shared with others. I didn't think Mr. Wood would punish Luke if that was the case but I didn't know how it worked.

"How are you enjoying your time on the island?" Mr. Wood asked after a minute, his eyes intense on mine as he waited for my response.

"I'm enjoying it," I said, not wanting to elaborate on why.

Mr. Wood continued to take me in as if trying to read more out of my comment. After a moment, he smiled. "That's good. We want the women here to be happy while being obedient. We set this society up to benefit both sexes. This society won't work without the women wanting to be here. None of us believe in forcing women to submit. We want to bring out a woman's natural tendency to submit which will ultimately make her happy, too. I hope you're finding this the case."

I nodded. "Yes, I am, Mr. Wood. I enjoy submitting. It feels natural."

"That's good because it is."

Mr. Wood turned his attention to a knock at the door, telling them to come in. A woman I didn't recognize with short red hair and big tits that strained against her white blouse sashayed in on high heels, swiveling her hips for maximum effect as if she were on a catwalk. She walked towards Mr. Wood and handed him a white envelope.

"This just arrived for you, Mr. Wood," she said.

He took it from her and opened it. She stood there waiting as he read it. I noticed a cloud pass over his eyes. He put the letter back in the envelope and set it on his desk.

"Thank you, Cheryl, you may go."

Cheryl looked disappointed as she sashayed herself back out of the office, closing the door behind her. I wondered if this was one of Mr. Wood's new girls.

I wanted to ask if everything was OK but I knew better not to initiate conversation. Instead, I sat on my heels and waited to be instructed.

"Lean forward and rest your left cheek on the carpet," Mr. Wood instructed. "Keep your hands behind your back, ass up."

I did as I was told. The carpet was scratchy against my cheek, my ass in the air. My heart quickened at not knowing what Mr. Wood intended to do. I felt myself get aroused from not being in control. Even though I wanted to be with Luke, I still belonged to Mr. Wood.

He slapped my ass, lightly at first but then with more force. I bit down on my lip as he dipped his fingers into my wetness. I felt embarrassed but knew I had no reason to be. Before I could give it more thought, he slapped my ass again, harder this time, pushing my cheek into the carpet.

He continued his assault my ass, slapping in an irregular rhythm, until my ass felt on fire. My body hummed, craving a cock to sink itself into me. I wanted to beg for it, to convince him to fuck me, but I kept silent and submissive, taking whatever he gave me.

"I want you to stay this way while I have my meeting," Mr. Wood said. "I don't want you to move unless one of the men wants you to move. Otherwise, stay put."

"Yes, Mr. Wood," I said, mortified by the prospect of being in this position in front of more people.

I didn't have to wait long before there was a knock at the door and four men dressed in suits entered. One of them let out a low whistle at the sight of me, saying something about how kind it was for Mr Wood to provide them with a snack. I felt myself blush against the carpet as I struggled to maintain the position. It wasn't the most natural or comfortable position and it took concentration to hold it.

One man slapped my already red ass, laughing as he made contact.

"Is she available for play?" one of them asked.

"Yes," Mr. Wood said. "Be my guest."

One of them spread my ass cheeks before dipping a couple of fingers into my sopping pussy. I wanted to groan and push into it but I didn't dare move. He flicked my clit on the way out before pushing his fingers into my ass, causing me to gasp. He pushed in deep, wiggling his fingers around, chuckling at my predicament. He was enjoying it, I could tell, and all I could do was take it.

Another man came over and stood in front of me while the man behind me continued to finger fuck my ass.

"Suck my cock, slut," he said.

I raised my head and pushed myself up onto my hands and knees so I could take his waiting cock in my mouth. He pushed it in without mercy until it hit the back of my throat. I opened myself to it, willing myself not to gag, as he grabbed my hair and pushed himself in deeper. Behind me, the man kept his fingers buried in my ass while his cock slipped into my aching pussy.

They impaled me from both ends, filling me completely as they sank in as deep as they could. They moved in a sporadic rhythm, causing my mind to spin. Arousal threatened to overtake me as they pumped into me. My body felt on fire.

Someone grabbed my tits and pulled on my nipples, causing an electric current of pain to wash through me. The cocks continued their assault while more hands found their way on my body. Some pulled my hair while others pulled and pinched my nipples. Someone smacked my ass as the cocks pounded into me.

The man behind me yelled "Oh God" before pulling out and releasing himself all over my lower back. He pulled his fingers out of my ass, smacking me, before another cock slipped into my wet pussy.

The man in my mouth quickened his pace before pulling out and releasing himself over my face and hair, causing me to close my eyes. He gave my face a little slap before another cock took its place.

The new cocks fucked me harder as if they had something to prove, moving in and out at a frantic pace. I was nothing more than sensation and arousal, taking everything they had to give, being nothing more than a placeholder for their greedy cocks.

Someone smacked my ass a few times while the fucking continued. My body didn't know what to do with all the sensations. I felt overwhelmed as the pressure built. They pinched and pulled at my nipples. It was all too much. My body erupted as I came with a fierceness that made me light-headed and afraid I would pass out.

The cock in my mouth came first, spraying itself over my face. The cock in my pussy pulled out a minute later and came over my ass, leaving me empty and gaping. I managed to keep myself up on my hands and knees, afraid of the consequences of letting myself fall to the floor. My limbs felt like jelly and all I wanted to do was collapse.

One of them smacked my ass one more time before saying, "That was great. Thanks for the ride, Lance. This slut is tight. Next time I want to take her ass."

"That can be arranged," Mr. Wood said.

They officially started their meeting, moving off to the round table in Mr. Wood's office. Their words floated above my head. I was too wrung out to comprehend. I kept my position as best as I could, somehow holding myself up, as I waited for them to release me.

Randomly one of them tweaked a nipple or smacked my ass while they talked, startling me. I had a feeling Mr. Wood was putting me back in my place, showing me that women are meant to be shared and used, since I've had it so easy at his brother's house. I knew Mr. Wood wanted me to understand that my true purpose here was to be obedient and submissive, nothing more than holes to fill.

TWENTY

I lost track of time while they talked, my mind blank. My arms and knees ached. I felt like a statue that was meant to stay like that forever. The random gropes had stopped while the men got down to business, leaving me feeling forgotten. It was amazing how quickly I felt useless when I wasn't being used.

After a while, the meeting ended. The men smacked my ass on the way out, thanking Mr. Wood for their morning snack. Only once the men left with the door shut behind them did Mr. Wood acknowledge me.

He stood in front of me and chuckled.

"You look like a well-used slut," he said. "Did you enjoy being used like that?"

I wanted to open my eyes and look up at him but had come all over my face. I nodded. "Yes, Mr. Wood. Thank you for arranging it."

"I had given my brother explicit instruction to make sure you were well used but it seems like he preferred to keep you to himself."

I blushed because I knew it was true.

"I'm not sure if I should have you return to him or take you back. What do you think I should do?"

My heart plummeted at the thought of not returning to Luke but knew better than to say that to Mr. Wood. I knew it'd only make things worse and I didn't know how Mr. Wood would react. Instead, I said, "Whatever you think is best, Mr. Wood. I trust your judgment."

Mr. Wood chuckled. He probably expected me to say that.

"In that case, I want you to return to my brother's house after work but I don't want you to clean yourself. You can clean your eyes so you can see—I noticed that you're afraid to open them—but nothing else. I need my brother to see what a proper slut looks like."

"Yes, Mr. Wood," I said, relieved to be returning to Luke.

"You may go clean yourself up now and then get to work."

He ran a wet washcloth over my eyes, wiping away the come, before helping me to my feet. My legs wobbled, taking me a moment to stand on my own. Mr. Wood held me up until he felt confident I could stand unassisted. Once I had my footing, he returned to his desk without another word. I knew that was my cue to leave.

I went straight to the restroom, grateful to only have a couple of guys catcall me on the way. I knew I looked too much of a mess for them to touch me with come all over my face and dripping down my legs. I used the bathroom, careful not to wipe any more come away than necessary, washed my hands and looked at myself in the mirror. Mascara ran down my face, leaving me looking like a well-used raccoon. Come caked in my hair and on my face. Mr. Wood had done a decent job washing away the come around my eyes so I didn't need to do anymore there. I knew the more come I left on my face, the better off I'd be.

I returned to the desk in front of Mr. Wood's office and got to work. A couple of notes were left on the desk explaining what needed to be done. None of it was complicated, just answering emails and organizing things. There was also a stack of files waiting to put away in the office file room.

I got to work, wanting to get as much done as possible, showing Mr. Wood that I was dedicated to him and this job. I liked coming into the office even if that meant being used by the men there. It gave me a sense of purpose beyond being something to fuck. It gave me a shred of something else to hold on to.

I stopped for a quick lunch of yogurt taken from the break room. A few of the regular women were in there eating but I didn't feel like chatting.

"Looks like you had a fun morning," one woman said, nodding to the come in my hair. "No wonder the men have been more low key today."

The other women chuckled as I went into the fridge for my yogurt. I knew I looked a mess but that was part of my role here. This was how Mr. Wood wanted me so this was how I was going to stay.

The rest of the afternoon passed uneventfully. Mr. Wood left sometime around two, telling me he wouldn't be back but to return in the morning. I was grateful to have time to myself even though I spent that time working.

I saved filing for last since I wasn't looking forward to walking to the file room at the front of the office. Men catcalled as I made my way over, thanking me again for their morning snack, laughing among themselves. My cheeks reddened as I walked, happy that the day was almost over. I was happy I was returning to Luke's but had a feeling it might not be for long.

The file room was empty. I let out a sigh of relief and got to work, wanting to finish as quickly as possible so I could get home to Luke. I had no way to contact him and, even if I had, I knew better than to reach out. I needed to trust that Luke would do what he could to buy me from his brother. I hoped that Mr. Wood would let me go.

I was busy filing when a guy from the meeting earlier wandered in.

"We meet again, slut," he said, eyeing me up and down.

I wasn't sure how to respond so I said nothing. I gave him a nod and continued filing. My tits were out thanks to the earlier tryst and since Mr. Wood hadn't told me to put them away, I had left them out.

He came behind me before wrapping his arms around me so he could pinch and pull on each nipple. I stopped filing as I let him play with my tits. He squeezed each one as if measuring its heft before pinching and pulling on them again. I started to get aroused despite myself. I wasn't in the mood to be used again but knew I had no choice. I wondered if Mr. Wood had put him up to this.

His hand slid down my ass and in between my legs, slipping two fingers in my wet pussy. I gasped at the intrusion as he pushed his fingers in as deep as they could go while his other hand pinched hard on one nipple.

"You're such a slut," he purred in my ear. "I can see why Lance keeps you around."

I knew I was a slut but hearing it at that moment made me feel confused. I didn't know what I wanted to be anymore.

He pulled his fingers out before unzipping his pants and instructing me to bend over.

"Grab your ankles," he commanded before pushing his hard cock in my wet pussy. It slid in without resistance, filling me completely. He grabbed my hips as he pumped in and out, fucking me hard and quick.

"I didn't get a chance to fuck you earlier," he explained as he pounded into me, "so when I saw you with the files, I thought here's my chance."

I said nothing as I let him fuck me. I gave in to the feeling of being nothing more than a slut for his pleasure as he pounded into me again and again. My pussy felt open and willing, happy to be filled. It was different to be fucked by some guy I didn't know and didn't want to know. I let my mind go blank as he used me.

It didn't take long before he came, pulling out to squirt on the back of my thighs, marking me like a dog with a hydrant.

He smacked my ass before zipping up and leaving me to finish my filing. I wasn't surprised he didn't say anything more. I slowly straightened once he left, not feeling compelled to stay like that since he didn't own me. I finished the filing as quickly as I could, aware of the come dripping down the back of my thighs.

I SCURRIED BACK to Luke's place, grateful that I had gone mostly unnoticed. I looked a mess with come in my hair, on my face and dried up on my thighs. I'm sure that was deterrent enough to keep hands off me. There were a few catcalls but that was it. Riley was in the kitchen cooking something at the stove when I walked in.

Her eyes bugged out when she saw me.

"Wow. Looks like you've had quite the day."

I gave her a half laugh. "You could say that."

"Where were you?"

"At Mr. Wood's office. I have to go in tomorrow, too." I didn't want to think about going in tomorrow so I pushed it out of my mind. "What are you making?"

"Homemade sausage and tortellini soup. Family recipe. It's just us tonight. Luke had to go out."

My heart plummeted. I was hoping to see him right away.

Riley must have caught my look because she said, "Don't look so glum. I doubt he'll be out that late. I'm just about done with the soup. Why don't you sit down and have some."

I knew Mr. Wood wanted Luke to see me a mess so I slid onto a stool opposite Riley. She ladled soup into a bowl and pushed it in front of me with a spoon. It looked good—thick and rich. My stomach growled.

The soup tasted incredible and felt warm going down. It only took a few minutes to finish the bowl. I only looked up when I finished to see Riley smiling at me.

"Want more?" she asked.

I nodded.

She filled me up before pouring herself a bowl and joining me at the counter.

"I wish Luke would let me work at the office or leave the house on my own," Riley said after a minute. "It gets boring being home alone all the time."

I wanted to tell her not to wish such a thing but who knows, maybe it'd be exactly what she wanted. Each woman had to make her own decision about what was a fulfilling way to live. Riley may love it.

I finished most of the second bowl before working up the nerve to ask Riley what was really on my mind. "Where did you disappear to last night?"

Riley smiled. "My room. Luke told me to stay there and not come out until morning. I heard you guys going at it. I can't say that I wasn't jealous but I was happy that he likes having you around because I do, too."

My heart warmed. I liked being around, too.

"Do you think you'll be staying?" Riley asked.

That was the big question.

"I honestly don't know," I told her. "I belong to Mr. Wood so it's up to him. He wants me back in the office tomorrow so who knows. I know he had acquired new girls and wanted Luke to take up my training for a while so he could focus on them. Who knows how long that'll take."

"Didn't you get here not that long ago?"

I had to think a minute. I had lost track of time. How long had I been here? I could barely remember a time when I wasn't here. What was my life like before I came to the island? I had just finished up college, had dated a couple of college guys, nothing spectacular and nothing close to this.

"A few weeks," I said, thinking that was close enough. "I honestly don't know. The days have blurred together. It's easy to lose track of time here."

Riley laughed. "I'm figuring that out."

She got up and cleared the empty bowls, washing them out and sticking them on the drying rack. She put a lid on the soup and moved it towards the back of the stove.

"I'll leave this for Luke in case he's hungry when he gets home," Riley said. "He seems to like my cooking."

I had no doubt. It was delicious.

"Thank you for sharing some with me," I said, feeling sincere. "It was amazing."

I saw her blush. "Of course. What are slut sisters for?"

I couldn't help but laugh.

TWENTY-ONE

I went to my room and waited on my knees for Luke, having used the bathroom but not cleaned myself off. I was tired and felt disgusting with the dried come clinging to my hair and skin. I wanted nothing more than to take a hot shower and sink into my soft bed and sleep forever. But I held my head up as I sat on my knees and waited. Even if word never got back to Mr. Wood about how obedient I had been, I would know and I was pleased with myself for withstanding the discomfort to follow instructions.

I waited for what felt like forever, my mind drifting before getting quiet, like a white fog. I leaned into it, happy not to think, to have this new ability to shut my mind off. It felt almost like sleeping but without dreams and without losing consciousness. I heard Riley downstairs and then later moving up the stairs. I had hoped for a minute it was Luke but the steps were too soft to be his.

It startled me when the door opened. My eyes went straight to him. He looked a bit wild and out of control. He came to me and scooped me up, planting a kiss on my lips as his arms went around me. I kissed him back as his tongue explored my mouth, drinking me in, tasting me, not seeming to mind that I was covered in other men's come. He kissed me with a passion that took my breath away before pulling away and staring at me. His hands gripped my shoulders, helping to hold me up as my legs started to wake.

"He wants you back in the office tomorrow," Luke said, looking uncertain.

I nodded. "I know. He told me."

"He's talking about taking you back. I sent him a note this afternoon telling him I wanted to talk about you and then he had every man in the office fuck you. I met with him this evening and he told me about your day. He told you not to wash because he wanted me to see you covered in come, reduced to the inferior slut you're meant to be here."

Luke took in a deep breath. My eyes widened, not knowing what to think. I should have known Mr. Wood wouldn't let go easily. He seemed to be a man that hung on to what he wanted.

"I wish I could take you away from this place but I can't," Luke said, his eyes pleading. "My livelihood is too entwined with my brother's to risk it."

My heart sunk even though I wasn't sure I wanted to leave this place yet but I knew I wanted to be with Luke, whatever way that looked.

"Is he going to take me away from you?" I asked, my voice small.

"I don't know. I think he's playing with me as much as he's playing with you. I told him this evening that I wanted to buy you, to make you a permanent part of my household, even joking with him that he was right about me needing more than one woman, but he knew there was more to it than that. He knows me so well that I couldn't lie to him. I told him I was falling for you and wanted you to myself."

I blinked at him. Those were the last words I expected.

Luke gave out a weak laugh. "The men here aren't supposed to fall for the women or at least it's not what they do. But I've never bought into the lifestyle my brother is developing here. I'm not opposed to it but I'm not sure it's the right lifestyle for me. I want more than a casual fuck. I want substance and love. I want it all. Is that something you want, too?"

He looked hopeful as his eyes searched mine. At that moment, I had no idea what I wanted. I wanted to be with Luke, I knew that much, but I wasn't sure if I was capable of love. I knew I didn't want to go back to my old life, to casual dating and hookups. I craved something more, something deeper, but I wasn't sure what that was. I wasn't sure how to communicate this to Luke who was looking at me as if I could deliver a miracle to him.

"I'm not sure what I want," I admitted, "but I know I want you to be a part of it."

He closed his mouth on mine, drinking me in. I gave myself over to the kiss, allowing myself to float away on it, to take it in, to make it mean everything even though I had no idea what.

He pulled away to look at me. "I will make you mine. Do you have the patience to bear with me? I think once my brother sees my determination he may let you go."

I nodded. "I'm patient. Tell me what I need to do."

He kissed me again before saying, "Continue to be your sweet obedient self. I need to show my brother that I can treat you how he thinks you need to be treated to fit in here. I need to be more dominant and share you more—show him I can be detached."

I nodded. It made sense. I was here to be used and the men were usually detached. I wasn't sure I could give Luke exactly what he wanted but I would allow him to use me however he wanted. I trusted him. I wondered how Riley would play into this but I didn't want to ask. I didn't want to bring her into it. If Luke was going to do what he thought his brother wanted then I was sure Riley would need to be a part of that. And the funny thing was I didn't mind.

———

I WAS BACK at the office the next day. Luke had me shower in his bathroom with him after our talk. He took special care in scrubbing away all the come and washing my hair. He wanted every reminder of the men who had taken me washed away. He wanted me clean and new. I thought he might fuck me in the shower but he dried me off and carried me to his bed, placing me down gently on the crisp white sheets.

He looked me over as if he couldn't believe I was there before he came at me like a jungle cat, all stealth and determination. He captured my mouth with his as his hands roamed over my body. It didn't take long before his cock was inside me, fucking me, as he kissed me senseless. I felt alive and on fire. Explosive. It didn't take long for me to come, to clamp down on his cock, forcing him to come with a fierceness I've yet to experience.

He roared in my ear as he came, continuing to plow into me through his orgasm. He fucked me until I came again, until he slipped out, spilling his seed down my legs and onto the clean sheet.

He held me in his arms until we fell asleep. It startled me when I woke up alone. Luke had left me a note on the pillow next to me.

Annabelle—

Have an amazing day at the office. Slip into your green evening dress when you return. I'm taking you out this evening.

x Luke

I stared at that x for a long time. Men on the island didn't show affection. With Luke, it was something different, something deeper, something I could easily tumble into and never return. I needed to tread carefully.

The office felt different now that I felt like I was navigating between Mr. Wood and Luke. I wasn't sure how to act but figured I needed to act like nothing unusual was happening. For all Mr. Wood knew, I didn't know Luke wanted to acquire me. It was a delicate balance.

I brought Mr. Wood his coffee first thing as usual. I knocked on his door and waited until he said to come in. He was alone sitting behind his desk. I approached with my eyes lowered, my steps steady. I placed the coffee on the coaster then paused, waiting to see if he needed anything else.

He looked me up and down as if he were weighing what he would say.

"How did my brother respond when he saw you last night?"

I failed at hiding my surprise.

"All he said was that you wanted me in the office today."

It wasn't a lie but it wasn't everything. I hoped Mr. Wood couldn't tell.

"Kneel."

I sank to my knees.

Mr. Wood slapped my face, startling me.

"You're nothing more than an inferior slut," he said as he circled me. "You are nothing more than property here, to be owned and used as I see fit. I've been too lenient on you, not seeing to your training as much as I should have. You need to be put back in your place, to understand your purpose here, to fulfill your potential. Do you understand?"

I nodded. "Yes, Mr. Wood."

"This is for your benefit," Mr. Wood said as he stopped in front of me. "In order for you to obtain the full freedom and submission you crave, you need to be here fully, to accept your place fully, not have fantasies about it being some other way. I know my brother can be overly accommodating and I thought sending you to him would help him to see how a woman needs to be treated. You're a natural submissive. You need strict guidance and discipline to obtain your true potential. Not all women are as naturally submissive as you are. You stand out in that way."

I took in his words. They resonated deep inside me. I knew what he was saying was true—that I was submissive and that I needed to submit to be truly free. I wondered if Luke could give that to me. I knew Mr. Wood could.

"I'm going to give you a mantra I want you to repeat out loud the moment you wake up, while you're getting ready in the morning, before every meal, whenever you're walking somewhere and before you go to sleep. You'll repeat the entire thing at least ten times each time you recite it, more if you feel you need it. This will help you get back into the proper mindset and to forget about life being any other way."

"Yes, Mr. Wood," I said. I knew I had no other choice than to leave. Maybe it would be good for me. I had felt lost the last couple of days. I no longer knew what I wanted or who I was.

He seemed pleased by this.

"I've printed it up for you," he said. "There's a copy on your desk. If you should misplace it, until you have it memorized, ask me for another copy. You won't be punished for losing it. It's of vital importance that you use this mantra. It will make your life here easier."

"Thank you, Mr. Wood," I said, interested in what the mantra would say and how it would change me.

"You're dismissed. Start with the mantra as your first task and then continue with the work that's been left for you."

"Thank you, Mr. Wood," I said, pushing myself up before leaving his office, closing the door behind me.

I let out a sigh of relief as I sank into my office chair. I thought he was going to punish me, see through to the truth of what was going on between Luke and me. I knew I needed to get back on track with the true reason I was here and not let Luke distract me. As much as I craved being with Luke, maybe he wasn't the answer. His hands seemed tied as much or even more than mine. I could leave anytime but he was tied up with his brother and needed to please him almost as much as I did.

I picked up the paper with the mantra on it and read it out loud, testing it on my tongue.

"I am an inferior slut. My only purpose is to obey and please men. I am nothing more than three holes meant for use. My mind is meaningless. I accept my role here. I submit happily."

I looked up to see a couple of secretaries looking at me. I wondered if they needed mantras, too. I felt like a remedial student falling behind in my studies.

I repeated it again, this time with more conviction.

"I am an inferior slut. My only purpose is to obey and please men. I am nothing more than three holes meant for use. My mind is meaningless. I accept my role here. I submit happily."

It felt better this time, more real. I liked the orderliness of it, the simplicity. It was direct and told me everything I needed to know.

I repeated it eight more times as per Mr. Wood's instructions. I didn't want to mess this up. I wanted more than anything to obey and please.

I felt more aligned with my truth when I finished. I tucked the paper under the pile of work that was left for me, hoping I didn't forget it at the end of the day.

I lost myself in the work, grateful not to be thinking about Luke and my life here and how it was all going to play out. It was out of my hands which was a huge relief. In the past, I would have wanted to control the situation, to debate about what I could do to sway it to how I wanted it, but here I was powerless. There was nothing I could do and in a way that felt wonderful, like a huge relief.

Mr. Wood called me into his office during the afternoon. I had just gotten into a flow, feeling almost like I was at a regular office, feeling productive, when he called me and told me to come into his office.

"Would you like a cup of coffee?" I asked.

"No, that won't be necessary."

I hung up the phone, got up and knocked on his closed door. He called for me to come in. I stepped in, unsure what to expect, closing the door behind me.

"Come here then kneel."

I complied, walking to the front of his desk before dropping to my knees, lowering my eyes. I was grateful for the soft rug he kept there. I wondered if it was placed there exactly for this reason—to cushion the women who he had kneel before him. I knew I wasn't the only one.

He came around the desk and slipped a blindfold over my eyes, plunging me into darkness. I didn't like not being able to see but knew better than to say anything. I drew in a deep breath as I prepared myself for anything.

He slapped me across the face, startling me. My cheek stung from the contact.

"Repeat your mantra," he commanded.

I swallowed, afraid I wouldn't be able to remember it exactly but I knew I had to try.

"I am an inferior slut," I started. "My only purpose is to please and obey men."

I paused, trying to remember.

He slapped my face, the other cheek this time.

"Continue."

"I am nothing more than three holes to be filled," I said, hoping I was getting it right. "I accept my role here."

He slapped me again, startling me.

"You missed a sentence."

I thought hard. Fuck. I couldn't remember.

"I'm sorry but I can't remember, Mr. Wood," I said, hoping he wouldn't slap me again.

He didn't. Instead, he let out a sigh and fed it to me.

"My mind is meaningless," I repeated. "I accept my role here. I submit happily."

"Again."

I repeated it again, this time not messing up. He had me repeat it eight more times until it rolled off my tongue, becoming a part of me.

"Good," he said when I finished. "Do you believe these words?"

I nodded. "Yes, Mr. Wood."

I could feel him smiling. It pleased me that I had pleased him Maybe this was all my life was meant to be, on my knees pleasing men.

I heard his zipper and opened my mouth before he could command it open. His cock slipped into my mouth, filling it, pushing against the back of my throat. I worshiped his cock with my tongue, opening my throat as much as I could as he pushed in deeper. He didn't use his hands to guide me, simply thrusted further in, impaling me completely. I welcomed the feel of his cock on my tongue, filling me making me complete. It had been a while since I had his cock in my mouth.

It didn't take long for him to empty himself down my throat. I sucked in every drop, licking him clean before he pulled out. He petted my head before retreating to his office chair. He got back to work, making calls, typing on the computer, as I stayed kneeled, waiting to be released.

After a while another man came in and met with Mr. Wood, ignoring me as if I were another piece of furniture. As their meeting wrapped up, I heard him move towards me. I opened my mouth automatically. The man chuckled. Instead of sliding his cock down my throat, a few minutes later he sprayed my face and open mouth with his semen. I held my mouth open, taking in what I could while he coated my face and hair. He said more words to Mr. Wood and then left, closing the door behind him.

This went on for some time—random men coming in, meeting with Mr. Wood then coming all over my face and hair. I kept my mouth open the entire time, my hands face up on my lap, thinking this was the most receptive position. I swallowed what semen I could while most of it landed elsewhere.

By the end of the day, I lost track of how many men deposited themselves on me. I knew I looked a mess, covered with come.

"You are a slut," Mr. Wood said after a long time. He removed the blindfold. I blinked against the light. "Go back to my brother like this. You're dismissed."

"Thank you, Mr. Wood," I said before lifting myself. My legs were stiff and asleep but I didn't hesitate to leave the office. Most of the others had left already and I wondered how long Mr. Wood had kept me in his office. Not that it mattered. My life was no longer my own. I was realizing this.

TWENTY-TWO

Luke was home when I came back. He took one look at me and smiled.

"I see my brother's at it again," he said with a laugh. "Go shower. Wear the green dress I had Riley lay out for you. We're going out."

The water felt amazing, loosening my tense muscles, washing away all the garbage of the day. I repeated the mantra while I washed, letting it sink into my psyche. I knew Mr. Wood was right that I'd be better off if I accepted my place here. I had signed up for this. I wanted to be here. I wanted to know what life would be like if I gave into my internal desire to submit to men. I needed to embrace it, to be it, to see if this was where I was meant to be.

I slipped on the green dress as instructed, happy with how it hugged my curves and accentuated my breasts. It was sheer, showing everything, but looked glamorous and almost discrete. I adorned myself with a pair of sparkly dangling earrings that I picked up on my trip to town with Riley and made sure my hair and makeup were perfect before descending the stairs to the kitchen.

Riley was at the stove cooking. Her eyes widened when she saw me.

"You look amazing," she said. "I'm so jealous you're going out with Luke."

"You're not coming?" I asked, already knowing the answer.

She shook her head. "No, he told me to stay home. He wants this to be a special night for you."

I smiled. My heart warmed. I felt special but tried not to let it show. I knew what it was like to be jealous.

Luke walked in a moment later looking amazing in a dark suit with a crisp white button-down and burgundy tie. He smiled when he saw me, warming my heart. I was happy he was pleased. I wanted nothing more than to please him, to have him happy to have me on his arm, to show me off.

"Wow, you look amazing, Annabelle," he said as he made his way over to me. "I'm one lucky man."

I blushed.

"Ready to go?"

I nodded. "Yes, Luke."

We walked arm in arm like we were walking the streets in some old movie in Paris. I loved the claim it gave off, keeping the other men from touching me as we made our way through town. Luke was in charge and I was happy to fall in line.

"I'm excited for tonight," Luke said on the way over, stopping so he could look at me, "but I need to know before we go any further if you want to be with me."

His eyes were serious. I smiled at him.

"Yes, I do. That would be amazing."

"Do you want to stay on the island and continue with this lifestyle?"

I swallowed as he kept eye contact with me. I hadn't thought I'd need to be making that decision so soon. My head swam with the possibilities. I didn't know what I thought.

He must have seen me struggling because a slow smile spread on his lips.

"You want to stay, don't you? It's OK if you do. I could get used to it here and it would make life with my brother easier but I want to be sure you want to stay. At least for now."

He was giving me an easy out and I was grateful. He was giving me room to change my mind.

I nodded. "I want to stay if I'm able to stay with you."

"And you don't mind being seen as a man's property?"

"I enjoy being of service," I admitted to him and myself. "There's freedom in giving myself over to someone else, to have the choices taken away. I've been more relaxed here than I've been in years. Each day is unique and I don't have to worry about anything. I've always loved sex so that hasn't been an issue for me."

Luke broke out in an enormous smile and hugged me before planting a kiss on my lips. He didn't sink into me but held my lips with his for a moment. Electricity sparked through me. I felt like I had just made a monumental decision and my heart fluttered. Maybe I was finally where I needed to be.

"You're amazing," Luke said when he pulled back, his eyes wide and bright. "Thank you for being you, Annabelle. I think tonight will be amazing."

I felt like I was walking on a cloud the rest of the way. I added a little extra sashay to my step, happy to be walking next to Luke, to be part of this amazing life. My heart felt like it would burst. I felt part of something better than myself.

We walked into a fancy restaurant off the harbor with expansive views of the ocean and open-air seating. The men wore dark suits while the women wore long elegant sheer gowns or nothing at all with jewels hanging off them. Crystal chandeliers twinkled above, casting a warm glow.

Luke led us to an area that bordered the outer deck that reached out towards the sparkling blue water. Tables were situated around a raised platform. Luke guided us towards a table that was filled except for two chairs.

My eyes locked on Mr. Wood right away with Zoey at his side in a sheer white gown. He smiled at me as Luke pulled out a chair for me. I quickly lowered my eyes, my heart pounding, unsure of how to act. Was I under Luke's direction at the moment or would I need to defer to Mr. Wood? I said a little prayer, hoping it'd be obvious.

The men greeted Luke as he settled in next to me. The waitress came around, her breasts on display with a tiny apron tied around her waist, and took orders from the men. A glass of white wine was put down in front of me. I sipped it, knowing it'd go straight to my head.

Luke leaned over and slid his hand under my gown so he could cup my breast. He pinched the nipple and whispered in my ear, "Welcome to the rest of your life."

A shiver ran through me.

The sun set as our dinners arrived. Luke had ordered a steak for himself and a chicken dish with a white sauce and mushrooms for me. After receiving a slight nod from Luke, I dug in, starving. I had to control myself from not overdoing it so I paced myself, taking one small bite at a time, setting my fork down between bites.

The men talked business, things I knew nothing about. I took in the lush surroundings, happy to be out of the office and out of Luke's place, happy to be adapting to this lifestyle. I tried catching Zoey's eye, to communicate with her, to ask her how life was going for her, but she kept her eyes lowered and focused on eating. I felt disappointed.

The waitress cleared the plates as soon as everyone finished. She replaced empty wine glasses with short glasses of bourbon for the men and port for the women.

Mr. Wood held up his glass. "To another successful deal and to Wood Enterprises."

The men held up their glasses, offering their support and happiness over the success, clinking glasses before drinking their bourbon. The women didn't raise their glasses but took delicate sips of their port, eyes lowered, acting as if they weren't part of the conversation which they weren't.

My head swam from all the alcohol. I wasn't used to drinking. A warm buzz crept through me, making me feel liquid and loose, a feeling I gladly sunk into. The men talked around me but I wasn't listening. I had learned when I needed to pay attention and when I didn't.

I wanted to talk with Zoey or even the other women to ask how their life on the island was going. It seemed like most of the women embraced their role here. I felt like I was about to make a major decision and I could have used some female support.

I felt Luke's hand snake up my thigh while he talked with the men, nudging my legs open. His fingers slipped inside me, causing me to squirm. He continued talking but I noted a small smile on his lips. He was pleased to be playing with me at the table like this.

I kept my eyes lowered and my face neutral as I wondered what other women at the table were being played with while the men talked. It wasn't like they needed to keep it secret but keeping it under the table added a level of mischievousness to it that thrilled me.

Luke pushed deeper, spreading me wide, as he circled my clit with his thumb. I wanted to buck against the sensations but tried to act as if nothing was happening. I had a feeling he was seeing how far he could push me before I had no choice but to make a scene.

I bit my lip as he tickled my clit, his fingers buried deep inside me. I wanted to push into his hand, to get him deeper, but I resisted the urge. I finished my port, happy with the warmth and distraction it provided.

"Strip," Luke said into my ear. "Pull your dress down so you're topless."

My face reddened at the command even though my dress offered no modesty. I did as I was told, slipping the thin straps of my dress off my shoulders and letting the sheer fabric pool around my waist. Luke pulled on each nipple with his free hand while his other hand played with my clit. I knew all eyes were on me which made me want to explode even more. I kept my eyes lowered as Luke pulled on my nipples.

"You're going to be the dessert tonight," Luke whispered in my ear.

I had no idea what he meant but before I could think, he was pulling me to my feet. My dress slipped off and onto the floor before Luke picked me up and set me on the now empty table. I felt mortified as he told me to lay back with my ass on the edge, my legs pushed open, on display for everyone.

I closed my eyes, wanting to block out everyone, but Luke told me to keep them open. He wanted me to see what was happening and not to escape inside myself as he had seen me do many times.

The tables must have been made for this type of thing because it took my weight easily without so much as a wobble. Luke buried his face between my legs, teasing my clit with his tongue, while the other men took to pinching and pulling my nipples and sticking their fingers in my mouth. I opened myself up to all of it, allowing the sensations to wash over me, overwhelming my senses.

I stared up at the ceiling, keeping my eyes open as instructed, taking in the faces of the men as they leaned over me, their hands on my body. It didn't take long before one man slipped his cock in my mouth, practically straddling my face to do it. I opened my throat to accommodate him, happy for the distraction.

Luke's tongue continued its assault on my clit, causing me to buck my hips, wanting more. Hands clasped my ankles, holding me down, making Luke's assault that much more intense. I wasn't going anywhere and was forced to lay there and take it.

My body felt on fire as it flooded with pleasure. I knew I was close to coming but I wanted to hold back as long as I could, knowing it'd make things easier for me if this evening went on for a while. Luke seemed to sense my reluctance to come because he intensified his tongue lashing while easing a finger into my ass, making it all too much.

I came with a fierceness, swallowing the cock in my mouth in the process, causing it to shoot its load down my throat. Hands held my wrists flat to the table as my body convulsed as if I were electrocuted.

I heard Luke's deep chuckle before he gave my clit one more suck and kiss. The cock in my mouth was replaced by another as I felt a cock slide into my wet pussy. I opened myself wide for both cocks, happy to be occupied and used, feeling full and loose. Hands grabbed and pulled at my nipples as others held my wrists and ankles down, keeping me immobile and open, on display for the whole restaurant.

I had no idea where Luke went after I came on his face but it no longer mattered as cocks slid in and out of me, having their fill before being replaced by others. This went on for what felt like forever. My jaw ached from being held open by cock after cock and my pussy hummed with each thrust. If there had ever been any doubt that I wasn't made for this, it slipped away as my mind drifted into a happy fog, happy to be filled and used and filled again.

When the last cocks came down my throat and deep in my pussy, pulling away from me, I felt empty and abandoned. The sounds of the restaurant rushed in, pulling me out of my fog, reminding me of my predicament of being spread out for all to see. I felt the come dripping out of my pussy and onto my ass. I didn't come again but my body buzzed from being thoroughly fucked and part of me craved more.

Hands pulled me up and it wasn't until I was standing on wobbly legs that I realized it was Mr. Wood who had helped me. He looked pleased, a smirk on his face.

"Nice show," he said, his voice low and smooth.

I met his eyes.

"Thank you, Mr. Wood," I said. "It was fun."

"I'm pleased by how well you've adapted to this place," Mr. Wood said. "Not all women do no matter how submissive their nature. It takes a special woman to adapt here. Do you think you'll be staying with us after your six-month trial?"

I blinked at him. I had thought little past today but staying intrigued me. I wasn't ready to give this place up yet and I was curious how things would play out with Luke.

"I'd like to stay, Mr. Wood," I said, feeling the weight of the words and knowing I meant them. "I feel like I'm meant to be here."

Mr. Wood smiled. "I couldn't agree more. You're the best slut I've seen in a while."

I blushed under his praise, letting the words sink in. I felt proud of this, knowing that Mr. Wood had put me through a lot, especially lately, and I came through it all a stronger, more determined woman.

"What's your mantra?" Mr. Wood asked.

I heard the restaurant around me as I took in a deep breath. I'd been saying the mantra regularly as instructed and had finally memorized it.

"I am an inferior slut. My only purpose is to obey and please men. I am nothing more than three holes meant for use. My mind is meaningless. I accept my role here. I submit happily."

"Again."

I said it again and again and seven more times until my body hummed with it. I felt eyes on me but I didn't care. That part of me that used to care about what others thought had disappeared. I felt liberated and more confident than I had in years, like I was where I belonged. I relished in the role I had chosen for myself, knowing it was the best place for me.

"Good," he said before sliding something underneath my collar. "I want you to go back with my brother and obey him as if he were me. He'll let you know whether he wants you to continue to work in the office and anything else. I am relinquishing my ownership of you."

My heart dropped. Even though this is what I wanted, I didn't know what it meant. Was I without an owner now or did Mr. Wood just tell me that his brother was my new owner? I tried not to get my hopes up and I didn't want to look overjoyed in front of Mr. Wood.

I tried to keep my expression neutral as I looked up at him and said, "Thank you, Mr. Wood."

"You'll do well," Mr. Wood said. "Don't disappoint me."

TWENTY-THREE

Mr. Wood left me with the restaurant swirling all around me. I felt light-headed and a little dizzy. I could hear our party breaking up and watched as the waitresses continued to serve meals and drinks to other tables. I stood there unsure what to do without instruction. I felt like I had been cast out to sea without oars. I was in uncharted waters.

I took in a few deep breaths, willing myself to stay calm and focused. Mr. Wood had praised me and told me I was free of his ownership. My body tingled at the thought of belonging to Luke but I didn't want to let myself go there until I knew for sure, until I heard it from Luke himself.

Everyone in the restaurant ignored me as I stood there waiting for what was next. Waitresses cleared the table behind me as I waited, not paying me any more attention than if I were a chair. It was interesting to be ignored while standing in the middle of a restaurant naked with come dripping down my legs. It should have been my nightmare but it wasn't. It was my new way of life.

I let myself slip into a haze while I waited, drifting on a white fog.

It startled me when Luke appeared in front of me, all smiles.

"Ready to go?" he asked.

I nodded. "Yes."

"Great. Let's go."

He led me back to his place with no fanfare. My mind tried to grasp on to what had shifted but I couldn't land on anything solid. I needed Luke to be the one to tell me, to spell it out.

Riley wasn't around when we returned. Luke didn't say a word but led me straight to his bedroom. He closed the door before leading me to the bathroom where he ran a shower, pushing me into it once the water warmed. I thought he might join me but instead he washed my front and my back from outside the shower, instructing me to turn, to bend, so he could reach all the places. He washed my hair, too, adding a conditioner that smelled like summer.

Once he was satisfied, he turned off the water and took his time towel drying me, going over every inch of me with the plush towel. He smiled while he did it but didn't say a word. I knew I couldn't ask him, couldn't break the silence, so I didn't. If he was my new owner, I didn't want to start off on the wrong foot. I didn't think he'd be as strict as Mr. Wood but I couldn't be sure and I didn't want to test him. I wanted him to take the lead. I needed to resign myself to not knowing anything until he was ready to tell me.

When he finished, he unclipped my collar, letting it fall to the floor. I sucked in my breath as my eyes met his. He smiled at me as he slipped a new collar around my neck without a word. He fastened it, locking it into place, before moving before the floor to ceiling mirror.

I almost cried when I saw it. It was white.

Luke kissed my cheek, moving my hair off my shoulders.

"Today was the last day any other man fucks you," he said, his eyes meeting mine in the mirror, "unless you want other men to fuck you but I'd prefer they didn't."

Tears filled my eyes. He wanted me to be his. I almost couldn't comprehend it. No more random fucks. No more random blow jobs. This collar put me off-limits.

"I bought you this evening," Luke said, turning me so we were face to face. "That's why you had to wait in the restaurant for so long. I was ironing out the details. My brother wanted one last hurrah and for me to prove to him that I could handle your training but what we do together from here on out is up to me. The deal is done."

I couldn't keep from smiling. My heart felt like it would burst with happiness. I couldn't believe he had gone through with it, that I was his. It felt like getting engaged but even better. He owned me, body and soul, for as long as I wanted to stay which at that moment felt like forever.

"Can I hug you?" I asked, unsure if I should talk.

He laughed. "Yes, of course."

He wrapped himself around me, pulling me in tight. I felt his heartbeat as I laid my head on his chest. I felt safe and secure as I snuggled into him, his powerful arms solid around me. This was everything I wanted and more. He was everything I wanted.

He pulled back a little to look at me, his arms tight around me. "Annabelle, listen to me. I want you to have as much freedom and autonomy as you want. When you're inside this house, feel free to talk to me, to do whatever you want, to sit anywhere you want, to be how you want. I want you to feel relaxed and at home here."

I smiled at him, my heart warming. "Yes, Luke. I'd like that."

"At the same time I know you came to this island to experience what it was like for men to be in control of women," Luke said. "I know you're a natural submissive and I want to honor that. I'm not keen on sharing you, at least not right now. If you'd like to have that type of lifestyle, we can negotiate a different collar color for you but for now, I'm not sharing."

I beamed at him. I loved his possessiveness. I liked belonging to him.

"You're mine now, Annabelle. Are you ok with this?"

I nodded. "Yes. God, yes. It's all I want."

Luke captured my mouth with his, drinking me in as he continued to hold me tight. His mouth was warm and demanding, sending waves of emotion through me. I felt overwhelmed. My head spun as I tried to grasp at what this meant. Suddenly I had some control over my life here while also being able to be fully submissive. I wasn't sure how it was going to work but I was sure we'd find a way. Even though Luke wasn't as dominant as his brother, he still had a dominant nature I appreciated. The difference was he wanted to please me as much as I wanted to please him.

He pulled away, leaving me breathless. His eyes searched mine as he smiled at me. My heart skipped and felt full.

"I don't have all the answers right now," he said, "but we'll figure them out together. I want you to be a part of this, a part of me, as much as you want or as little as you want. If you want me to be more dominant, I can do that for you. If you want to be more of a partner, I can do that, too. The most important thing is that I want us to be together in whatever way that ends up being. I want you. It's as simple as that."

I blinked at him, hardly believing what I was hearing. This powerful man wanted me in whatever way I was willing to give him. My heart filled with the love he was showing me, handing me. I couldn't believe my luck. I wanted all of him, too.

He scooped me up and took me into the bedroom. I clung to his neck, breathing him in, my heart bursting with joy. I had everything I wanted at this moment and I couldn't believe it was happening. I felt like I was dreaming and didn't want to wake up.

Luke kissed every inch of my body as if claiming me with his mouth before he slowly sank into me. His cock felt amazing as it filled me. I clamped down and held him there, relishing that this man was all mine and that I was all his. He kissed me with a fierceness that took my breath away as he slowly fucked me, claimed me, made sure I understood that I was his.

It didn't take long before I was exploding all around him. He smiled down at me as he increased his pace before spilling deep inside me. For a moment I wished that I wasn't on the island's high potency birth control. I liked the idea of Luke planting himself inside me. Maybe one day. My head spun with the possibilities. I never knew I could be so happy.

He kissed me after he came, his cock buried inside me. I wanted to keep him there, keep him close, and was disappointed when he slipped out. He fell down next to me before taking me up in his arms, pulling me on top of his chest. I rested my head there, satiated, before falling into a deep happy sleep.

———

THE NEXT MORNING Luke was gone when I woke up. I stretched like a lazy cat, excited to start my first day as Luke's. I still couldn't believe Mr. Wood agreed to sell me to Luke. I thought for sure he'd put up a fight. It made me think Mr. Wood was too busy with his latest acquisitions to be bothered with me anymore. I wondered what Zoey thought of all this or if she even cared. We had never clicked as I had hoped.

I had no idea what to do with my day. After using the bathroom, I wandered downstairs to the kitchen. I was surprised to see Riley in the kitchen making breakfast. She smiled at me as she scooped eggs from the frying pan.

"Congratulations, Annabelle," she said as she put the eggs on a plate. "Luke told me the great news. I'm so happy for you and me."

I felt a little dumbfounded. I had forgotten about Riley and how she'd play into this new dynamic.

I forced a smile, not feeling it, as I sat at the counter.

"I can hardly believe it," I said. "It doesn't feel real."

Riley brought her food over to the counter and started eating.

"Does this mean you're done with the training?" Riley asked.

Good question. "I have no idea," I admitted. "All I know is that I'm Luke's now. We didn't get into the details. I was hoping he'd be around this morning."

"Oh, he left early," Riley said as if it were nothing.

"Did he leave anything for me?"

"Sorry, no. Was he supposed to?"

I had no idea. I felt a little uneasy. I didn't know what I was supposed to do.

"Do you want me to cook you anything?" Riley asked.

I shook my head. I wasn't sure I could stomach anything.

"No, I'm OK," I said before getting up and heading back upstairs.

I went straight to Luke's room hoping I'd find a note somewhere but after a thorough search, I came up empty. I checked my room but didn't see anything from him there either. I couldn't believe he'd leave without giving me any instruction around how he wanted me to spend the day.

My head spun. I sank to my knees on the plush carpet next to my bed and cried. I knew I should have felt happy and overjoyed with my new found freedom but instead I felt lost and overwhelmed. I had no idea what was expected of me now and I had no idea what to do with my day. I wished Luke would have left me some instruction, something, or at least an idea when to expect him back. I had hoped to spend the day together, preferably in bed, cuddled in each other's arms, then I wouldn't have to deal with all this.

I tried muffling my crying since I didn't want Riley to hear and find me a mess on the floor. I knew I was being ridiculous but I couldn't help it. All the pent up angst and confusion over the past few weeks came to the surface and needed to be released. I couldn't hold it in any longer. I had no idea what I was doing here or what I wanted anymore.

Part of me knew I'd have a hard time returning to normal life while another part of me had no idea what my life would look like being here now. I had been living in a fantasy world, allowing myself to be controlled, allowing myself to give in to this place, and now that Luke was offering me an out, I no longer knew my place.

I leaned forward until my head rested on the carpet, my arms at my side, in a naked child's pose. I took in deep breaths as I willed myself to relax, telling myself that it was going to work out. I knew I was better off with Luke than anyone else and he'd create any type of relationship that would work for both of us. He knew I had needs and was willing to fill them. I wished he was here to guide me.

I cried until I fell into a blissfully deep sleep. I woke up feeling refreshed and more relaxed. I wandered into the kitchen, my stomach alerting me that I needed to eat. Riley wasn't there this time. I went straight to the fridge for a yogurt, devouring it in a couple of bites before discarding it in the trash.

I listened for any noises in the house, any signs of life, but there was nothing. Maybe Luke was out with Riley. The thought didn't turn my stomach like I thought it might but instead left me wondering how I fit in with their dynamic. Earlier I had worried about how she'd fit in with us but now I realized that she was here first and I was the third party entering their relationships. Did he feel the same way about her as he did about me? Did he want her to be part of us, too?

I went back to my room, unsure what else to do. Even with my new white collar, I didn't feel like venturing out. I wasn't sure I'd know how to act with this new symbol of freedom. Would the men smirk at not being able to touch me? Would the women be jealous? I didn't have any money to spend in any of the shops. At least that would have made me feel a little bit more normal. And I couldn't show up at the office without an invitation. I assumed my job there was over.

I kneeled on the plush carpet on the side of the bed with my hands in my lap. I hadn't bothered to get dressed this morning—I had become accustomed to being nude and didn't mind it. I sat up straight, arching my back slightly so my tits were on proper display even though there was no one to see them. I wished I would have thought to put on a blindfold, allowing me to block out the world for a while, but I closed my eyes instead and sunk into a deep and calming meditation.

I felt feather touches on the tips of my nipples before I opened my eyes to see Luke standing over me smiling.

"There's my baby girl," he said before pinching my nipples, making me swoon. "Have you been in here long? You know I don't expect you to wait for me like this anymore."

I blinked at him, feeling the tears starting to form. I felt a deep sadness which surprised me. Wasn't he offering me everything I wanted?

Luke look confused as he sensed my sadness. He put out his hands to help me up. I stood on shaky legs, unable to look him in the eyes. I felt lost and confused. I didn't know how to explain it and I knew he wanted to ask. I kept my eyes lowered.

"I think I know what's going on," he said, his words surprising me.

"You've been under such strict training and suddenly I'm offering you all this freedom and it's too much. Am I right?"

I nodded, unable to say the words.

He hugged me to him. "I get it. I do and I'm sorry for springing it on you like that. I should have known better but this is new to me, too. I'm not used to women wanting me to have this level of control."

I breathed in his clean scent as my body relaxed against him. He felt solid and secure. He wrapped his arms around me and held me as I rested my head on his shoulder, allowing myself to lean into him, to be held up by him. It felt good and right to be supported by him. It was something I craved and now I knew needed. I needed him to be in control of me. I needed him to take charge.

He kissed the top of my head before pulling back enough so he could look at me. I met his dark green eyes and bit my lip. He'd be so easy to get lost in, to do anything for. I wondered if he had any idea how much he could control me and how much I'd love it. I wished there was a way I could communicate that to him without saying a word. I didn't want to admit that this was what I needed, this was why I came here. I just wanted him to know, to feel it, to see it in me.

He studied me as he held my gaze. He traced my lower lip with his finger before slowly slipping it in. I opened my mouth to him, welcoming him, happy to taste the saltiness of his finger, to let it play on my tongue.

He slipped a second finger in and then a third. I sucked on his fingers as if it were his cock, keeping his gaze the entire time. He stared at me with intense eyes as he pushed his fingers in deeper, sliding them up and down my tongue.

I felt myself becoming aroused. My nipples hardened. I sucked in his fingers, swirling my tongue around them, lapping at them. I saw a hint of a smile on his face as he watched me. I was sure he could tell I was enjoying this, loving having him in my mouth, enjoying pleasing him.

He pulled his fingers out before capturing my mouth with his. He devoured me, exploring my mouth with his tongue, drinking me in. I opened myself up to him, kissing him back with everything I had. My body hummed. I wanted more. I wanted everything.

His hands found their way up my body. One hand cupped my ass, pulling me in closer until I felt the hardness in his pants, while the other roamed over my breasts, grazing and pinching my nipples. He stroked and played with me while he kissed me, his kiss hard and demanding. My body was on fire for him, alive and pulsing.

The hand on my ass slipped lower until a finger slipped into my wet pussy. He thrust in one finger before adding more, filling and stretching me, as his mouth stayed on mine, claiming me.

I melted into him, happy to be filled, happy to be taken. I forgot my worries as my mind emptied into the moment. I was nothing more than pure sensation and pleasure.

He increased the pace with his fingers, causing my breathing to go shallow. He released my mouth and trailed his lips down my neck. I threw my head back, my body quivering with need, wanting him. He sucked on my neck, driving me crazy.

Abruptly, he pulled his fingers out and pushed me back on the bed. My legs automatically opened for him, anticipating, showing off my glistening pussy. He smiled at my invitation, dropping his pants and pulling out his hard cock.

I licked my lips. If I wasn't so desperate for him, I would have wanted to take him in my mouth first, savor his taste, drive him a little mad. But I didn't think I could wait another minute for him to fuck me. I needed him and I wanted him to know it.

He must have read my mind because he wasted no time sliding his thick cock into me. I sucked in my breath as he flexed his hips, pounding into me with urgency, like he couldn't get enough. I hung onto his muscled shoulders as he pounded into me, throwing my head back as an orgasm ripped through me. I screamed and clamped down on his cock, causing him to chuckle and increase his speed.

He continued fucking me, his eyes intense on mine. I felt like a wild animal, feral and raw. I wanted more of him, more of this. I couldn't think and I didn't want to think. Another orgasm started to build deep in my abdomen as his cock claimed me.

It was like he could sense it building. He grabbed my hips to pull me in closer as he slammed into me again and again. I screamed and threw my head back as another orgasm ripped through me. I shuddered as my world exploded.

He fucked me through my climax before emptying himself deep inside me. He collapsed on top of me, his breathing fast in my ear. My head was spinning. I felt like I was somewhere else, like I had left my body and was floating on the ceiling. Euphoria snaked through me. I had never felt so satisfied and wiped out in my life.

"God, Annabelle," he said into my ear. "You're amazing."

I blushed at his compliment. I had never thought of myself as amazing.

TWENTY-FOUR

I must have fallen asleep because the next thing I knew I was cuddled up with him, my head resting on his chest, as he stroked my hair. I felt content and happy in a way I had never experienced. If I were a cat, I'd be purring and content to stay like that forever.

Luke must have felt me up because he brushed the hair off my face before kissing my forehead.

"Welcome back, little girl."

I glowed under his endearment, heat spreading through me. I cuddled in more, not wanting to move, not wanting to leave the warmth of his side. I had no idea what the future held for us and I was in no rush to find out.

"Are you a good little slut?"

I nodded, warming to his use of the word slut. It was something Mr. Wood called me but Luke hadn't used it before. It felt like a turning point in our relationship.

He ran his hand over my ass until his fingers found my wet pussy and pushed in. I welcomed him, spreading my legs for easier access. He chuckled in my ear as his fingers found my clit and circled over it, driving me insane.

"I thought about it while you were sleeping and determined that you need me to continue with the structure and discipline that my brother started. Isn't that right, my little slut?"

I nodded as his fingers continued to play with me, circling over my clit. Heat rose through my body as my pussy pulsed with need. I enjoyed the torment and wanted more.

"Women like you are a unique breed and I am very fortunate to have you. I came to this island not sure what to expect and I never thought I'd end up falling for one of the women here but I have."

He gave me a moment to absorb his words while his fingers drove me mad, playing with my clit, making it hard for me to focus. He increased the pace, causing my body to squirm. He chuckled.

"I think we could have a lot of fun together, don't you?" he purred as he increased the pace, milking an explosive orgasm out of me. I screamed and jerked against his hand as he slid his fingers deep inside me, fucking me with them until another orgasm ripped through me. He laughed before pulling his fingers out, bringing them up to my mouth to suck which I did willingly.

"You don't want to be in control, do you?" he asked, his eyes finding mine.

I shook my head. It was the truth. I needed to be controlled. I had finally realized this was part of me.

"You want me to be in control of you, don't you?" he asked.

I nodded, feeling a warmth spread through me.

He smiled.

"I would like that, too. I don't know what it is, Annabelle, but you bring out something primal in me that I hadn't tapped into before. You make me want to dominate you, to control you. I think part of it is because you are a natural submissive and need me to be that for you but I think you bring out a part of myself that I've kept buried for most of my life. I thought it was ridiculous when my brother first told me about this place and what he was trying to accomplish here but now I'm thinking it might be exactly where I need to be."

My heart felt like it might burst as I looked into his eyes and saw the sincerity there. Maybe this was destined to work. I had no idea when I came here that I could meet a man like this—both caring and dominating. I thought it had to be one or the other and I had been ready to give up caring to get the domination I needed.

"Please say something, Annabelle," he said, his eyes searching mine. "Do you want to stay here on this island and try this out with me? I'm not sure what it will look like exactly but I promise you I'll care for you and give you all the discipline you need."

I threw my arms around his neck as I said, "God, Luke, yes. This is all I ever wanted." And I meant every word.

WANT MORE?

Annabelle and Luke's story continues in Sweet Submission - The Island Series Book Two. Sign up for eroticwritergirl's email newsletter so you don't miss out at www.eroticwritergirl.com.

CONNECT WITH EROTICWRITERGIRL

THANK YOU SO MUCH FOR READING MY BOOK. I HOPE YOU LOVED IT!

Please take a moment to leave
a brief review on Amazon and/or Goodreads.
I'd truly appreciate it.

Books Two and Three are now available.
Don't miss out! Sign up for my email newsletter at
www.eroticwritergirl.com to stay in the know.

Email me at connect@eroticwritergirl.com.
I'd love to hear from you.

ACKNOWLEDGMENTS

I am so grateful for each and every one of my readers but this book (and series) wouldn't be possible without the continued support and understanding of my amazing husband. He has encouraged me every step of the way, wanting me to pursue my passion for writing, and without him, none of this would have been possible. He's given me the time and space I've needed to write without abandon. He's my sunshine and I'm his blue sky.

I also want to thank my amazing beta readers but especially Anne who has been with me every step of the way through this series. She has been my greatest cheerleader, helping me overcome my doubts and provide insights into my writing that I didn't even see. She has helped me to keep moving forward, in believing in my dreams, and for that I'm eternally grateful.

Thank you to my wonderful friend Tonya for her insights along the way and for being one of my first readers. Her support and insights have been invaluable.

ABCUT THE AUTHOR

eroticwritergirl is the pen name of a super introverted and creative writer who loves to explore women's submissive nature in super sensual, romantic and surprising ways. She wrote her first full-length romance novel at age 13 and has been writing ever since. She writes contemporary romance along with erotic romance and loves to push boundaries and explore human nature through her writing.

When not writing, eroticwritergirl reads everything from YA to the steamiest erotic romance, spends time at the beach (she's a total water girl), dances around to her latest playlist, plays her electric guitar and paints using her intuition.

She grew up outside of Detroit, has lived in Chicago and currently resides back in Michigan off the shores of Lake Michigan with her husband and two spoiled cats.

- instagram.com/kinkyinkpress
- facebook.com/kinkyinkpress
- amazon.com/eroticwritergirl/e/B08FYXJHBZ
- youtube.com/@eroticwritergirl